Delphi Embassy

Series
Book Eleven

Bob Blanton

Cover by Momir Borocki
momir.borocki@gmail.com

D1732921

https://www.facebook.com/StarshipSakira/

Table of Contents

Chapter 1   Princess Catie

"I am so tired of Princess Catie!" Catie hissed as she pulled her bag out of the closet and tossed it onto the bunk in her cabin, the captain's cabin. She started packing her things.

"Do you want some help?" Morgan, her personal bodyguard, asked.

"I can do it," Catie said.

"I know you can, I'm just offering to help."

"Sure, if you'll pack up my clothes, I'll go take care of the head."

"Got it." Morgan had brought another bag to take care of the extra things they'd had made for Catie after the mission began. She had needed extra clothing that was more appropriate for a princess than her typical uniforms that she had brought with her when she was just the captain of the Roebuck.

Morgan folded the gowns with extra care. She didn't understand why Catie hated wearing them. She was beautiful when she did. But who could figure out a teenager, especially one like Catie? At almost seventeen, Catie was just becoming a woman, but she'd lived a life only few could dream of. Following her father's discovery of the Starship Sakira, she'd experienced one adventure after another, including a war where she'd been instrumental in Delphi winning. She'd even been awarded the Delphi Cross for that. But now she was going to have to play Princess Catherine of Delphi and Ambassador to Onisiwo, the planet they'd just rescued from being conquered by the Fazullans.

Morgan picked up the jewelry box. She paused to admire it. It was beautiful in its own right, but the jewels that it contained were gorgeous, things she could only dream about having. Catie had loaned her some a few times when she had a big event to go to. That's one of the things she liked about Catie and all the McCormacks, they were completely indifferent to the fact that they were some of the richest people on Earth, and now in the galaxy. Morgan decided that she'd just carry the jewelry box across, no need to risk damage by packing it. She grabbed the bag and walked across the passageway with the jewelry box tucked under her arm. It was only two meters, but she knew to Catie it would be miles, from the captain's cabin to the owner's cabin. Morgan knew it was killing Catie to have to turn over command.

"Sergeant, is there a problem?" Lieutenant Suzuki, the first officer of the Roebuck, asked.

"No, ma'am. Just moving a few things."

Lieutenant Suzuki nodded an acknowledgment to Morgan and continued to the bridge. Suzuki wondered why Captain McCormack needed to use the owner's cabin as well as the captain's cabin. *"She probably has too many dresses to fit into the wardrobe."*

"First Officer on the bridge," Roebuck, the ship's AI, announced as Lieutenant Suzuki entered.

"Status?" Lieutenant Suzuki asked.

"We've been ordered to rendezvous with a Fox that's heading this way. It just started its deceleration to match velocities," the ship's navigator announced.

"That's unusual. It would have had to do a very high G profile to catch up with us."

"Yes, ma'am. It was doing a twelve G profile to catch us. Not very comfortable for the pilot."

"Hmm, must be something important. When will it match velocities?"

"Four hours, ma'am."

"Very well, carry on."

◆ ◆ ◆

"Commander," Catie greeted Commander McAvoy at the airlock to the flight bay. "Welcome aboard."

"Thank you, Captain. Shall we proceed to the bridge?"

"Of course, follow me. My aide will take your bags to your cabin."

"Thank you," Commander McAvoy said, giving Catie a nod and a reassuring smile.

"Captain on the bridge," Roebuck announced as Catie and Commander McAvoy entered.

"Captain," Lieutenant Suzuki said as she jumped to attention from the captain's chair.

"At ease. Please prepare for an all-hands announcement," Catie ordered.

"All-hands, all-hands, standby for an announcement," the Roebuck blared over the ship's speakers.

"Commander," Catie said.

Commander McAvoy pulled out a parchment and read: "By order of Admiral Blake McCormack of the Delphi Space Forces, Commander Tegan McAvoy is hereby ordered to assume command of the DSS Roebuck." Commander McAvoy folded the parchment and turned to Catie. "Captain McCormack, I relieve you."

"I stand relieved," Catie said as she saluted the new captain of the Roebuck.

"Princess," Captain McAvoy said as she saluted Catie.

Catie turned and left the bridge through the main entry instead of the entry that would take her to the captain's day cabin. The owner's cabin was identical to the captain's cabin except for that one feature, direct access to the bridge.

"Status!" Captain McAvoy demanded.

Once Captain McAvoy had gotten an update on the current status of the Roebuck, she and First Officer Suzuki went to the captain's day cabin to go over more details.

"Are there any changes to the standing orders that you would suggest?" Captain McAvoy asked.

Suzuki paused to think. "I'm not sure, possibly limiting the Onisiwoens from accessing some areas of the ship more; they seem to have free rein."

"I see, and how would you do that?"

"Restrict them from level B." Level B was the bridge level.

"That would make it difficult for them to speak to the captain or the princess."

"They could be escorted."

"Hmm. Captain McCormack was trying to establish a personal relationship with them, as part of the process we need in order to open trade with their planet. Her evaluation on you says you're a good first officer."

Suzuki suppressed a snort. "That's nice of her."

"Lieutenant, you seem to have a problem with Captain McCormack. Would you please explain?"

"She's just a figurehead. They put her in charge of this ship to impress the Onisiwoens. They sent you to take over once they could and it really counted."

"And how did you reach this conclusion?"

"She's not even seventeen."

"Alexander the Great and Augustus Caesar were only eighteen when they led their first campaigns."

"I doubt they were really in charge," Lieutenant Suzuki said.

"Well, let me clarify some things for you," Captain McAvoy said.

"First, let there be no doubt that when Catherine McCormack is in charge of something, she is in charge.

"Second, they sent me here not because they needed a more experienced officer to take over, but to free Captain McCormack to step into the role of Princess Catherine and our Ambassador to Onisiwo. She is now in charge of the entire mission in the Onisiwo system. She is in fact in charge of all Delphi assets in this system. She is my boss, and even Admiral McCormack's boss while he is in the system.

"Third, when the admiral came to me and asked if I would take this assignment, he specifically stressed to me that Catherine McCormack would be in charge, that it would be unlikely that she would tolerate any failure on the part of the Delphi Forces that would compromise this mission. He wanted to make sure I felt up to the task.

"So, tell me. Am I making a mistake by not relieving you and sending you to the Victory?"

Lieutenant Suzuki gulped. "No, ma'am. I can and will do my job."

"Let's hope so. Because with me, you only get one strike."

"Princess," Captain McAvoy greeted Catie after Morgan let her into Catie's day cabin.

"Catie, please."

"Then call me Tegan," Captain McAvoy said. "We haven't met; I was on the Victory during the war, and for most of the time after."

"I know," Catie said. "Please be seated."

"Thank you. I wanted to meet, to make sure that you had everything you needed and to find out if there was anything specific you might wish me to do," Captain McAvoy said.

"You know our goals. Separate out the slaves from the Fazullan ships and put those ships in isolation in another system until we find a home for them. That part of the mission will mainly fall to Captain Clements. We also need to set up an embassy on Onisiwo. See what we can do to involve them in the economics of resettling the Paraxeans, the Aperanjens, and eventually the Fazullans. And of course, we have to do all that without upsetting the balance of power on Onisiwo or within the Delphi League."

"Sounds simple." Captain McAvoy gave Catie a smile.

"I wish. You should know that I've offered the Onisiwoens that we freed from the Fazullans, refuge on the Roebuck until they're ready to return to the planet. Especially the women might wish to wait for the media storm to settle down before they return home."

"I can understand that."

"Is there anything else about the Roebuck you need me to explain?" Catie asked.

"I don't think so. I've reviewed your standing orders and the ship's log. If I do have a question, I'll be sure to ask. Well, I do have one question, Lieutenant Suzuki?"

"Ah, our intransigent first officer. I think she's a fine officer, but it seems she has a chip on her shoulder. I haven't spent very much time researching her background to try and figure out where the chip comes from, but I don't think it's gotten in the way of her duty."

"Not even when she challenged you to a sparring match?"

"I think that was Morgan," Catie said.

"*Moi?*" Morgan feigned surprise.

Captain McAvoy gave Catie a quizzical look.

"Morgan couldn't help herself. I think she saw the opportunity to teach the lieutenant a lesson and make a mint off of it by betting with the crew."

"I was only taking cues from my captain," Morgan said.

"Hmm, about half the crew thinks you got lucky," Captain McAvoy said.

"Good, we wouldn't want to undermine the first officer's authority by having the whole crew think she got slammed by a sixteen-year-old girl."

"Your uncle warned me to never underestimate you."

"I think he was trying to keep me from having any fun at your expense. But I would never do that," Catie said, "at least not while you're the captain."

"Thank you for that." Captain McAvoy had heard about Catie's penchant for playing tricks on her peers, and especially her penchant for getting even. She was relieved that Catie was giving her a pass on that. "Now if you don't have any special instructions, I'll get back to running the ship."

❖ ❖ ❖

"Hi, Uncle Blake."

"Princess," Blake replied, giving Catie a salute. Fist over heart, the new Delphian salute they'd adopted from the Aperanjens.

"Uncle Blake!"

"Okay, hi, Squirt."

Catie just sighed. "I thought you wanted to chat, not tease me."

"Can't I do both?"

"Obviously."

"The Paraxean carriers are heading home. We'll leave the Victory here until you finish moving everyone to their new planets, and until we can get one of the new frigates out here, we'll leave you the Sakira as well."

Catie just nodded her head, taking it all in.

"I assume you'll be bringing the Fazullan ships into the system one at a time before you move them over to the next star system."

"I've been thinking about that. What do you think about leaving them where they are?" Catie asked. "They're too far away from Onisiwo to cause any problems."

"I agree, that sounds easier and probably safer. Good idea, but what about the ones on the other side of the wormhole?"

"I thought I should ask Captain Clements to move them into this system but beyond the fringe like we did with the ones trying to invade, except this time without any velocity. He can use the Sakira to move the wormhole."

"I agree, and approve, although you're the boss, so you don't need my approval. Now, once the first frigate arrives, you'll be free to send the Roebuck off to check out the new planets. That is assuming we find what we're looking for."

"I'm sure we will."

"I'll keep the Enterprise out on the fringe of Earth's system, so she can be here in a few hours if you need her," Blake said. "And of course, we're all just a phone call away."

"I know."

"Don't worry, you'll do just fine. Do you want me to send anyone else out this way?"

"No, not now. I'm sure we'll be rotating crews before this is over. But for now, I think we should minimize the change."

"Your will," Blake teased, using the Fazullan acknowledgment of a royal command.

Catie just waved at him as she cut the Comm channel.

"I want to thank everyone for joining me," Catie said as the leaders of the Onisiwoen mission gathered with Captain McAvoy and her staff in her cabin for dinner. "I wanted to have a chance for Captain McAvoy to meet all of you and for you to provide us more information about Onisiwo before we arrive on the planet next week."

"Thank you, Princess," Charlie, the captain of the Onisiwoen mission, said. Commander Zaragaxia, the lead female of the mission, just nodded to Catie.

"Zoey," Catie greeted her. Captain Zaragaxia had selected Zoey as her familiar name. "I've asked Captain McAvoy, Major Prescott, and Lieutenant Mischeff to join us."

Kasper, Major Prescott, and Captain McAvoy used the new hand-over-heart salute to greet everyone, giving a slight bow to make it more formal.

Catie nodded to her steward to serve drinks.

"I'm sure we will all benefit from understanding the situation on Onisiwo as you remember it," Catie continued. "Charlie, can you explain your system of government?"

Charlie finished taking a sip of the wine he'd been served before he began. "Our planet has a unified government, but that can be misleading. There are actually six different major governments, one for each of the five continents and one from our space colonies and space stations. Each government selects its representative to the Planetary Council. The Council has a Chair who leads it. That position rotates among the six representatives, with a new one stepping into the role of Chair every two years. The current Chair is from my home, the Northern Coalition. Zoey's home coalition will provide the Chair for the next session which starts in another year."

"Are they elected?" Captain McAvoy asked.

"No, each representative to the Council is appointed by their sponsoring nation. I think in all cases they are appointed by the coalition's president and confirmed by their legislature."

"That is how I remember it," Zoey said. "I'm sure that's true for all members of the Council."

"So, they don't have much power?"

"No, they do," Zoey said. "Their appointment to the Council is for twelve years, so each one will be Chair six times before their appointment ends. Their decisions carry a lot of weight and it takes a ruling by our planetary supreme court to overrule them, or all six governments must agree with a supermajority from their legislature."

"How does the Chair influence the Council?"

"The Chair controls the agenda and has an extra vote in case of ties," Charlie said.

"I see. What about your military?"

"Each nation still maintains a separate military. There have been attempts to eliminate them and form a single planetary military, but they've all failed. No nation wants to give up the power that the threat of military intervention gives them," Zoey said.

"What about the colonies and space stations?"

"They are demilitarized," Zoey said. "The lunar colonies aren't really permanent; since the gravity is low, the people on them rotate every five years. Some rotate to the space stations, others come home to their nation."

"So, does that mean that the space stations are the real power for the sixth nation?" Catie asked.

"That is correct; before we left, they were maintaining a neutral stance. Since they were all established as a shared planetary mission, they have ties to all five coalitions on the planet's surface. Historically, they have been a stabilizing influence."

The dinner continued with the Onisiwoens asking questions about Earth, and Captain McAvoy and Catie asking questions about Onisiwo. By dessert they had moved on to questions about the various forms of entertainment the two planets enjoyed, giving Catie the feeling that the dinner had been successful.

Chapter 2 Sorting Them Out

"Hey, Catie, how's it going?" Liz asked.

"Slow. But I'm ready to go over shipping schedules with you."

"Okay, shoot."

"I want to redirect the Dutchman to Onisiwo instead of Artemis. We'll trade the Onisiwoens a couple of pods worth of appliances, but mainly we'll just pick up a load of Paraxeans from the Fazullan ships. The Dutchman will then head to the newest Paraxean colony world; they say they'll be happy to take the stuff we were shipping to Artemis since they generally have the same needs. It'll take us two days to swap containers and load up the colonists since we'll only have the one Skylifter."

"Okay, so how many colonists will we be able to send out on the Dutchman?"

"Forty-five to sixty thousand, depending on the number of children."

"And how are we paying for this?"

"You mean how are we being paid for this."

"Yes, or who's paying."

"The Paraxean colony will buy the cabins from us with our standard markup. Paraxea is paying one thousand Auroras per colonist, but I told them we wouldn't charge for children, anyone under sixteen."

"Wow, there is a heart under that financial calculator," Liz said.

Catie stuck her tongue out at Liz, making Liz laugh.

"Don't worry, we all know you're really a sweetheart."

"Right!" Catie said. "Now, back to our plan. Once the Dutchman reaches the first colony, we can start the loop. The Dutchman will go to Paraxea from there, then Onisiwo, and then to the second Paraxean colony, and repeat. That's one load of colonists every twelve weeks."

"What will we be carrying from Paraxea?"

"The colony will ship ores and grains to Paraxea. The Paraxeans have agreed to buy that from us and then ship a load of gravity drives and a load of high-end appliances here to Onisiwo to start up the trade triangle. They're also going to ship a bunch of colonist cabins for the Paraxeans we need to relocate. The Onisiwoens are just starting to manufacture them so we'll only need ten pods worth from them on the next run, after that they should be able to keep up. The Paraxeans will also make four Skylifters so we can leave two at Onisiwo and two at Paraxadux, the second colony. The Onisiwoens will start making basic furniture and appliances for the colonies as well as the cabins, but we'll have to learn how far up the chain we can move them."

"How long will all this take?"

"Thirty weeks. The Resolve starts next month; it'll come here to Onisiwo and then head to the Paraxeans' third colony planet. We'll have her bring the high-end trade from Earth, the Dutchman will continue to bring it from Paraxea. After we finish with the Paraxeans, I think we should be able to move all the Aperanjens in one trip."

"That's still seven months!"

"I know, but it should mean I'll make it back home in time for Yvette's graduation. Besides, we're getting paid, shipping cargo, that's what the company does."

"I know, but I was worried about the poor Paraxeans and Aperanjens," Liz said.

"Most of them are in stasis. The ones who aren't will go out on the first trip."

"What about the Aperanjens here on Delphi Station?"

"Once we find a colony planet, we'll send them out on the Sakira. They can start building the infrastructure so they can handle the rest of their colonists. I'm not sure they'll have selected a planet before we're finished with relocating the Paraxeans. But as soon as they do, we'll set a timetable to send the rest of their people. We might have to delay a little to give them time to get ready."

"I hope not. That would delay you getting home. What about the Fazullans?"

"They have their own ships. Once we find their planet, we'll start setting up the jump points. Once they're ready we can start jumping them to their colony after the slaves are removed from their ships. They can sort out their own infrastructure."

"What are you going to do about the ships you hold back with the Paraxean and Aperanjen slaves?"

"I'm not doing that. I don't want to move the stasis chambers," Catie said. "So, I'm planning to leave them in the stasis chambers with the people in place until we're ready to wake them up and send them to their new planet. It makes things a lot easier."

"It would; do you think the Fazullans will agree?"

"I'll find out when I talk to the empress. I don't see why not; we probably won't have the jump points ready until we've relocated all the colonists anyway. How are you doing training the Aperanjen colonists?"

"We've had to modify a few tools, and we're getting ready to make a few from their own designs. They're pretty amped about getting the rest of their colonists back. Not only are they excited because they're alive, but they don't have as many skill gaps to deal with, so they're feeling a lot better about their colony mission."

"That's great."

"They've also expressed interest in sending someone to Onisiwo to help when you start to wake the Aperanjens up."

"That's probably a good idea. We should talk about it at the board meeting next week."

"Okay. I'll let you get back to doing princessy things. Ta-ta!"

Catie gave Liz a special wave as she closed the call.

◆ ◆ ◆

"Empress." Catie greeted the Fazullan empress as they started their Comm meeting.

"Princess, what can I do for you?"

"I'd like to change the process we agreed to for separating the captives from your ships." Catie had decided to refer to the formerly enslaved aliens as captives instead of slaves. Saying slaves made her wince.

The empress frowned, or at least Catie thought that was a frown.

"What change would you like to make?"

"I would like to leave the ships in their current location until we're ready to wake the captives up. The ones on the other side of the wormhole will be moved here to Onisiwo, but well outside of the gravity well."

"What is the purpose of this change?" the empress asked. She knew she didn't really have a choice, but knowledge was power.

"The major benefit is we won't have to move the stasis chambers which will be safer for the captives and your people since we would have to move your people to make room for the captives. It will also place less strain on your shipboard resources. It also means that it's likely that we will allow you to keep all of your ships and stasis chambers."

"That is most generous of you." The empress gave Catie a warm smile. Catie had figured that she would like the idea of getting to keep all the stasis chambers, especially since it would include the ones they had taken from the Paraxean ship.

Catie was surprised when she noticed that the empress had normal teeth, not the sharp alligator-like teeth that the men had. The empress's big smile made that obvious and Catie's shock must have shown on her face.

"You seem disturbed at something," the empress said. "I hope I haven't done something to offend you."

"No, I was just noticing your teeth. They seem more like ours. The men I've seen all have pointy teeth."

The empress shook her head. "Idiots. The men of noble birth all sharpen their teeth as a rite-of-passage when they reach maturity. It is barbaric. I've banned the practice in the future, but what can we do? I would have them all pulled, but then how would they eat?"

"We replace teeth." Catie gave a big grin to emphasize the point.

"With false teeth? That never works well for Fazullans. They always get damaged, we're a little aggressive when we eat."

"No, we can replace them with real teeth. It takes two days for them to stabilize, but after that, they're as strong as the original teeth. Essentially, each tooth is a clone of the original. Or we have a process where they stimulate the root so the tooth grows. You have to grind it down every so often. It works for a chipped or cracked tooth. That might be better; I could have our doctor look into it if you wish."

"I would be very grateful. It would help to erase the memory of our recent past more quickly."

"I'll have them look into it and report to you."

"Thank you, Princess."

Board Meeting – Nov 7th

"This meeting will come to order," Marc said. "First, some breaking news. I'm happy to announce that Gavril has finally decided to plead guilty."

"Gavril?"

"The guy we arrested for running that prostitution ring on Delphi City."

"That's great, so did all his friends plead as well?" Catie asked.

"Yes, so that clears up that case. But it also means that the court will stop paying for the girls and Celia to stay on Delphi Station. Catie, I assume you're planning to cover their cost?"

"Yes, I already told them I would. Celia even has a job at Deogenes." Catie turned to Dr. Metra, "This should mean we can start treating the triplets, right?"

"Triplets?"

"That's what the twins started calling them. It's an easy handle. The three of them are about the same age, they look alike, and they live together. Since they don't have the same last name, triplets makes it easier to refer to them as a group."

Dr. Metra gave a light laugh at the description of the three girls. "We have already started the treatment. I've been told that they are responding well."

"I'm glad to hear that," Marc interrupted the dialog so he could move the meeting back to the agenda. "Fred, anything on the business side we need to discuss?"

"You know there is," Fred said. He'd sent a note to Marc to explain the problem, but he understood the need to introduce it. "We've discovered an issue with our printers. The products being printed have started having higher defect densities. We reviewed the results with the Paraxeans and learned that they just replace their print heads in their printers every two years as a matter of course. Nikola looked into it on the technical side and determined that the wear was in the palladium components in the print head, which probably explains why the Paraxeans are ordering so much palladium. It seems every part you print leaves with a little palladium sprinkled on it."

"So, what's the bottom line?"

"Since palladium is so rare, we need to accelerate our efforts to minimize the use of printers. We also have to push harder to use standard manufacturing processes for most of the components we need, as that will reduce the consumption of palladium. And we have to go through and replace lots of print heads, especially the medical ones. Those aren't so bad since we can manufacture most of their components."

Nikola tapped the virtual table with her hand. "This highlights the need to continue to break the Paraxeans and their colonies from the 3-D printers."

"Agreed. Fred, do you need us to do anything?"

"No, just be aware of it."

"Okay. Now, how about the status of our condo sales?"

"They sell as soon as we put them on the market. It has improved recruiting, getting a contract that says you can buy your condo after six months makes our job offers look better."

"Kal, what about your guys?" Marc inquired, looking for a more complete status update, especially since it was one of Kal's Marines who had brought the issue up.

"Those who can afford it are buying. Those who can't are thinking about drinking less so they can. So overall, it's been good for us."

"Blake, anything on your plate to discuss?"

"Not much. We're moving the forces back to their home stations. The Victory and Sakira are staying in Onisiwo to support Catie. We're still waiting on the first frigate to come off the line. It should be ready for a test flight in three weeks."

"Kal, any update, besides your guys are drinking less?"

"We're doing well. Recruiting is better with condo ownership in the mix. We've had to filter out more people due to mixed allegiances. The various superpowers keep trying to get people on the inside. But the psych profile seems to be taking care of that."

Admiral Michaels, tapped the table indicating that he wanted to speak. Kal gave him a nod so he knew that he was finished.

"It's to be expected that they would be trying to get some of their people on the inside. The formation of the Delphi League was a big deal. It's still playing strong in the news. It even seems to have given a shot in the arm to forming a unified planetary government here on Earth, but it doesn't seem to have done anything to reduce the petty politics."

Catie laughed. "The Onisiwoens say they have the same issue. I'm compiling a report on what we're learning from Charlie and his team. I'll send it to everyone next week. I'll update it once we have more experience with the current government."

"I'll be very interested to look at it," Admiral Michaels said.

"What about the current conflicts in Africa?" Marc asked, pushing the agenda back to Admiral Michaels' update.

"It is amazing what removing easy access to weapons has done. Things are slowly calming down, and we're seeing civilian protest becoming more effective in forcing the government to listen."

"Also, the fact that these political dictators are finding their offshore accounts suddenly being seized," Kal added. Kal had been the biggest cheerleader of Admiral Michaels' new process of having ADI find and appropriate the hidden offshore accounts of the various politicians who were stealing from their countries. The money was funneled back into the country via the U.N. and other aid organizations.

"Yes, when you realize you can't afford to run away and hide, you're more committed to solving the problems at home," Samantha said.

"That's good. But, now to our main agenda item. Princess Catherine, what's the status in Onisiwo?"

"Daddy, give the princess thing a rest." Catie rolled her eyes at her father. "The Dutchman will be here next week. I'm sure you heard that the Paraxeans are sending an ambassador."

"Yes, we heard. I think that's a good thing," Marc said.

"You would!"

"It shows their commitment," Samantha said. "Once you get past the reception, things will settle down."

"I hope so. We've pushed the reception off until after the Paraxean ambassador arrives. The Onisiwoens wanted to have two, but we told them we needed at least a week to ensure that it was safe for us to be on their planet without being in a spacesuit."

"They must have liked that."

"Yeah, they did. We're going to construct a bubble in the hotel so we can be on the surface and meet. We'll have a room separated by polyglass so we can see each other and pretend we're breathing the same air."

"Good for you," Samantha said.

"Now back to our plans," Catie said. "We've started to wake the Paraxeans we'll be sending out on the Dutchman. The Victory is going to house them in one of their flight bays until we have cleared out the tower in the hotel we're using. Then we'll send them to the planet so they can move into the cabins before we lift them. It's a bit of a mess, but things will get better once we get ahead on the cabins.

"The Paraxeans are going to ship two Skylifters here to Onisiwo which will help speed things up. They'll ship another two for Paraxeadux on the next trip. We've given the Onisiwoens the design for the cargo pods and agreed to give them the license for making polysteel; we won't charge them a license fee as long as the products are for the colonies. We've also provided them the designs for furniture and some of the appliances that they can make here."

"I've noticed that most of the manufacturing seems to be concentrated in the Northern Coalition," Samantha said.

"Yes, we've started looking into that after Charlie and Zoey explained how their government works. We'll be trying to find ways to more equitably distribute the orders so there's a positive impact in all the countries."

"How are you doing with the government?" Samantha asked.

"Every time I talk to anyone it's all about the reception and the embassy. I have to use an avatar, pretending to be my aide, to get anyone to spend time on trade discussion, and even then, the conversation is dominated by the embassy and reception."

"Sounds like the Onisiwoens like to party," Liz said.

"Or maybe not talk about things that might point to questionable activities," Samantha suggested.

"That makes sense. They're trying to train us to let them manage the details," Catie suggested. "Anyway, the Resolve should be ready in another month. Hopefully, we'll have found a colony world for the Aperanjens by then, but if not, we'll focus on getting the Paraxeans all resettled.

"One last thing: Liz says the Aperanjens would like to send someone out here to help when we wake their people up. I think maybe in two months," Catie finished.

"That sounds like about the right timing," Marc said. "Blake is sending you the Oryxes you've asked for. He'll send the Aperanjens on another Oryx when you're ready for them."

"I've had him include some cargo to help set you up for a prolonged stay," Samantha said.

"Let me guess, more dresses."

"Yes, but there are also foodstuffs, furniture, and some fixtures you might like to have when you set up residence on Onisiwo."

"Thanks, I think."

"Oh, and one last thing," Marc said while giving Catie a big smile.

Catie sighed, "What now?"

"We need to report the events in Onisiwo. I have Sam and Blake working on a press release, but the first thing that will happen after that is the press will start hounding us for an interview."

"SO!"

Marc chuckled as he threw Samantha under the bus. "Sam thinks you should give Sophia an interview."

"I just mentioned that Sophia would be the first one demanding an interview!" Samantha defended herself.

"Same thing. Well, Catie, what do you think?"

"I think I should run and hide."

"Well, you're essentially going to be doing that for the next few months. So?"

"Alright, but let me read the press release before it goes out. After that, I'll give Sophia a call."

"That's my girl. Everyone, good day."

After the press release, Catie called Sophia.

"Catie, why didn't you give me some of this before?!"

"Because it was classified."

"Ah, come on, once you guys told Earth about the Fazullans, you could have told me more. The Gazette needs a few exclusives to maintain its prestige."

"Sure, well, do you want an interview or do you want to scold me?"

"Okay, an interview. And can you arrange for a few more with some of the other people involved?"

"Sure, I'll bet Sergeant Takurō would love to give an interview."

Sophia's article the next week made world-wide news. "Delphi League wins first interstellar war. Princess Catie tells us the inside story."

Although Catie was not happy with the title, the story was good. And Sergeant Takurō had been a good sport during his interview.

Chapter 3   Embassy

The Onisiwoen President had assigned the second tower of one of their best hotels to be the Delphinean Embassy until they had time to find a permanent location. The ambassador's residence would be the top floor. They had had a crew working on it for three weeks, ever since they knew they would be accepting a delegation from the Delphi League.

Morgan took a team of construction engineers down to prepare the place, isolating the airflow, creating the bubble which would allow the Onisiwoens and Delphineans to work in view of each other without contact or sharing the same air. Morgan also had a few special modifications she wanted made.

The embassy, with the help of the hotel, would host the big reception when the Paraxean ambassador arrived and the Delphinean doctors declared the air was safe.

"Hello, Zoey," Catie greeted the Onisiwoen commander. "Please have a seat."

"Thank you, Princess," Zoey said as she took a seat in front of Catie's desk.

Catie rolled her eyes at being called Princess but knew she had to get used to it. Princess or Madam Ambassador, neither felt right to her. "What can I do for you?"

"You offered to allow the members of our mission to stay on board the Roebuck after we made orbit," Zoey said. "I'd like to understand more about that option?"

"Of course. Basically, once we make orbit, we'll put the Roebuck in a stationary position over Onisiwo's North Pole. That will allow us to maintain gravity in the ship while it is only one thousand kilometers above the planet."

"Why the North Pole?" Zoey asked, ever the scientist.

"To maintain gravity, we can't be orbiting the planet. If you're going to be stationary at an altitude of one thousand kilometers, you want to be out of any traffic lanes for satellites or launches. The North Pole is a convenient location for that."

"But how will you maintain altitude if . . . oh, I keep forgetting about your gravity drives. They're such a foreign concept to us."

"I understand. Anyway, that will allow us to maintain eighty-five percent gravity, which should be comfortable and eliminate any health risk of staying on board."

"Good, what about the air? We've been told it's okay, but then we heard that you're asking for another week before you break isolation."

"We need to make sure there are no pathogens in the planet's atmosphere or water," Catie said.

Zoey looked at Catie skeptically.

"Okay, but don't tell on me. I'm using it as a delaying tactic. I don't want to have to attend two different big reception balls, so we're stalling until the Paraxean ambassador arrives. Our satellite sent probes down to sample the water and air weeks ago. We know it's safe. Morgan is also using that as an excuse to do some work on the hotel to improve security."

"Your secret is safe with me. The team would like to take you up on your offer. We've elected Charlie to go down and face the hordes of reporters and officials. And all of the women would like to stay on board until after they give birth plus a few weeks for the baby to have a chance to grow stronger before we attempt to enter Onisiwoen society."

"I understand. We won't have a problem accommodating that. And later when we've established our embassy, you're welcome to come stay there while you acclimate to full gravity and . . . whatever."

"Thank you."

"So even the men are too chicken to go down right away?"

"Too chicken?"

"Sorry, afraid. Chickens on our world are birds that seem to be afraid of everything. If you go 'Bawk Bawk,' it sounds like a chicken and is the same as calling someone a coward."

"I see. Yes, they are chicken. They would like to let Charlie take the first barrage from the press and other government officials. After that, I'm sure more of the men will join him. Also, I think some of them want to stay with us women to provide company and help with the children."

"That's nice of them. I'm sure Charlie will appreciate getting all of the attention," Catie said.

"Well, he is the captain."

"That's true. I'm glad to hear that the men are helping out with the children; it must be hard to look after a toddler while you're pregnant. They always have so much energy."

"It is, but we all help each other. Anyway, I'll let you get back to your work."

"It's not a problem. Please come by anytime."

"We're ready," Morgan announced. The Roebuck had taken up position over Onisiwo's North Pole two days before. Now it was time to move to the embassy and officially take up residence.

"Okay," Catie said. She was in an exosuit and carrying the helmet. They had to carry on with the charade about the air, so they would all be in full exosuits until they were inside the hotel's sealed environment on the top floor, plus Morgan liked having the armor.

"The Lynx will land on the roof," Morgan explained. "We'll have two Foxes close by providing cover and four up high just in case."

Catie nodded and boarded the Lynx, followed by Charlie, Morgan, and six other bodyguards. *It should at least impress the Onisiwoens,* Catie thought.

It took them two hours before they were hovering over the hotel. They had been assigned the top floor of the second tower. This one was two stories shorter than the first tower, which had a pool area and an outdoor garden on its roof for the hotel guests. Apparently, the hotel wasn't willing to give up those facilities to the embassy.

There was a film crew and reporters to record their arrival. The Onisiwoen Council, as well as the president of the hosting nation, were there as well, each vying for a position in front of the cameras. Everyone waved as the Delphineans made their way through the crowd to the elevator.

When the elevator stopped at the top floor Catie saw that Morgan had had an airlock installed where they exited the elevator. Catie recognized it as an entry port for security, but saying you needed an airlock wasn't as offensive as saying you didn't trust the Onisiwoens.

"Okay, Catie, you've got two hours to get all dolled up for the first press conference," Morgan said.

Catie rolled her eyes and followed Morgan to her room. One of the other guards had her suitcases. Her other luggage would follow the next day. A third guard led Charlie to his room so he could change and join Catie at the press conference.

Catie and Charlie met outside Charlie's room. "Are you ready for this?" Catie asked.

"Hey, we train for this. Dealing with the press is the hardest part of the training to be an astronaut."

They walked into the room that had been set up for the news conference. They had half of the room to themselves; well except for security guards that Morgan had posted. They were behind a polyglass panel which separated the room in two. Their side was connected to the rest of the floor, while the other side was isolated and only had access to the second bank of elevators. The Onisiwoen delegation was seated with their backs to the panel, with space left in the center where Charlie and Catie would be seated on their side of the panel so that everyone faced the cameras and the press.

Lord Lexisen, the Chair of the Council, stood to address the audience. "Everyone, I would like to welcome Princess Catherine of the Delphi League. With her is Captain Margakava Charmaxiam, the leader of the mission to Ditubria which was captured by the Fazullan aggressors. I want to again express our gratitude to the Delphi League for rescuing our astronauts and returning them home to us."

After a surprisingly short speech, Chair Lexisen turned to Catie and asked her if she would make a brief statement.

"I would like to welcome the people of Onisiwo to the Delphi League. The League was formed to help foster trade and security among the starfaring civilizations in our galaxy. Your world has been on the brink of breaking out among the stars for many years. It is unfortunate that it was the aggression of the Fazullans that forced us together, but it had the benefit of cementing the creation of the Delphi League to prevent such things in the future."

After a few more statements, Catie sat down. She assumed that it would be more efficient to provide information by answering questions; reporters never seemed to take what you said at face value anyway. They were always going to ask questions.

Charlie stood up and spoke next. "Again, I want to thank our rescuers, the Delphineans. They have gone out of their way to help us, and when they realized that our homeworld was at risk, they immediately came here to protect all of Onisiwo. They are a true example of friendship." Charlie added a few more comments before he sat back down.

One of the reporters stood up, a young-looking woman. "Princess Catherine, I'm Lois Lane from the Daily Planet. Can you tell us about your homeworld?"

Catie was stunned for a second. How was her translator coming up with Lois Lane from the translation of the Onisiwoen reporter's name? She realized it must be ADI playing a joke on her. She coughed to cover her surprise before answering.

"Our homeworld is eighty light-years from Onisiwo. It is similar in size; we both have a yellow dwarf for a sun. My planet is about seventy percent water, our measurements show that yours is sixty-two percent water, so they are very similar."

A second reporter got Catie's attention, this time. "I'm George Will with the Washington Post. Could you tell us how you've managed to become so proficient in our language?"

This time Catie wasn't surprised, *"Very funny, ADI,"* she messaged.

"I'm not speaking Onisiwoen," Catie said. "My words are being translated into your language by my Comm. It is approximating my voice. Your words are being translated into our language and I'm hearing them via speakers in my ears."

"That's incredible!"

"It is. It takes a very large and powerful computer to create the translation program. Then it is able to run on our Comms, which are themselves very powerful computers despite their small size." Catie pointed to the Mini-Comm she was wearing as a pendant.

An older reporter had been standing with his pen tilted up to indicate he wanted to ask a question. Catie called on him.

"Thank you, Princess. I'm Walter Cronkite with CBS News. Can you explain how you are able to travel such great distances, and why it has taken so long to reach our planet after the war ended?"

Catie laughed. "It is funny that we can travel eighty light-years in minutes, but it takes us two weeks to travel thirty thousand light-seconds or eight light-hours. The secret is a dimension tunnel through space-time that we call a wormhole."

"So, they exist. Our theory of gravity predicts them but it seems like a fantasy."

"Yes, they do exist. That is what put your planet at risk. You are near a terminus of a natural wormhole that extends from the Fazullan system to yours. It crosses about one hundred light-years of space. Fortunately, it is only in Onisiwo for a few months every year or so. Delphi has learned how to create an artificial wormhole that we can use to travel between star systems, which is how we are able to reach your planet so fast. But the wormholes can only exist outside of a gravity well, so once we get here, we have to travel to your planet by more normal means."

"If it's normal means, then how can you traverse eight light-hours in a matter of weeks?"

"Our ships are powered by fusion reactors," Catie said, leaving out the fact that they actually used antimatter reactors to power the ships once the fusion reactor had started up the process. "Because of that, we are able to maintain constant acceleration or deceleration during our trip. . .. and before you ask, we don't generally use reaction mass, instead, we use gravity drives that work against the gravimetric waves coming from your sun."

"And, it takes two weeks to get here?"

"We can make it in less time depending on the mass of the ship and the medical condition of the passengers. We came here using a low acceleration profile since we weren't confident of the medical condition of everyone on board."

An older woman had been impatiently trying to get Catie's attention during the conversation about travel time. Catie pointed to her.

"I'm Murphy Brown with FYI. I understand that the Delphi League has decided to help the Fazullans. How can you provide aid to such a barbaric people?"

"The barbarity of the Fazullans was due to the people in power, not their inherent nature," Catie said. "A rebel faction of the Fazullans took the opportunity of this conflict to rise up and take over their government. It was their revolt that allowed the Delphi League to neutralize the Fazullan fleet with minimal loss of life. Without their help, it is likely that we would have lost thousands of spacers and Marines during the conflict."

"But still!"

"We see them as potential allies and trading partners for all of us. The empress has done everything in her power to make things right, to atone for the mistakes of their former rulers."

"The empress, you mean that they are still under the same rulers?"

"The previous Fazullan regime treated their women little better than they treated their slaves. The empress is the wife of the former emperor, she was the one who formulated the rebellion. We are indebted to her, and are going to help them find a suitable planet to colonize."

"What was wrong with the one they had?"

"Their planet was part of a binary star system. Planets in such systems have unstable orbits. Over decades or centuries, their orbit can change. Theirs changed and made the planet very inhospitable."

Chair Lexisen stood up to get everyone's attention. "Let's please move the questions beyond the Fazullans and the war."

At this point all the reporters scrambled to be recognized. They all wanted a chance to get on record for interacting with Princess Catherine.

"In the earlier press release, it says that Captain Charmaxiam was held in a stasis chamber, can you explain?"

"A stasis chamber puts your body into something approximating suspended animation. They were developed to allow people to travel between stars. Those early missions took decades to accomplish," Catie explained. "That's all I know; I've never been in stasis, although our doctors use it sometimes when they have to treat someone with severe injuries." Catie pointed to another reporter.

"Gwen Ifill with Washington Week in Review. What types of technologies are you planning to share with us? Those Comms for instance?"

"We and the Paraxeans will be sharing quite a bit of technology with you. Some we will give you, some we will license or sell to you, and some you will be given access to, but we won't always give you the design or technology. This is a Mini-Comm," Catie said, again pointing at her pendant. "I have a company that manufactures them. Their sale is definitely in the offering; we'll have to determine when. We will be talking with your government about what technology you need and want, as well as what technology you have that we would like to have access to."

Ms. Ifill followed up. "What would you want from us?"

"You have a very advanced intrastellar economy, one of the most advanced that we're aware of. We are very interested in your space-based manufacturing. You've been doing it for decades, far longer than we have. The Paraxeans have a longer history of it, but they did not invest as much into it as it appears you have."

Catie called on a posh looking reporter who'd been raising a pen a few times.

"I'm William F. Buckley with the National Review. Are you going to share your wormhole technology with us?"

"We may eventually provide you access to it. But we're not sharing our jump drives, as we call them, with anyone at this time."

After a few more questions, Catie closed the conference.

"ADI, that was really mean!"

"Oh, you handled it okay. I know how bored you get during press conferences, so I wanted to liven it up."

The Paraxean ambassador arrived three days later aboard the Dutchman. That meant it was time to give up the charade about isolation. Which was a good thing since Captain McAvoy and Captain Clements wanted to send members of their crews down to the planet for shore leave.

Morgan had the construction guys remove the polyglass separator and the entry bubble, but kept the airlock as a security measure. Catie had thought that ending the charade would mean that she could go outside to run, but Morgan disabused her of that notion immediately.

"Ambassador Betzag, how was your trip?" Catie greeted the ambassador on the roof of the hotel where his Lynx had landed. She had left things vague with the Onisiwoens so there was no reception committee to deal with.

"It was excellent, Princess, although a bit long." The ambassador looked around as though wondering where the reception committee was.

"Let's get you settled in. We have a short reception with the Onisiwoen Planetary Council this evening. It'll give you a chance to meet them before the big reception tomorrow."

"That's very thoughtful of you," the ambassador said, apparently relieved that he was at least important enough to warrant a reception.

His aide grabbed his luggage and followed Catie down to the embassy residence. Catie walked with them to their room, then left them to get ready for the reception.

"He seemed disappointed not to be mobbed by reporters and dignitaries," Morgan said.

"I thought I was doing him a favor."

"Not everyone is as shy as you are."

Councilor 1: "My country would be very interested in discussing how we can aid your efforts to help the refugees. We have significant industries that could provide some benefit to those efforts."

Councilor 2: "The CEO of one of our larger communication companies would love to talk to you about a licensing deal for your Comms. He would also be interested in having you on the board of directors for the company. He is sure that they would benefit from your insights."

Councilor 3: "My country would love to be the first to test out your fusion reactor design. We would be able to idle one of our powerplants while your people made the change."

"I thought your planetary council was supposed to advocate for the entire planet," Catie whispered to Charlie.

"They're politicians, what did you expect?"

"I didn't expect to be continuously lobbied for special treatment."

"You think this is bad, wait until the big reception this weekend," Charlie whispered back.

"Ambassador Betzag has fielded twelve entreaties for special treatment," ADI informed Catie.

"How did he deal with them?"

"He told them he would get back to them. He seemed very interested."

"Great, now we have to worry about the Paraxeans messing things up."

"Derek, how is the loading going?" Catie asked. Derek had come down the day after the Dutchman made orbit. He wanted to visit with Catie in person while the crew was finishing up with all the colonists.

"We're almost done with the loading. It's getting all the colonists on board that's taking so much time."

"Well, they are the primary reason that you're here."

"It would be more efficient if you had a better way to get them into orbit once we arrive," Derek suggested. "Maybe we could build a transportation pod to bring them up. Something bigger than an Oryx, but that would fit into the flight bay, or attach to the airlock for the cabins."

"I'll work with Ajda on a design. Maybe we'll have it ready for when you get back," Catie said. "Of course, by then most of the cabins should be built here on Onisiwo, so you'll just take them up in their cabins."

"True, but it's still a good idea."

"Yes, it is. Ajda should have our new shuttle ready soon, but it's not designed to carry that many people."

"But it would be cool to have one. Then we'd be able to fly out of the Dutchman without having to wait for the flight bay to decompress. Are you going to have them retrofit the Roebuck and our other starships with your iris?"

"I was hoping that once they see it in action, they'd demand it."

"Oh, you want to make them pay."

"Of course. We're in business after all."

"I want you to wear that cobalt blue silk dress with your turquoise jewelry," Samantha said.

"Okay!" Catie rolled her eyes at Samantha. She could never get used to Samantha telling her what she had to wear.

"With the tiara I sent. The one with turquoise."

"Really?!" Catie groaned.

"You're Princess Catherine. You have to look the part."

"Alright, but no sash!"

"Okay, no sash. Just pick shoes to match. And your diamond ring."

"No nose ring?"

"Funny. Now behave yourself."

"I'll try. Can you believe I got over twenty offers about special trade deals at the little reception we had when the ambassador arrived?"

"I'm not surprised. Just be polite and tell them to refer their friends to your trade minister."

"Who is that?"

"You and your father. But they don't need to know that."

"Won't they want to meet this minister?"

"I guess. Why don't you pick one of the Marines from the Roebuck and assign them the job? And not Ensign Racine, she doesn't have the right temperament."

"Oh, you're no fun. It would be perfect if she was it. They'd be scared to death as soon as she gave them her special look after one of their stupid offers."

"I know that would be fun, but it's not what you're there for."

"*Okay.* . . . Are you going to inspect my outfit before I go?"

"No, I'll trust Morgan and ADI. Have a good time." Samantha waved to Catie before she cut the transmission.

"Are you ready?" Captain McAvoy messaged Catie.

"I think so, come on in," Catie replied.

"You look lovely," Captain McAvoy said when she saw Catie.

"You think so? Not sexy though."

"I think the purpose of having you wear a Greek-style dress was for you to look young and innocent, not sexy and on the prowl. I assume Cer Newman selected the outfit for you."

"Yes, she always selects my official outfits. Did she tell you what to wear?"

"Of course. I would not be wearing a long skirt as part of my uniform if I had my choice."

"But you look so lovely," Catie cooed. "And all those medals, you must really be brave."

"You're hilarious. Now, where is Morgan?"

"Coming!"

Morgan joined them from her adjoining suite; she was wearing the enlisted version of the uniform that Captain McAvoy was wearing.

"Were you able to find enough places to hide all your weapons?" Catie asked.

Morgan snorted. "The only good thing about wearing a long skirt is that there are plenty of places to hide things. Now let me tell you about the layout. Six of the servers are our people. Plus, we have an honor guard that will be standing around the room against the wall. They'll look like decorations, but they'll be watching everything. We've got the room wired with cameras and mics, so ADI and Roebuck can keep track of things."

"You're not really worried about someone trying something, are you?"

"The Marine Corps motto is 'Semper Paratus', always prepared," Morgan said.

"I thought it was 'Semper Fi', always faithful," Catie said.

"Delphi Marines prefer to be prepared. You can only be faithful if you're alive."

"Ladies, our escorts await," Captain McAvoy interrupted.

Major Prescott was waiting outside to escort Captain McAvoy, Kasper was there to escort Catie, and Takurō was there as Morgan's escort. They took the elevator down to the fourth floor where the ballroom was. When they exited the elevator, there were two Marine sentries on each side of the bank of elevators. They looked great in their dress blues, but the weapons at their shoulder clearly stated that they were not there for decorative purposes. Major Prescott nodded to them as he led the party to the ballroom.

"Are you ready for your speech?" Kasper teased Catie.

"Just don't snore," Catie told him before making her way to the front of the room and the podium.

◆ ◆ ◆

"Welcome to the Delphi Embassy. This reception is being held in honor of your planet becoming a new member of the Delphi League of Planets." Catie ignored the fact that the embassy was for Delphi Nation, not the Delphi League, there was no reason to confuse the audience; besides she was confused about where one ended and the other started.

"Today, Onisiwo stands with the Delphi League on the brink of a new era. An era that will herald an unprecedented expansion of colonization into the galaxy and with that an unprecedented expansion of interstellar trade.

"Thwarting the invasion of Onisiwo was the catalyst that formed the League, the event that raised everyone's awareness of the value of cooperation and trade over conquest. Today the members of your mission are free from their captors. Today the Paraxean colonists are free to continue their mission to one of Paraxea's colonies. Today the Aperanjens are free and waiting for a colony world of their own. And yes, today the Fazullans are free from their despotic and corrupt leaders, free to move to a new world, free to prove to the Delphi League that they are worthy of membership. . . .

"As we move into this new era, let us focus on the ways we can help each other, learn from each other, make each other stronger and better people. . . .

"And finally, let me say that all this is possible when we respect life, respect the individual no matter their form, and respect the rights of others as we expect them to respect our rights. To the Delphi League!"

Catie left the podium and was immediately greeted by Chair Lexisen of the Onisiwoen Planetary Council. "Princess, an excellent speech. I hope we can all live up to its ideals."

"I'm sure we can," Catie said.

"I see that our women have decided to stay on the Roebuck."

"Yes, they're still dealing with health issues related to their pregnancies. Our doctors are working with them. They also want to protect their children from any publicity."

"As do we. I wanted to introduce you to one of our business leaders. He is the head of our largest steel manufacturer. He's interested in hearing more about polysteel," Chair Lexisen said. "Princess Catherine, may I present Lord Vortagax, Lord Vortagax, Princess Catherine of Delphi."

"I'm pleased to meet you," Catie said, extending her hand. Lord Vortagax took it and touched it to his forehead as he bowed. Catie had learned that this was the Onisiwoen equivalent of kissing your hand.

"I'm honored to meet you."

After what Catie felt was an hour, but which ADI assured her was only twenty minutes, of boring questions about polysteel and how its manufacture could be integrated with the existing steel industry, Chair Lexisen returned. "Lord Vortagax, we cannot have you monopolizing the Princess's time. Possibly you'll be able to find time to come to her embassy and continue your discussion later." Lord Lexisen then whisked Catie off to talk to another business leader, this one from his country, the Northern Coalition.

"Princess Catherine, Lord Constaxinavia, Lord Constaxinavia, Princess Catherine."

After the greeting, Catie immediately realized that for the next span of time she would get to learn the ins and outs of the Onisiwoen communication system.

"We feel we should come up with a trade agreement for a license for your Comms. I'm sure we could find an arrangement that would be mutually beneficial. We are the largest supplier of personal communication devices in the world. If you would join our board, we would all benefit from the relationship."

"He just made the same offer to the Paraxean ambassador," ADI informed Catie.

"And what did the good ambassador decide?"

"He decided that there was likely to be a very beneficial arrangement to be had."

"I don't think it would be beneficial to introduce our Comms with you right now," Catie said. "Possibly next year would be better timing."

"Oh," Lord Constaxinavia said, uncomfortable at being refused. Shortly he excused himself from Catie's company giving her a curt nod goodbye instead of the hand-to-forehead thing.

"So, you're going to wait for a year to introduce Delphi Comms?" ADI asked.

"No, I thought we'd wait a few months then introduce them using Onisiwo's second-largest supplier of individual communication devices."

"You must not have liked Lord Constaxinavia."

"No I didn't, he's slimy."

"You do know that the CEO of the second-largest supplier might be just as slimy," ADI said.

"True, but he didn't rub any of it on me today."

"Hello, Charlie," Catie said as he walked over to greet her.

"Princess, are you enjoying yourself?"

"I'm surviving." Catie paused and looked at Charlie. "Hmm, something about your uniform is different."

"Ah, you've noticed. I've been promoted to the rank you would call captain. You've called me captain ever since we've met because I led the mission, but I was only a commander. They promoted me yesterday."

"You deserved it, it was over five years, after all."

"But you do realize, that to me, it's only been a few months. I was in stasis for the rest of the time."

"True, what about Zoey and the other members of the mission?"

"They'll all receive promotions, but it doesn't seem quite fair for the women since they've been awake most of the time."

"Has your government decided what to do about the women and their children?"

"They still want to keep it quiet. Since the Fazullans might be our trading partners in the future, they don't want to stir up too much public resentment against them. Keeping us as slaves is one thing, breeding us another."

"Isn't that going to be hard? How are the women going to keep it quiet? Their children have to go to school, socialize, have friends."

"I would agree. We'll have to see how it goes once all the hullabaloo, is that the right word, dies down."

"The word is perfect. Here comes a waiter, do you want a drink?"

"Champagne. I hope you don't run out of it."

"Samantha sent plenty. It seems your people really like it. We'll have to start bringing it in as part of our trade goods."

◆ ◆ ◆

"How are you handling the princess thing?" Kasper asked as he and Catie danced.

"I'm doing okay. It's a hassle, but tonight has to end sometime."

"I liked your speech, by the way."

"Good, you can thank Samantha for it. She wrote most of it."

"But you gave it."

"True. How are you doing on the Roebuck? Are you and Captain McAvoy getting along?"

"I'm doing fine. Captain McAvoy is an excellent captain, and you can tell her I said so."

"Ass kisser."

Kasper laughed. "Maybe, but she is a good captain. Almost as good as you."

"Now you're really piling it on."

"Hey, I'm trying to get promoted. I've been a lieutenant for too long."

"Aren't you already on the promotion list?"

"I am, but I want to stay there. I notice you're not on it, so I'm a bit worried."

"Don't be. I haven't spent enough time on active duty. Besides, Liz and I are focused on StarMerchants."

"Are you sure? You know you'll probably get another Delphi Cross for that trick of yours." Catie had come up with the idea to use the Roebuck and the Sakira to move the end of the wormhole so the Fazullan ships would be stranded out beyond the fringe. That and the help from the empress's rebels had ended the conflict with almost no loss of life on the Delphinean side.

"I doubt it. It wasn't dangerous, so probably just some other commendation. In fact, I'll make sure Uncle Blake knows how I feel."

"I'm sure he does."

"Princess, may I have this dance?" Charlie asked. Catie smiled at him. She was glad he'd picked a waltz. At least she knew what to do as long as he didn't screw up the lead. "Oh, will you be leading?" she asked after she realized that maybe the custom was different on Onisiwo.

"I'll be happy to. We don't have a rule about who leads. But we've all been practicing your various dances," Charlie said. Four of the Onisiwoen men had come down with Charlie to the reception. The other three and the six women were still pleading trauma and ill health. Catie noticed that the four men were spending a lot of time lined up at the bar, getting their Champagne glasses refilled.

"Are you supposed to be lobbying me?" Catie asked.

"Of course, but I know better," Charlie replied. "I hope you haven't been too offended by our various politicians and business leaders."

"Not too much, they've mostly been very subtle."

"Who wasn't subtle?"

"The guy from the communication company."

"Oh, very new money. He's not very polished. He's always, how do you say it, sticking his foot in it, at press conferences."

"Perfect phrasing, you're becoming quite good with our idioms," Catie said as Charlie and she glided across the dance floor.

"Good morning, Catie. I see you've survived the festivities," Captain McAvoy said as she joined Catie at the kitchen table.

"Hi, Tegan. I see you survived as well. Did you send Major Prescott home in one piece?"

Captain McAvoy laughed. "Major Prescott was perfectly safe and he was a perfect gentleman the whole night. He headed up to the Roebuck as soon as we left the reception."

"Maybe he didn't think he was safe," Catie teased.

Captain McAvoy ignored Catie's comment. "Did you accomplish much in the way of diplomacy last night?"

"After my speech, I spent the rest of the night fending off subtle hints that we could reach a 'mutually beneficial' arrangement on some aspect of trade or another." Catie used air quotes to emphasize mutually beneficial.

"That's to be expected. I was never at a high enough rank to have to deal with that kind of politics. The Roebuck is the first ship I've actually commanded."

"Hmm. Uncle Blake certainly thinks a lot of you."

"You think so?"

"Of all the people he could have sent to take over the Roebuck," Catie said.

"I guess that's right. I wonder how he arrived at that opinion? We've only worked together a few times."

"Admiral Blake reviewed your entire service record, both from the U.S. Navy and Delphi Forces," ADI said. "He also had me do a deep behavioral analysis on you."

"Ohh, should I feel impressed or violated?"

"A little of both," Catie said. "ADI!"

"I only do what I'm ordered to do," ADI said.

"I guess it's to be expected," Captain McAvoy said. "Do you realize how lucky you are?"

"I think so, although sometimes I don't feel so lucky."

"Your parents, I guess mostly your father, have scripted your whole life. He's made sure that the people you work with are the finest there are. This mission is probably the first time you've had to deal with people with questionable integrity. Well, except for that kidnapping thing."

"That and there were a couple of people at the Academy, but I get your point. But sometimes it's not so fun to have everything scripted for you."

"Well, you've certainly had plenty of adventure, it was just with the best people. You'll need to keep your guard up while here. Politicians and business leaders tend to behave like sociopaths."

"I know, and I also know that some of them are actually sociopaths. But I've got ADI to help me out. She observes everyone and cues me in on things I might miss."

"I'm her guardian angel," ADI said.

"And sometimes pest. She's always telling me to adjust my posture, eat slower, laugh at lousy jokes."

"Oh, so that's how you pull it off," Captain McAvoy said.

"Pull what off?"

"Decorum. It takes years of training for royals to achieve the proper level of decorum. To know exactly how to behave in each situation. I always wondered how you seemed to pull it off."

"It's ADI . . . and she's a real nag."

"I beg your pardon!"

"See?"

Chapter 4   The Trade Loop

"Princess."

"Catie," Catie corrected Captain McAvoy.

"Catie. How are you doing? Why are you working in here, is there a problem with your office?"

"No, I was just feeling claustrophobic, so I thought I'd work here in the dining room for a while. Am I in your way?"

"Not at all. Do you want some company?"

"Sure," Catie said, swiping the documents closed that she was working on and leaning back in her chair.

"Would you like some coffee or some utywala?" Utywala was an Onisiwoen tea that they usually drank in the morning.

"Coffee, please. I really don't like utywala, although if I keep trying it, I might develop a taste for it."

"The Onisiwoens like our coffee. I'm not sure utywala is suitable to the human palate."

The captain returned with two cups of coffee. She set one down in front of Catie, then took a seat across from her.

"That should be a trading opportunity."

"You're right," Catie said. "How was your tour of the city?"

"It was interesting, it's almost the same as Sydney, but not quite. The architecture feels strange, and all that blue hair just drives my eyes crazy."

"You're not going to dye yours blue?" Catie teased.

"Not in this lifetime. What were you working on?"

"Load balancing for the Dutchman."

"Is that interesting?" Captain McAvoy asked.

"No! It's pretty boring."

"Then why don't you have someone else do it?"

"Because Liz says it's my turn."

Captain McAvoy laughed, she'd heard about the sister-like relationship between the princess and Commander Farmer. "You know you could hire someone to do it."

"Then we'd have to pay them to do something that I can do in a few hours."

"Are you really that cheap?"

"Frugal," Catie corrected. "And StarMerchants is a new company. We can't afford to just keep hiring people. We still need to add two more crews."

"Then why don't you make one of the crew do it?"

"We'll probably have the captain start doing it. But that's still Liz and me; Derek is just learning so it's a bit much to put on his plate right now."

"Why the captain? It seems more like something a cargo master would do and then the captain would approve."

"Hey, that's a good idea," Catie said. "And we already have two cargo masters. I'll suggest it to Liz."

"I'm glad I could help."

"Me too. Are you staying for dinner?"

"If I'm invited."

"You're always invited. Especially if you keep coming up with good ideas."

"How can we swap the crews out without having to be at zero velocity at the fringe?" Derek asked. "That adds another two weeks to the trip." Liz, Derek, and Catie were meeting to discuss how to rotate crews.

"No, you can use the trick we used against the Fazullans. Jump into the system, do a microjump so your vector is cutting a small chord across the orbit, swap crews, then when you hit the fringe you jump out."

"But what about the crew? They're now heading out of the system at 0.1C."

"Yes, but they can use the same trick. When they hit the fringe, they have the jump ships send them on a microjump which reverses their velocity vector so they're heading into the system. That means it only takes them eight days to get home or to reach the ship so they can swap in."

"Okay, but that only works in systems with jump ships," Lieutenant Payne said.

"Right, so Earth or Artemis. If the crew wants to go someplace else, they can hang around on board until you get there. I guess that would be important if we had Paraxeans on the crew that wanted to go home for their break."

"We'll deal with that problem when we have to," Liz said.

Gavril woke from his first night in prison which was located in the airport section of Delphi City. His accommodations were not nearly as nice as the ones he'd had while in jail awaiting trial for his prostitution ring. His new cell had a door to it just like a regular room. A toilet, shower, and a sink were crammed into a two-meter square section of the room. His bed was along one wall, then a TV and a desk were along the other wall. Today would be his first chance to interact with the other prisoners, to let them know who was boss. He'd been issued uniforms when he arrived and he now dressed in one. He pulled at the necklace he was forced to wear. It had a Comm device embedded into it. He'd figure out how to remove it later.

He reported to the orientation room where he was to attend the class. They had a light breakfast sandwich which he was supposed to eat while listening to the first set of rules. *"Rules, screw them,"* he thought. He would figure out which rules he would impose on his fellow inmates; he wasn't interested in following anybody else's rules. He spent the entire day mostly ignoring the lecturers. *"What a waste of time."*

Now he was going to dinner in the cafeteria where all the inmates ate. He collected his tray already loaded with food; apparently, there wasn't any choice about what to eat. He headed over to one of the tables where some of the guys who used to work for him were sitting.

They all were wearing the Comm collar. *"What sheep! They couldn't even be bothered to remove the damn collars."*

"Move over!"

The other prisoners slid over to make room for him. They shook their heads wondering what he was up to.

"What is this crap?"

"Porridge. It's not bad. You need to get used to it; we get it every day. At least until you can afford to buy your own food."

"You mean we have to eat porridge, a roll, and a piece of fruit every day?!"

"So far. We get the same thing for breakfast and lunch too."

Gavril looked around the cafeteria, everyone looked like they were eating the same thing. "Why are you putting up with it?"

"What do you think we should do about it? Go on a hunger strike?"

"Why not?"

"You really want to be fed through a tube?"

"They can't do that for all of us."

"I'm pretty sure they can. Anyway, by next week I'll be making enough money that I'll be able to get some food from the pay line."

"Don't you have friends that will send you money?"

"Any money from the outside goes to pay the victims until we've covered all their costs and reparations."

"Then how will you be able to make enough money to buy meals?"

"They only take half of what we earn at our jobs for the victims, so eventually, once you get a couple of raises, you're making enough to pay for your room and board and have a bit left over."

"We have to pay for room and board?!"

"Didn't you just go through orientation?"

Gavril slapped the guy on the back of the head. "What the . . ." Gavril gasped as an electric shock coursed through him.

"No touching other prisoners!" was announced via his earwig as he received a second shock.

"Hurts, doesn't it?" the prisoner said as Gavril rubbed his head. He had really enjoyed the look on Gavril's face when the shock hit him.

"Princess Catherine, what can we do for you?" Chair Lexisen asked. Catie had asked for a meeting with the Planetary Council to discuss how the contracts for the supplies for the colonies were being managed.

"Chair Lexisen, I'm concerned that it appears that all the contracts for the cabins we're having constructed for the colonists have been let in the Northern Coalition."

"Yes, we're also concerned about that," said the delegate from the Eastern Coalition. The other delegates were nodding to each other.

"We erred on the side of expediency in order to meet your schedule."

"The expediency of getting the money into your pocket," someone whispered. Catie's Comm had picked up the whisper and translated it for her. She doubted that anyone else had heard.

Catie raised her voice and dropped it half an octave, "I think it's critical that we distribute the contracts among the six nations. That is what the Delphi League originally promised and what you agreed to."

"Yes, Princess, we will certainly do that as we continue to build cabins and buy materials to furnish them. It just takes time."

"I see." Catie wasn't satisfied but didn't know what she could do. "I am also looking for permission to buy and trade directly. It will be more efficient if we purchase certain materials and goods directly. Then we can put them into orbit ourselves."

"What will you use for funds?"

"I'm assuming that our first load of goods we're bringing to Onisiwo will generate a surplus compared to the cost of the cabins and goods you are providing."

Chair Lexisen and the other delegates looked unhappy at this suggestion. "We assumed we would be trading for equal value."

"It seems unlikely that you would be able to achieve equal value for items of higher quality and sophistication from Paraxea. The items we are shipping on to the colonies are generally lower cost, and part of the loads will be foodstuffs, so again, I can't see why we wouldn't see a surplus."

"Of course, Princess. We'll make sure that any excess value gets credited to an account that you can use to purchase whatever you like."

"Please send the information to my assistant. Good day." Catie closed the call, frustrated at dealing with the politicians.

"ADI, can you believe how slimy those delegates are?"

"They do seem more concerned about their own welfare," ADI replied.

"Princess," Dr. Moreau nodded to Catie as she entered her office.

"Hello, Dr. Moreau. Please have a seat. Now, what can I do for you?"

"I'm here to discuss what of our medical technology we can start to share with the Onisiwoens."

"And?"

"Based on my discussion with my colleagues here, I would suggest that we start creating an organ growing system and organ bank like we have on Earth. They have a long waiting list for organs, and with their more advanced vehicles, they don't have very many traffic accidents, so they wind up losing a lot of patients because an organ is not available in time. They are using artificial hearts and such, but those come with their own set of problems."

"I can dedicate a small printer to you so you can print organs. However, I would like it to remain on the Roebuck."

"That shouldn't be a problem. What should I tell the Onisiwoens?"

"Just tell them we can grow organs from donor cells, you don't have to mention how we grow them. How long will it take you to prove out the process?"

"Three to six months. We could do it faster, but their studies and review processes are quite lengthy."

"Okay. Is there anything else?"

"I would like to give them our tests for blood and saliva that they can use to isolate bacterial and viral infections. Their current tests are slow, and they have to develop a new one for every virus. Like Earth, they have occasional pandemics, and having our fast testing will allow them to control them before they spread and very many lives are lost."

"ADI, is there anything proprietary in those tests?" Catie messaged.

"Nothing of significant note," ADI replied.

"Doctor, go ahead and release the tests. Tell them we'll provide an open license to them."

"Thank you, Princess. One last thing. Their birth control is very good, but it creates some undesirable side effects. I'd like to start testing our method?"

Catie sighed. "Go ahead, but we will have to deliver it like we do on Earth. We don't want to introduce them to nanites yet."

"I understand. I'll leave you to your work." Doctor Moreau stood up and prepared to leave Catie's office.

Catie motioned for her to wait. "Doctor, I want to thank you for working so hard. I know it is frustrating not being able to do everything you know we could. Please let me know if there is anything I can do to help you or the Onisiwoens."

"Thank you, Princess."

Catie was studying the trade loops they would need to make to distribute all the Paraxeans to Mangkatar and the three other Paraxean colonies. They would need to include a few pods of food with each delivery to allow each colony to absorb the new colonists without impacting their existing food supply. Fortunately, Onisiwo was like Earth, and had an adequate supply of food, plenty of which was available for export.

Their farmers would be happy to sell their surplus crops. Onisiwo's population was just under four billion. They had managed to get control over the birth rate over fifty years ago, and now they were reaping the benefits. The various economies of the five nations on the planet were healthy, and their citizens all benefited from a good standard of living. Much about Onisiwo modeled what her father hoped Earth would evolve to.

Catie identified four suppliers in the other coalitions where they could acquire the types of appliances and machines that the colonies would need and want. The weather pattern and seasons would determine where she could buy the crops she would need, but that would help all the farmers since it would deplete the stockpiles and allow them to sell at better prices once they were ready to harvest.

The problem she had was that Chair Lexisen had outmaneuvered everyone by getting the manufacturing for the cabins set up in the Northern Coalition. Trying to move or redistribute that work would take more time. Time they could not afford.

"ADI, can you map out the supply chain they're using for the cabins. I'm looking for where we can push work and purchases out to the other coalitions."

"Yes, Cer Catie. I have done that already. Unfortunately, Chair Lexisen had his friends make orders that extend out for six months. It will be difficult to redistribute those orders."

"What a scuzzbag."

"An appropriate assessment. Unfortunately, he is a smart scuzzbag."

"Hi, Catie," Liz said as she and Catie started their Comm chat.

"Hi, Liz. How are things going back in Sol?"

"Good. I just sent you a video of the triplets and the twins playing in the obstacle course. The triplets loved it. The twins have promised to take them every time they come up."

"They don't have to wait for the twins."

"No, but for now, it's a social thing. The twins are going to use working with the triplets to guilt Kal into allowing them to come up twice a month."

Catie laughed. "Those two are always working every angle."

"True. The triplets did great. They might be able to rival the twins after a year or so. Anyway, how are you doing?"

"Busy, we're sending the first load of Paraxeans off to the closest Paraxean colony tomorrow. The Dutchman should break orbit tonight.

Since the Onisiwoens only made some of the cabins, they've been shuttling the rest of them up all day."

"Where have they been staying?"

"Here at the embassy; it's a hotel after all."

"You must be excited."

"I am, but then I think about managing the next four loads and all the work and coordination necessary. Makes my eyes roll up to the top of my head. It's all I can do to not scream."

"Well, I've got some good news, the next StarMerchant is ready for its space trials."

"Oh, great. I thought it would be ready by now. I didn't have a chance to check in with Ajda. She's been ignoring my status requests."

"That's because you're asking for an update every day."

"So?"

"So, quit being a pest. Now that it's ready, we need to name it."

"Oh, I've picked out a name already. The Resolve, if you're okay with it?"

"What's that, another ghost ship?"

"Yep, it was found floating off Newfoundland back in 1884. It was actually named the Resolven, but that's Gaelic for Resolve."

"Okay, that works for me. I reviewed your trade list; it looks okay to me."

"Great," Catie sighed. "What a boring job."

"You complain too much. Jobs can't all be exciting, some of them are just work."

"I know. Captain McAvoy suggested that we have the cargo master do it, and then we captains will just need to review and approve it."

"I'm good with that. It's not my favorite job anyway. How are you doing with the rest of your assignment?"

"Okay. You know that Daddy stuck me here just like sending me to another year at the Academy. He's making me do all this work just because he thinks it'll be good for me."

"And, it will be good for you. You have to learn how to run a billion-dollar business."

"Why? That's Fred's job."

"I'm talking about StarMerchants. With the Resolve, we'll have over half a billion in assets and they're going to be trading continuously for the next two years. And that's before all the business we'll be doing once we start trading with the other civilizations the Paraxeans know about."

"True, but aren't we going to hire someone like Fred?"

"Yes, but we still have to understand what they're doing so we can manage them. And don't you think it's good to learn all this stuff before you show up at some new civilization's fringe and start asking them about trade? You'll be dealing with politicians and corporate bigwigs then, too."

"Yeah, I guess you can't get away from those types," Catie sighed. "I'm just getting claustrophobic. I'm stuck in this embassy, and Morgan has a fit every time I suggest going out to explore Onisiwo."

"I can imagine. You need to wait until we get to know them better. I'm still not sure how trustworthy they are, especially after reading about how Chair Lexisen manipulated things to give his coalition an advantage."

"I guess."

"Hey! You've got that entire hotel. Bring some entertainment in, like the Four Seasons did with Miguel's band."

"Speaking of Miguel, are you guys dating?"

"We did. He's off on tour in Europe, but he's going to move to Delphi City, so we'll see each other when he's not touring. We'll see how it goes."

"Has anyone built a recording studio?"

"No, and no I don't think you should do it. Let someone else get a jump on a new business."

"I was just thinking of Mariam Beaulieu; she's into music and engineering."

"Give her a hint and we'll see what she does. You know she's out there on the Victory?"

"Yes, I'll send her a message."

"Great. Hey, guess who sent me an email asking about joining Delphi Forces?"

"Who?" Catie gave Liz a shrug to indicate that she had no idea.

"Commander Questa Bastien."

"Oh, from the ISS? Why didn't she contact me?"

"She probably did. I just got it, so you'll probably get one on the next data dump."

Once the jump gates were in place between Earth and the various planets, the Delphineans had placed a satellite into each system. It recorded all of the data from that system, and every twenty-four hours they would open the wormhole so they could send a relay to Earth, while another relay probe would jump from Earth. Each would do a data dump from the satellite on the other side of the wormhole to the satellite in the system with them. That kept the satellite in each system synced with the data from Earth. Eventually, the data from all the various worlds would make it to each of the other worlds via Earth. It was like a digital mail system that would keep all the systems in sync. The quantum relays just didn't have enough bandwidth to handle all the information that needed to be transmitted between systems.

"Commander Questa's message is in your inbox, Cer Catie," ADI informed her.

"Why does Commander Questa want to join us?"

"She's hoping to go on one of the next exploration missions."

"Well, she'd better hurry. She needs to go through Uncle Blake's fast Academy first."

"I know that and I told her. There's a class starting next month, so if she comes now, she'll be able to get in, I assume you'll recommend her."

"Sure, but all she needs is your recommendation."

"Maybe, but to sneak into the next class might require more than just my recommendation, there's a pretty long waiting list."

"I'll tell Uncle Blake. But I'm jealous, I'll still be stuck here when they start that mission."

"Probably. And I think they're going to swap the Roebuck for the Sakira, so they can use the Roebuck for the mission."

"No, I think the first frigate will be ready before then. They'll probably send it here and have the crew swap over, Uncle Blake wants to keep the Sakira close."

"That's probably right, I forgot about the frigates. Anyway, I'll talk to you later."

"Bye." Catie closed the channel, then crossed her arms across her chest as she sat back in her seat.

"Cer Catie, are you depressed?" ADI asked.

"No, ADI. . . . Maybe a little. I can't believe we're going to send out an exploration mission and I won't be able to go."

"There will be many such missions in the future. You will probably start finding them boring."

"Not as boring as this." Catie went back to reviewing all the requests she was getting from the Onisiwoens about trade opportunities.

◆ ◆ ◆

Three days later, Catie was awakened by the song 'Happy Birthday'.

"ADI, thanks, . . . I think."

"I wanted to be the first to say happy birthday. I know that you won't be able to hold your usual celebration."

"That's okay. I'm happy to avoid any big princess-themed birthday parties. I hope Sam doesn't have any surprises planned."

"I'm confident that she doesn't."

◆ ◆ ◆

Later that evening Catie got a call from Captain McAvoy. "Princess, Zoey is asking if you can come up and discuss some things with her."

"We can't do it over a Comm channel?"

"I'm sure you could, but she seemed to want to do it in person."

"Alright, I'll be there in an hour."

"Thank you."

"Morgan, I have to go up to the Roebuck. Do you want to go with me?"

"Hey, bodyguard," Morgan said pointing at herself, then she pointed at Catie and said, "body."

"Very funny. I'm leaving in twenty minutes. If I'm lucky, I'll lose you on the way to the roof."

"Just try."

When their Lynx landed in the Roebuck flight bay, they had to wait for the bay to repressurize before exiting it.

"Hey, aren't you supposed to be designing a shuttle that can land in a flight bay without depressurizing the whole bay?" Morgan asked.

"I've designed it. I just need to get enough priority to build one. But my plan was to get Uncle Blake to buy them for Delphi Forces Starships by putting one on the Dutchman to rub their noses in it."

"Well, rub their noses in it by using it as a personal shuttle for the embassy."

"They have to install the iris for it to be useful."

"Well, the iris must be cheap compared to a shuttle. You should give that to them for free."

"Good idea. . . . Pressure's equalized. Let's go."

Captain McAvoy was waiting for them by the airlock. She must have been waiting inside the airlock for the pressure to equalize to already be inside the bay. "Welcome aboard, Princess."

"Catie."

"Okay. Welcome aboard, Catie. If you'll follow me, Zoey is waiting in the lounge."

Catie and Morgan followed Captain McAvoy into the airlock, cycled through it, then took the elevator down to the rec level. At that point, it was a long walk along the passageway through engineering to get to the lounge.

"Hey, why don't we have those cool lifts like on Star Trek?" Morgan asked.

"What do you mean?"

"You know, the ones that move you laterally as well as vertically. You always get off at your destination, none of these long walks."

"Sounds like an inefficient use of space."

"That was TV, they didn't want to waste time having you watch people walk," Captain McAvoy pointed out. "Too much dead airtime."

"Still, it would be cool."

"Just visualize that you're still on the lift while you're walking. Then you can pretend you're just as cool."

"Here we are." Captain McAvoy opened the door to the lounge and stepped back.

"Happy Birthday!" everyone in the lounge shouted out.

The lounge was crowded with Onisiwoens, a few Paraxeans, and lots of the crew. Kasper was standing in front of the door with two glasses of Champagne.

"We couldn't have you spending your birthday alone." Kasper handed Catie one of the glasses. "And what seventeen-year-old wouldn't want to get a little drunk on her birthday."

Catie teared up as she took the glass. "Thank you."

"No, thank you. They guard this Champagne like it was gold. This was the only excuse we could come up with to requisition a few cases."

Catie laughed. It helped her to stop the tears.

Kasper raised his glass and offered a toast. "To Princess Catherine, Captain McCormack, Lieutenant McCormack, Catie, Cadet MacGregor, and whoever she is today!"

"To Catie!"

"Thanks everyone. I hope you don't expect a speech."

"No speeches. We've cleaned your cabin, so plan on staying up here tonight," Captain McAvoy said. "Now go have fun."

Catie enjoyed the evening, and for the first time since her celebration after the victory over the Paraxeans, she didn't count glasses of Champagne. Her friends and parents all called in to wish her a happy birthday. All in all, it wasn't a bad birthday for being eighty light-years from home. Different people kept coming up with reasons to have a toast, and Catie joined in all of them.

"Thanks, guys!"

"Morgan planned it. We just jumped on board," Kasper said.

"Thanks, Morgan, sorry I wanted to lose you earlier."

"No problem; you get a pass since it's your birthday."

Catie took Liz's advice and talked to the hotel about bringing in some form of entertainment. They told her that the lounge in the other tower had a nightly music act. Catie insisted that they needed something inside the embassy's tower, and after a bit of negotiation, the hotel agreed to help reconfigure one of the conference rooms into a bar. They would schedule acts to come in and play as long as the Delphi Embassy covered the minimum charge. They also agreed to configure the ballroom so that it could host plays. The city's local repertory theater agreed to stage a few shows.

Captain McAvoy came down for the first play. Charlie, who had been posted to the embassy as an official liaison officer also joined Catie for the play. A third of the Roebuck's crew came down, and along with guests from the other tower and employees of the embassy, they were a respectful audience of one hundred people.

Catie was curious about how their Comms would do translating the language of the play. It was set in early Onisiwoen history, so the language would be different than what the translation program had been based on. ADI assured her that the translation program would be up to the challenge.

Charlie explained the play as they found their seats. Of course, the Princess and her guests were seated in the best seats, a raised dais in the back of the theater with room for her and six guests.

"This play is about two young people who fall in love, but their families hate each other. But their love is so intense it transcends those barriers and, . . . that's the gist of it. You'll have to watch the play."

"Sounds like Romeo and Juliet," Captain McAvoy said.

"Romeo and Juliet?" Charlie gave Captain McAvoy a questioning look.

"It's an old Earth play about two young lovers."

"Well, you'll have to see."

"Okay. Now tell me, if you didn't know better, you'd swear that Shakespeare wrote that," Captain McAvoy said.

"It was almost the same, but different. The language wasn't quite Shakespearean. That made it more different than an alternate staging of Romeo and Juliet would be," Catie said.

"But if you staged Romeo and Juliet here, don't you think the audience would just assume it was an alternate staging?"

"Even if they're similar, if you told them the play was from Earth, they'd probably like it and see the differences," Charlie said. "Would it be possible for me to read this Romeo and Juliet?"

"Sure, I'll send it to your Comm," Catie said. "If you want, I can send all of Shakespeare's plays."

"Oh, that would be wonderful. My cousin is the artistic director of a small company down the coast. He might want to stage some of these plays."

"Really?"

"Yes, it would be a niche, 'Plays from Earth'. Earth is going to be a big draw for a long time."

"Well, at least the copyright has expired."

"That is even better. Do you have more plays that have expired copyrights?"

"Let me look and I'll get back to you."

Chapter 5   Board Meeting – Dec 5th

"Let's get this meeting started," Marc said as he sat at his desk. Everyone was on the Commlink. A few looked tired, syncing a meeting up among time zones on Earth and multiple planets, was problematic. "Fred, you have the honor of going first."

"Thanks, Pal, that just means they're all eager to chew me up."

"No way! We're eager to hear your news."

"Okay. Well, this week MacKenzie Discoveries became the richest corporation on Earth."

"All right!" Blake already had the bottle of Scotch ready. He passed drinks out to all the attendees on Delphi Station. "The rest of you guys have to get your own."

"Don't worry about us, it's too early to drink anywhere else."

"It's never too early."

"Is there anything else?"

"Yes, we're trying to figure out how to source the cabins for future colony missions. If we ramp up enough to keep up with the demand, we're going to have a lot of excess capacity pretty soon."

"Not really. I'm sure that we'll be sending more colonists to Artemis once we're done moving the Paraxeans," Catie said. "We don't seem to have a problem attracting candidates."

"Catie's right. We should plan on one load of colonists every one to two months."

"You're the boss. So, do we want to build them in Delphi City?"

"I think we should build them in Indonesia," Nikola said. "One of our assembly plants for the solar panels is there. I was talking to the owner last week and she indicated that she would like to expand her operation."

"Is building cabins a good complement to her existing business?" Fred asked.

"No, but she has a cousin who owns a small construction company. Building cabins is like building a house. She would provide all the electrical and plumbing and of course solar panels."

Catie got excited and leaned forward to get everyone's attention. "If we modify the design a little, it would be like building a manufactured home. Indonesia always suffers from housing shortages. The cabins would be a great starter home. And you might even want to use them as starter homes for the colonists when they start moving out to their land."

"You're sure excited, and you won't even be able to grab a piece of the action," Blake said.

"Hey, I just like finding ways to make the world a better place. Getting a piece of the action is just icing on the cake."

"If you approve, I'll assign an engineer to look at it," Nikola said. "And I'll have someone do research on rules for manufactured homes in Indonesia."

"Approved," Fred said. Everyone was surprised that Fred was the one to approve it. Things were changing.

"Okay, anything else?" Marc asked.

"The frigates, but Blake should cover that."

"Thanks, Fred. Our first frigate has just passed its space trials. We're crewing it up. It will be going to Onisiwo to trade places with the Roebuck so we can send the Roebuck on a planetary exploration mission."

"Are you going to swap the ships, or swap the crews?" Catie asked.

"We're going to let Captain McAvoy decide. She'll move over to the frigate, which needs a name by the way."

"I have a whole list of names," Catie said. "That is if you're interested."

"Sure, tell us."

"Well, we're going to have two classes of frigates, the explorer class, like the Roebuck and the fighter class. For the explorer class, I think we should follow the naming convention we started with the Roebuck, so

Bounty, Surprise, Beagle, and Aventurier are the names of famous explorer ships."

"I like that, although isn't the Surprise fictitious?"

"No, there actually was one, but most people know the name from Patrick O'Brian's Aubrey novels or the movie *Master and Commander*."

"Interesting, and for the fighting ships?"

"Ironsides, Comte, Merlin, Charon, Françoise, Romulus, Ulysses, and Drake. Although we could use Drake for an explorer ship if we need to. I've got a few more names of famous frigates if we need more."

"All of them are American or British," Samantha noted.

"Two are French, but most are British. They kind of owned the seas back in the age of sail."

"True, I guess it would be a problem if we named a ship the Yamamoto."

"You think?!"

"Moving on!" Marc cut off the sidetrack. "Anyone else have something important before we turn to Catie's update?"

"No!" Blake rubbed his hands with glee, giving Catie a hungry look.

"Be nice! I have a lot of stuff. It's been in my daily reports if anyone's reading them."

"We're busy."

Catie ignored the comment from Blake. "Okay, first, as you should all know, we sent the first load of Paraxean colonists off to Paraxea's first colony two weeks ago; it should arrive in three more weeks. We're accelerating the process of bringing the Paraxeans out of stasis in anticipation of the Resolve showing up next month."

"Resolve?"

"Yes, we named the second StarMerchant Resolve, after the Resolven, another famous ghost ship. The Onisiwoens are ramping up the cabin construction, so they should be able to handle the entire order by our third load of Paraxeans."

"That's good," Samantha said.

"Kind of. But the delegate from the Northern Coalition, who also happens to be the Chair of the Planetary Council, has managed to get most of the contracts to benefit the Northern Coalition. We're looking for places where we can redirect some of the work, but it's not easy."

"Oh, outmaneuvered."

"Uncle Blake!"

"Hey, don't sweat it, I'm sure he'd have outmaneuvered any of us. He's got home-field advantage. Are you planning on doing anything about it?"

"I am. He also managed to get the Paraxean ambassador to give him an exclusive on Comms. I'm going to give a deal on Delphinean Comms to the competitor, kind of an object lesson."

"Be careful that you don't teach the wrong lesson," Marc said. "But I'd do the same thing."

"Thanks, Daddy. Now, on to medical technology. I've given Dr. Moreau permission to give our fast tests for viruses and other pathogens to the Onisiwoens."

"Good."

"I've also told her to go ahead and work out an organ donor program with them. I assume we won't charge anything over cost."

"Right, but keep the printers on the Roebuck."

"I already told her that. And she's going to start testing the birth control nanites on Onisiwoens."

"Don't they have their own method?" Samantha asked.

"They do, but apparently it has some undesirable side effects, so why not? And before you say anything, I told her we would have to control distribution."

"Agreed."

"And before I give an update on the probes, I have a general issue. How do we deal with access to Earth's internet and deal with copyrighted material?"

"Why wouldn't we do the same thing we're doing with Paraxea?" Fred asked.

"We can, but what about stuff without copyrights, like plays by Shakespeare, or just junk on the internet. We're keeping Artemis and Earth synced up, and now Onisiwo. But that information has value. Should we do the same for Paraxea, and give them access to Earth's internet?"

"We should call it the starnet," Liz said.

"Or the galaxynet," Kal said.

"Name aside. That access has value. My question is, should we tap into it?"

"It also would help to bring the members of the Delphi League closer together," Samantha added.

"Earth's internet is government funded," Admiral Michaels said. "We should have the Delphi League fund the galaxynet."

"I agree . . ."

"Hey, what's wrong with starnet?"

"Galaxynet seems more accurate. Besides, it's bigger."

"Okay!" Marc said in a raised voice to grab everyone's attention. "But if we do that, we have to come up with some way to fund the League Government. Right now, it's just us paying for everything."

"Do the same thing as the U.N., have member planets contribute to the budget," Samantha suggested.

"Sam, I think I hate you," Admiral Michaels said.

Everyone laughed at Admiral Michaels' displeasure at being handed another thorny issue to bring up with Earth's various governing bodies.

"Sorry. But I'll work with ADI and the Paraxean president on defining a budget. Then we'll just submit the proposal to the League Council."

"That means we have to have a method of selecting delegates." Admiral Michaels rubbed his face as he thought about the politics and all the meetings he'd have to deal with to get Earth to align on a method of selecting a delegate.

"Well, each world will have to come up with its own method," Samantha explained.

"That's why I hate you."

"Okay, you guys can figure that out later," Catie said. "Now our probes. The first explorer probe will jump into its target system next week. It'll take two weeks for it to get to the planet and start taking readings. We already know a lot about the planet from its first visit. But this time it will actually make orbit and send small probes to take samples."

"Okay, and our other probe?" Marc asked.

"It should jump into its system a week later. If things go well, by the end of the month we'll have two planets for the Aperanjens to survey."

"Shouldn't we just send the Aperanjen survey team out on the first frigate, so they can move to the Roebuck and leave from Onisiwo?" Liz asked.

"The Merlin."

"Sure, we can name it the Merlin. And yes, we could do that," Marc said. "It would save them a month. They can transfer to the Roebuck and just head to whichever planet is the best option. I'm sure they're willing to bet that one of the probes finds a suitable planet before they have to jump from Onisiwo."

"Catie, that means you have to get most of the cargo for the mission from Onisiwo," Samantha said.

"Oh joy!"

Chapter 6   The Merlin

"Now I have to rush and select the crew for the Merlin," Blake thought. *"Damn, Jackie and I were supposed to spend the week on the Mea Huli.* Call Jackie,"* Blake ordered his Comm.

"Hello, Jackie Drummond speaking."

"Hey sweetheart, something's come up and I won't be able to take the week off."

"What? Why can't you work from the Mea Huli?"

"I could try, but I'm afraid I'd wake up with the anchor rope around my neck trying to hang onto the dive deck."

"Oh, that's true, you probably would. Oh well."

"I'll call Caesar and cancel."

"Don't you dare!"

"Why not?"

"I've already set everything up with my staff so I can take the week off, so I'm taking it off. I'm sure I'll be able to find some friends to go out with me."

"Okay," Blake groaned. "Do you need me to do anything?"

"No, I'll take care of everything. I'll see you when we get back."

"Bye. . . . Call Kal."

"What's up, Bro?"

"Is that any way to talk to your commanding officer?"

"What's got your knickers in a twist?"

"Well, Liz's idea about the Aperanjens means I have to finish selecting the crew for the Merlin this week."

"Oh! . . . So, does that mean the Mea Huli is available?"

"No, Jackie's still going. She says she'll just invite some friends."

"Just a moment, I've got a call from Sandra. . . . How come your problems always come back to mess up my life?" Kal asked when he came back on the call with Blake.

"What, Jackie invited Sandra?"

"Yes."

"Great. Then you have time to come up and help me select the crew."

"What do I know about selecting sailors?"

"Probably nothing, but we have to pick a Marine contingent too."

"I usually delegate things like that."

"But you have all that time on your hands now. Come up and I'll buy the beer."

"Damn it, that's the second one I've lost to the Merlin," Liz complained.

"I'm sorry," Barty said. "Do you want me to see if I can get someone to come in early?"

"No, by the time you find someone, my next candidate will be here. I'll find something to do. ... Call Catie."

"Liz, do you know what time it is?"

"It's 1100."

"Well, it's 0230 here!"

"Sorry. I just lost two people I was interviewing for the Resolve to your uncle."

"Oh, he's crewing the Merlin."

"Right. Anyway, I had time so I thought I'd follow up about the shuttle."

"I thought Nikola was going to do that."

"No, she's doing the cabins."

"Oh, right. Okay, what do you want to know?"

"Do you have the design ready?"

"Pretty close. It's just a hover Lynx wrapped in a different shell. It's bigger, but all the electronics are the same."

"Send me the designs."

"Sent."

"This thing looks like a vitamin capsule."

Catie laughed. "It does, doesn't it."

"How can it fly?"

"Once it's out of the flight bay, the shell for the bottom third rolls up. It's just there so the iris will seal to it. Then wings and a tail can be extended. It's a bit more aerodynamic then, look on the last page."

"I see. That doesn't make it much more aerodynamic."

"It's not much worse than one of the old space shuttles. With the grav drives, it doesn't have to be that aerodynamic."

"Good thing. How many people can it carry?"

"Twenty-six, plus the two pilots."

"Okay, I'll talk to Ajda and see if she can squeeze in a couple. If she can, I'll send one out to you."

"Thanks."

"Go back to sleep. Sorry I woke you."

"Hey, if I get a shuttle, it'll be worth it."

Liz sent an email to Ajda with the shuttle designs.

Councilor Faroot, the leader of the Aperanjens on Delphi Station, paused at Blake's door. "Admiral Blake, may I have a moment?"

"Of course, what can I do for you?"

"I've been told that we are leaving at the end of the week."

"That's correct. Yesterday, we came up with a schedule that gets you to the first planet a month earlier. That is assuming you can be ready."

"We can be ready," Councilor Faroot said. He was clearly annoyed at having to adjust his plans. "I just would prefer to have things more organized."

Blake had to suppress a laugh. He definitely didn't want to piss the Aperanjen off; they reminded him of the 'Thing' from the 'Fantastic Four', rock hard with very big muscles. Of course, what did you expect from a race that came from a planet with fifty percent higher gravity than Earth?

"I apologize for the inconvenience. I'm having to rush to get things ready as well. But we assumed you would want to take advantage of the accelerated schedule."

"We will be ready. Are there any other changes we need to be aware of?"

"No, just the schedule change."

Councilor Faroot left Blake's office. Blake was glad that the doors were automatic and slid open and shut, he wouldn't want to see what happened when an Aperanjen slammed a door.

Catie was sitting in her office reviewing the relationship map she and ADI had made. It showed all the connections in the supply chain to make the cabins and their links to Chair Lexisen. Over half of them involved a man called Constaxinavia. Catie remembered him as the slimy guy from the reception given by Chair Lexisen. Catie decided to call him Constantine. He was one of the big business moguls in the Northern Coalition. He even had business in the other coalitions, and the parts of the supply chain that were outside of the Northern Coalition invariably intersected with his business interests there.

"Chair Lexisen is so crooked it's a wonder he can stand up straight," Catie hissed.

"Cer Catie, I still cannot find a direct relationship between him and Constantine," ADI said.

"There must be something. Does Lexisen own part of one of Constantine's businesses? Does he have shares in any of them?"

"Not that I can find. It would be easier if you would allow me to hack their systems."

"What happened to Ms. 'Due Process'?"

"I assume you're not going to press charges."

"You're right, I just want to know how to steer our future investments and purchases so that the money doesn't wind up in Chair Lexisen's pockets."

"We don't know that the money is making its way into his pockets."

"Yeah, right. How much did you say his net worth has gone up since he was appointed?"

"Approximately two hundred million dollars," ADI replied.

"That means he's crooked, but also smart if you can't see how he's getting paid off. And that's just the money he admits to having. He could have a few hundred million stashed away somewhere else."

Chair Lexisen had entered public service in the Northern Coalition parliament as a middle-class lawyer. He had quickly risen through the ranks of power and his wealth had followed a similar trajectory. He was now worth over one billion. All from shrewd investments, at least that was the story.

"I will keep researching their systems. Also, our trading account is doing well. I have developed a model that predicts the swings in their markets with seventy percent accuracy."

"Great. Just don't go crazy. We don't want to upset them, just develop enough capital for some things I want to do later."

"Yes, Cer Catie."

"Zoey, I wonder if you can help me?"

"Certainly, Princess Catherine."

"Catie, please call me Catie."

"I'll try. What can I do for you?"

"I've gotten tangled up in the local politics a few times. I'm looking for someone who can help me navigate it better. We want to be careful with how we introduce technology to Onisiwo, but everyone I'm dealing with right now is looking for how they or their coalition can benefit, which means I'm not getting good advice."

"I can see your problem. Let me think about who might be a good candidate to help. It might take me a couple of days to come up with the right name."

"Just call me when you have one."

"Kal, how does it feel to be a bachelor?" Blake asked.

"Not as nice as it used to. I like being around Sandra."

"Has she domesticated you already?"

"Hey, we're a couple. We like doing things together."

"Who cooks dinner?"

"We trade off. Who cooks in your house?"

"Whichever restaurant we call for takeout," Blake said.

"Can you at least make breakfast?"

"I'm good with cereal."

Kal just shook his head. He tossed Blake a list of Marines via his HUD. "These are the ones we have available. You can tell Colonel Bailey you're stealing eight of his people."

"We're replacing them. He won't care."

"Keep telling yourself that. I'm not sure he's going to buy the height requirement."

Blake sighed. "He doesn't need to. He just needs to trade out the people I'm asking for. Let's go to the Rusty Nail and I'll buy you a drink."

The Rusty Nail was four floors up and almost directly above Blake's office. One would think that they'd chosen their location to be close to their best customer. Blake signaled the bartender that he wanted two of the usual as he led Kal to a corner table.

"You spend much time here?"

"A little. Sometimes I have to get out of the office, and with a HUD, I can get almost as much work done here as I can there."

"Yeah, until the third beer."

"Fourth, I weigh more than you."

The waitress came over with their beers. "Anything else I can get you?" She gave Blake a big smile.

"We're good for now."

"Does Jackie know how much the waitress likes you?"

"She just smiles at me because she knows I'm a big tipper. She makes an effort to keep people from sitting next to me when I'm here, so I give her a big tip."

"I'll have to see if I can get a bar to open over by my office in Delphi City."

"Give me a break, you're a five-minute walk from the closest bar."

"But you're what, two minutes from here. And you don't have to go outside."

"Eat your heart out. How are you and Sandra doing?"

"Good. We bought a couple of horses last week."

"Why, aren't the ones at the stable good enough for you?"

"They're great horses, Catie didn't skimp on them. But if you want to get really good, you need to have your own horse. Sandra is thinking about competing again."

"Oh, that's a change."

"She competed when she was a kid. She says she could never break through to the top because they couldn't afford a great horse."

"So, what did you pay for the two you bought?"

"Seventy thousand."

Blake spit some of his beer out as he gasped. "Seventy thousand?"

"Each."

"Wow, I would have loved to be there to see you write that check. You get the shakes when you have to spend over two hundred for dinner."

"I know. But that's what the best horses cost. Besides, what's money for?"

"Does your mother know?"

"No! And don't you go telling her."

"Don't worry, I won't. We share too many secrets; I can't afford to have you rat me out to my mother. So, how's the riding going?"

"I'm getting better. Sandra has me doing jumps now. It wasn't so bad when I was riding one of the stable horses, but with this new one . . ." Kal shook his head.

"What?"

"I swear to you, that horse is laughing at me. The second time I rode him, we were in the ring going over some small hurdles. No problem for him, but I'm still getting used to jumping. Anyway, he hops over one and as we're approaching the next one, he turns his head to me and slows a bit. I swear he was thinking about just walking over the hurdle to show me how annoyed he was at the lack of challenge."

"Well, you'll have to take him over some bigger hurdles."

"Yeah, it's not him making it over the hurdle that's in question, it's whether I can stay on him when he does."

"Does Sandra laugh at you?"

"I don't think so. At least I've never caught her. I'm getting better. Maybe next month I'll be ready to handle the one-meter hurdles."

"If she laughs at you, you could give her an Aikido lesson?"

"You tell me when you give Jackie one and I'll think about it."

"No way. Like my mother says, you have to sleep sometime. And Jackie plays golf."

"You don't think you could handle a nine iron to the head?"

"Nope. I always make sure she's happy before we go to bed."

"You guys thinking about getting married?"

Blake sighed. He reached into his pocket and pulled out a small box.

"You bought a ring?!"

"I was going to propose this week while we were on the Mea Huli."

"Boy, when your plans get screwed up, they really get screwed up. Does she know you're planning to ask her?"

"Probably. That's probably why she got mad. It's okay, I'll find a good time when she gets back."

"How much did you spend on the ring?"

"Two horses."

◆ ◆ ◆

"The Merlin will be here tomorrow," Catie told Captain McAvoy.

"I know."

"Have you decided what you're going to do about the crew?"

"I'm going to have Lieutenant Suzuki stay with the Roebuck. She needs a new start with a new crew."

"Anyone else?"

"I asked if anyone wanted to stay with the Roebuck, no takers. With another eighteen Foxes, we'll pick up another thirty-six pilots and fifty flight crew on the Merlin; otherwise, we'll all move over to the Merlin. Do you know Captain Blackwell?"

"Never heard of him," Catie replied. "I hope Suzuki can get along with him."

"I'm sure she will. Did you know she's the only native Japanese officer we have right now?"

"No, but I'm not surprised. Most of the officers are from the American or British forces, with a few from Canada and Australia. Daddy and Uncle Blake didn't trust the other services."

"I don't blame them. The only other services big enough to draw from would be the Chinese and Russians."

"Yeah, and no way would they trust them. We have some at the Academy, so things will change in a few years."

"Too bad we don't know some that we can trust. I know your uncle is getting a lot of pressure from the Russians about having a presence inside of Delphi Forces."

"I wouldn't trust a Russian any more than a snake. . . . Well, I would trust Colonel Malenkov, from the ISS. He was a straight shooter."

"You should mention him to your uncle, maybe he can bring him in to give the Russians a presence, take some of the pressure off."

"I will. He's met him too, so I bet he'd trust him."

The next day, Catie flew up to the Roebuck for the change of command ceremony. It was a little sad to see the crew shift over to the Merlin, knowing that the Roebuck was going off to explore a new planet.

"Hello, Wolf," Catie said. She was meeting with the Aperanjen surveyors before they headed off. "Are you excited to finally get to check out a planet?"

"We are, Princess. It has been a long wait."

"I have good news. Our probe started to survey the planet. Right now, it looks very promising. Air samples and soil samples show a good environment. Of course, it doesn't have tests that are specific to your biology, but it's a good sign."

"That is good news. It could mean we're only a few months away from starting our colony."

"I'm sure all of you are looking forward to being reunited with the rest of your crew. Once we find a suitable planet for you, we'll send one of the explorer probes off to try and find your homeworld. Maybe you will be able to start trading with them."

"That would be nice. I do want to ask about the status of our people here."

"They're still in stasis. Once you find a planet, we'll start waking them up. We don't really have a good place to keep them now, and we're still overwhelmed with the Paraxeans."

"I'm sure they would rather sleep through it. My people do not do well with inactivity. Being here waiting would be intolerable. Also, we don't want them to atrophy in the low gravity. Stasis is best."

As Catie was leaving to return to the planet, she noticed that she seemed to be the tallest person on the ship. The Aperanjens were typically around 172 cm or 5 foot 8 inches. But that seemed to be the height of everyone she saw. She couldn't believe Blake would have crewed the mission with short people so the Aperanjens wouldn't feel bad.

"Uncle Blake, how come everyone in the crew is short?" she messaged.

"You noticed?"

"Yes."

"Because they're going to a 1.5G planet. We don't want their hearts having to pump blood up too high."

"Really?"

"Yes! The doctors suggested it and the fitness test for the mission confirmed it. Anyone over five-ten failed. And the ones who passed were pretty marginal."

"Hmm. Well, I never like being at 1.5G acceleration. It is exhausting."

"There you go. Now, anything else?"

Catie wondered why Blake was so testy. She opted to ignore it and say goodbye.

"Bye."

Blake just cut the transmission without saying anything.

"Princess Catie." Zoey's call came early the next morning. Catie started to remind her to not call her Princess, but decided that Princess Catie was at least a step in the right direction.

"Hello, Zoey. Do you have a name for me?"

"I do. Neloln Baxurian, she was a reporter when I knew her. She was also the communication director for an earlier administration. Now she is teaching at one of our universities."

"Hmm, what makes her the right person?"

"One, you need someone who understands PR. You want to make sure that the general population understands how it is benefiting from your technology. Two, she has the highest integrity of anyone I know. She's always spoken out against corruption and is a vocal advocate of the common good. And three, she is teaching a course on morality in government."

"Okay, that sounds promising; can you introduce us?"

"I'll send her a message and ask her to meet you at the embassy."

"Cer Baxurian, I'm pleased that you have agreed to meet with me."

"Princess Catherine, I'm happy to meet with you. But please call me Neloln."

"Only if you'll call me Catie."

"I can do that."

"First, let me give you a Comm, it will help with the conversation. Here, press your finger here and it will register to you. Now if you'll put these in your ears, they'll block out the sound of my voice, and your Comm will provide a translation. Mine will do the same when you talk. We've found that that works best."

Neloln gave Catie a cautious look as she put the earwigs in her ear.

"Hold your finger against it for eight seconds and it'll seal. Do the same thing and it'll come loose so you can take it out."

"Ohh, that feels funny."

"It does the first few times. You can leave them in and your Comm will adjust them so it doesn't interfere with your hearing except when it's providing translations. Our people typically always have one in one ear so that their Comm can easily communicate with them."

"They do work; it feels like we're both speaking the same language. Okay, now to why I'm here. Zaragaxia told me that this was a chance of a lifetime. A chance to achieve my goals for Onisiwo."

Catie winced at the description. "I hope Zoey didn't oversell the position."

"Position?"

Catie struggled to hide her surprise; apparently, Zoey had not mentioned that this was a job interview. "Yes. I'm looking for someone to help me, as well as the Delphi League, to navigate Onisiwoen politics. We want to make sure that our actions benefit the whole planet. Zaragaxia, I call her Zoey, suggested that you were someone I could trust and someone who understood the local politics. She says you were the communication director for President Zopeax."

"I'm not interested in being a communication director again."

"And I don't want you to be. I'm sure you can help me find someone who could fill that role. What I need is someone to help me decide what technology to introduce to Onisiwo and when to do it. As I said, we want to do these things in a way that helps the entire planet. And the help I'm getting from the Planetary Council seems to be self-serving."

"I'm not surprised at that. Okay, let's talk some more. This does sound interesting."

Chapter 7   Resolve to Ship

The Dutchman was subjected to a lot of fanfare when she arrived at the Paraxean colony with her load of colonists. The colonists were excited to be getting new blood, and they were especially excited that the colonists who had been lost in the attack had been recovered.

The colony was well established with over two million inhabitants. They'd spread out along the coast of the continent they'd chosen to establish their colony on.

The Dutchman was met in orbit by a delegation from the planet. They immediately asked that Derek and the head of the Paraxean colonists join them down in the capital city for a reception. There was to be a big press conference followed by a party as the whole planet celebrated the arrival of the new colonists.

As Derek flew down to the capital, he was amazed at how unlike Paraxea it was. Instead of the megacities of Paraxea, the cities seemed small and spread out. The buildings were low, ten to fifteen stories, unlike the one hundred to one-hundred-fifty-story wonders he saw on Paraxea. Of course, a planet with only two million inhabitants was far different than a planet with over six billion inhabitants. Their ship landed next to a huge dome that covered what looked like a park. *"That must be bigger than Central Park. I wonder what it's for,"* Derek thought.

"Welcome to our colony," the overdressed governor of the colony greeted Derek. He was wearing a tuxedo with a big red sash, a top hat, and medals. To Derek, he looked like a caricature, Mr. Moneybags from Monopoly but with more color.

"I'm happy to be here, Governor."

"Come this way, the Mayor and the leader of our new colonists will keep the reporters fed. We can use the time to get to know each other and to explore a little."

Derek watched as another man dressed much like the governor greeted the leader of the new colonists and steered him toward the boundary set up by security. A gaggle of what could only be reporters eagerly awaited them.

"They're welcome to it."

"Yes, some people love to get their name in the press. The local mayor is one. I think he wants my job. Now, you don't know how excited we are to finally have real contact with our homeworld. And to receive so many new colonists will breathe real life into the colony."

"We're just happy that we could bring them here." Derek followed the governor to the dome. "This dome is huge, what's it for?"

"Oh, it gets very cold here in the winter. We enclosed this park so everyone would be able to enjoy the outdoors year-round. Come, let me show you."

The governor led Derek into the dome. "We're holding the reception in here at the rotunda across the way. As you can see, we have sports fields for organized play and open park areas so families with children can let them run around."

Derek paused to observe the game being played on the field they were passing. It looked a lot like soccer, but there weren't enough players on the field. The goal was strange too. The center of it was closed off, you could only score by putting the ball into the right or left side of the net, and those openings were angled to the outside. It also looked wider than a soccer net. The poor goalie was forced to choose which side to defend.

"That looks tough."

"Oh, it is. The team has to funnel the opposition to one side of the net to allow the goalie to have a chance. The opening is narrow, so the opposition has to get a good kick off, but if they can get someone free on the other side, it's an easy score."

"Is it a popular game?"

"It's the national sport."

"Is it from Paraxea?"

"No, we developed it here. Somebody just dreamt it up and it took off. I think it's popular because it's not from Paraxea."

"Do people resent Paraxea?"

"No, not at all, but having something we can call our own is important, too. We miss our homeworld; the galaxy is a lonely place, or was. With your jumpdrives that will change."

"That's true. They will allow cargo shipments and easy immigration; and I guess people will do some visiting, though two weeks of travel time to get here will be a deterrent."

"Only two weeks, I thought it was five."

"For us. It will be five weeks until we place jump gates; that will take a week off of the trip. Then if you're not carrying so much mass, you can accelerate faster and get out of the system in just a week."

The governor shifted his eyes as he tried to remember something. "How can you make it in less than four weeks?"

"We save our momentum. That means we're accelerating the entire time when we leave a system and decelerating the entire time after we enter a system."

"I see, then how do you save another week, surely you cannot stand three Gs of acceleration?"

"It's uncomfortable, but we have a profile that lets us do that. But I guess tourists wouldn't put up with that; so that means it would be a four-week trip."

"That's still not too bad, considering the distance traveled. It would be like crossing the ocean back in the days of sailing. Now, mind you, I wouldn't be wanting to make a four-week journey, especially if I was faced with having to make another one to get home a few months later."

"Yes, I guess those video calls don't seem too bad when you put them up against that."

"They wouldn't, but we can't afford to have many of those. They're restricted to official business because the quantum relays have such limited bandwidth. That means that most people are out of touch with Paraxea. But I understand that you are bringing a way to solve that problem."

Derek laughed. "We are; we have a satellite with a copy of Paraxea's recent entertainment, movies, TV, and music. We'll put it in orbit tomorrow. We will also start to establish a jump gate here that will allow us to put a satellite at your fringe that will transmit a current copy of their digital internet. We're calling it Galaxynet. It will be a few months before that's up and running, but when it is, you'll be able to access anything within a day, two at the most."

"Excellent. That means we can actually email friends and family; we don't get responses to official emails in less time than that."

"You'll need to talk to Samantha Newman, the Delphi League Minister of State before we can set it up."

"I know, we've already talked. Just a small matter of taxes. Insignificant compared to the value." The governor leaned in and lowered his voice. "I understand you've also brought some delicacies from Paraxea with you."

Catie had made sure that Derek had stocked up on candy, liquors, wines, and any other luxury items they could acquire on Paraxea. She'd stressed that after all, they were in business to make money.

"We did. I've brought a case of your favorite whiskey. It should be coming down on the first load."

"Ah, we do miss things like that. We were hoping to produce it here, but the grain we need doesn't like this planet. We have substitutes, but they're nothing like the original."

The colony had been established approximately one hundred years ago. Most of the colonists had been brought out of stasis over the last forty years, so they still had fond memories of Paraxea.

It took an extra day to drop all the cargo pods on the planet. Unlike at Paraxea, they had to bring them all down to the planet instead of just leaving them in orbit. And they had to lift the new cargo pods since the colony hadn't had a SkyLifter to put them in orbit. Each of the cabin pods which were full of colonists was directed to a specific city or town. The leaders of the colonists had spent weeks discussing how to bring the new colonists into the colony. It had been decided that they would be distributed to the newer communities. Those communities were still establishing themselves and would readily welcome a new influx of colonists. And more importantly, they still had a small-town mentality where all members of the community helped to raise the children. This would be especially important since most of the women among the new colonists had six to ten children each. This was further complicated since the children generally had different fathers. The Fazullans had discouraged the formation of a family where both a mother and a father looked after the welfare of the children. The former slaves were still trying to establish relationships with each other while trying to recover from the years of slavery.

After a long day of shifting people and cargo, the Dutchman started her return voyage. It would backtrack toward Onisiwo since it would be able to jump to Earth by connecting with one of the jump points they'd put in place for Onisiwo. Then they'd be able to use the jump points between Earth and Paraxea to do the same thing.

"We're here!" Liz announced over Catie's Comm as the Resolve jumped into Onisiwo's outer system.

"Liz!"

"Hey, Girl. How are you doing?"

"I'm fine, but you're not really here, you're still two weeks out."

"Hey, that's closer than we were when we started out."

"How's the crew shaping up?"

"They're doing fine. Miranda's making a fine navigator."

"You never told me how you got her?"

"Horse trading with Blake. He's having trouble staffing the frigates and their flight crews, so we traded a few of our more experienced officers for some Academy grads. Miranda's a bit miffed at being pulled from the Foxes, but she's still a reserve pilot. We can't afford to have a bunch of pilots sitting around running simulations."

"What about Freddie?"

"He's happily flying Oryxes between Delphi City and Delphi Station. Those guys are in real demand since Blake has sucked off as many people as he can to fill out the flight crews for the Françoise."

"Maybe that's why he was so testy when I talked with him last."

"I don't think that's what it was."

"Spill, what do you know?!"

"A little elf told me that Blake was going to pop the question while he and Jackie were out on the Mea Huli. He had to cancel his time off to deal with all the staffing issues created by sending the Merlin out a month early."

"He was going to pop the question and he didn't tell me?!"

"Hey, he's supposed to ask Jackie first."

"I guess. Anyway, I can't wait 'til you get here."

Board Meeting – Jan 9th

"I call this meeting to order." Marc glanced at all the faces on his video feed. "It has been an eventful three months. We've repatriated the first of the Paraxean colonists, and Catie assures me she will be able to complete the mission by June.

"We have also achieved some notable milestones on our primary mission. Earth has seen one half of a degree drop in its average temperature, showing results from our efforts with fusion power, solar panels, electric vehicles, and reforestation. If the trend continues, we should start seeing a decline in ocean levels as well as a more marked drop in the CO_2 level. So, I want everyone to take a deep breath, relax, congratulate each other. We have a long way to go, but we have a clear path to get there.

"Now, Fred, can you update us on the business side of things?"

"Nikola can provide details, but we've reached an agreement with her friend in Indonesia to start manufacturing the cabins there. It will be a boost to the local economy, and as Nikola suggested, it segues well into the manufacturing of prefab housing. And of a much higher quality than comes to mind when most of us think of prefab housing."

There was a light round of applause for Nikola before Fred continued. "Our solar panels and fusion plants are continuing to drive our bottom line. And the Russians are continually crying for more of the small fusion reactors. Their sales of locomotives and cargo ships have skyrocketed. Soon over half of new locomotives put into service worldwide will be fusion powered and already half of new cargo ships are."

"Sounds like it's time to start selling those fusion plants to other countries," Samantha said. "Korea would be the next logical step, they're already a leading supplier of cargo ships."

"You heard her, Fred," Marc said.

"Noted. Moving on, we've moved all battery production to Malaysia to make room for our expanded production of Comms and other electronics based on our microgravity IC production. And finally, we've leased out a quad for Delphi City's third luxury hotel."

"Excellent news, keep up the good work. Kal, how are you doing?"

"I'm doing fine. Sandra and I bought a couple of horses and have been riding every day. . . ."

Marc rolled his eyes at Kal's blatant misinterpretation. "I meant your Marines?"

"Oh. Well, we've reshuffled our staffing so we can crew the frigates as they come off the line. We'll push to expand our recruiting to backfill, but that won't require too much. I've promoted Colonel Toliver to general. He'll be commanding our Space Marines."

"What does that leave for you to do?" Blake asked.

"I already said Sandra and I were riding every day." Kal and Blake were both having trouble stifling their laughs.

"Next! Admiral Michaels?"

"I'm still up to my neck in discussions on Delphi League, especially discussions about taxes. We continue to see progress in Africa. We'll be adding three fusion power plants, one in Kenya, one in Tanzania, and another in Egypt."

"That sounds promising," Samantha said.

"It is, but time will tell. The hope is that as their economies improve, those countries' economic gains will spill over to other nations on the continent. When we put a plant in the Congo, then you'll know we're making real progress."

"Good. Do you need anything else from us?" Marc asked.

"I think I've gotten all the help I can stand right now."

Samantha laughed and gave the Admiral a little wave.

"Samantha, you seem to have the floor."

"Negotiations with the colonies about taxes have gone surprisingly well. They're so excited about having easy contact with their homeworlds that the taxes are considered a minor issue. Not the same with Paraxea and Onisiwo, but we'll get there."

"Good to hear. Liz, how are you doing?"

"We're a week out from Onisiwo. We'll make orbit on Saturday. The new crew is shaping up fine. We've got Sam's latest shipment for Catie, as well as Catie's Comm shipment."

"Comm shipment?"

"I told you we were going to introduce them over the Paraxean sweetheart deal."

"Yes, but I thought you were going to wait longer."

"I am, but it'll be another three months before the Resolve makes it back, so we pushed hard to get them on this shipment."

Marc's eyes rolled up; he was obviously doing the math in his head. "I guess with the triangle route, it's a long time between hitting the same port. Okay Liz, go on."

"We have our first space shuttle on board. We have a few technicians finishing it up en route. But it should be ready to finish testing when we make orbit."

"Are you going to leave it with the Merlin?" Samantha asked.

"Yes, it's Catie's shuttle. We have an iris in our cargo hold that the Merlin can install in its smaller flight bay. We hope it proves so convenient that you'll order one for all the frigates."

"Geez," Blake exclaimed, "you're getting as bad as Catie."

"Hey, we're in business."

"We can tell."

"Okay, moving on! Catie, how are things going?"

"Before I start, Uncle Blake, do you remember Colonel Malenkov, from the ISS?"

"Of course, I do."

"Have you thought about bringing him into Delphi Forces?"

"No, but that's a good idea. We're getting a lot of pressure from the Russians to bring in some of their senior people. I'm pretty sure we can trust him."

"And I can test him," ADI chimed in.

"I'll send a note out to him."

"Done," ADI said.

"Now that that's out of the way, Catie, go on."

"Okay. One of our probes just reached the second planet we're considering for the Aperanjens. The initial survey looks okay but not as good as the first planet. I'm sure you all know that the Roebuck jumped into the first planet's solar system yesterday. They should be starting the aerial survey any day now."

"I heard. They're certainly excited. Now go on."

"We're working around the clock getting the Paraxeans out of stasis and ready for the Resolve. It'll be like that until June when we will finally be able to send the Aperanjens on to their colony. I'm pretty sure we'll have one by then."

"Are the Onisiwoens keeping up with the demand for cabins?"

"They're getting there. After the Dutchman does its next load, we'll be able to source all the cabins locally."

"Have you figured out how Chair Lexisen has been manipulating things?" Samantha asked.

"We've traced who benefits. This guy Constantine, I can't pronounce his real name, seems to be the one getting most of the deals. He's one of their richest people and he owns a lot of businesses. We cannot find a link between him and Chair Lexisen other than they attend the same parties."

"Can't you dig deeper?" Blake asked.

"We're trying, but unless you want us to break into their systems, it's slow."

"We don't want to break into their systems," Marc said. "Just keep at it. You'll find the link. What else?"

"We've started trading in their stock market. ADI has it pretty well figured out. We're keeping it small, but it will allow us to buy trade goods without relying on the government. That way we can control who benefits better."

"Just be careful," Marc warned.

"We will be."

"Anything else before we close the meeting?"

"I have one thing," Nikola said. "It's a licensing decision."

"For what?"

"Chewing gum and bubble gum."

"Do we have to discuss that here?"

"It is a licensing deal, and all licensing deals are supposed to be reviewed by the board."

"I want to hear about it," Catie said. She'd lived under the tyranny of her father's no chewing gum rule for her whole life. Now was the time for some payback.

"The head of the maintenance council came to me last year."

"Maintenance council?"

"Yes, all the maintenance supervisors have formed a council where they can share learning and best practices. Someone on the prime minister's staff came up with the idea."

"Okay, go on," Marc said, resigning himself to suffering through the presentation.

"Anyway, they told me that their single largest 'unnecessary expense' was due to chewing gum and bubble gum. People stick them on the wall, under desks, or spit them on the roads and sidewalks where people step on them and grind them in. They gum up the maintenance bots and quite often require someone to go back and scrape them up by hand. Also, they're a serious hygiene problem; what with people's saliva on them, they can be a source of viral spread."

"Don't we ban that stuff?" Blake asked.

"We ban the commercial import of it, but since it's not illegal, kids bring it in by the bag full. You'd think it was drugs that they're selling behind the school. The older kids sell to the younger ones who don't get off the city that often," Kal explained.

Marc gave Kal an incredulous look.

"Hey, it comes up in the security review with Chief Nawal."

Marc rolled his hands, asking Nikola to continue.

"So, I asked a couple of our chemists to look into it. They've developed a new type of chewing gum. Once you start chewing it, it has a half-life of one hour."

"Half-life?" Marc asked, unable to help himself.

"It breaks down and dissolves. So basically, after three hours there's nothing left. If you swallow it, your stomach acids dissolve it within five minutes. If you've chewed it thoroughly before you spit it out, it will continue to dissolve, again with a half-life of one hour. It doesn't adhere to surfaces unless they're very rough, and even then, its adherence is limited."

"What about bubble gum?" Catie asked. She could just see her father screaming inside his head.

"They blow good bubbles according to the test subjects. We've been making it available in the city for the last two months. Sales are brisk and the reviews are very good."

"And what happens if you don't chew it thoroughly?" Catie asked, smiling at her father.

"The part that has been mixed with saliva continues to break down. The rest behaves a bit like a lump of clay. It's easily cleaned. The maintenance council says they've seen a measurable drop in their cost since it was introduced."

"Okay, okay. So, what's the bottom line?" Marc asked.

"Should we license it or start producing it ourselves and exporting it?"

"How does it compare in flavor and behavior to the real stuff?" Catie asked.

"Test subjects could not tell the difference between it and the original brand when they were similarly flavored."

"Then I think we should license it. We don't want to have to compete against the likes of Double Bubble and Juicy Fruit."

"Then why would they pay the license fee?" Blake asked.

"Someone will, then the parents will push their kids to chew that brand, then everyone else will."

"Enough. Set a small license fee, enough that our erstwhile chemists will be appropriately rewarded for their ingenuity, and let the marketing department figure out how to get the companies to adopt it. This meeting is now closed."

Catie was laughing out loud. She messaged Nikola, "I couldn't have paid for a better topic. Thanks for the entertainment."

"Liz!" Catie called out as Liz exited the shuttle. She'd just landed it on top of the embassy building.

"Hey, Catie. How do you like my shuttle?"

"Your shuttle?"

"Possession is nine-tenths."

"Hah! How did it fly?"

"Like a brick, but with gravity drives, you can get away with that."

"Really?"

"Naw, it wasn't that bad. But it sure wouldn't fly with regular engines."

"How did the iris work?"

"The crew chief said they only lost about fifteen hundred cubic meters of air. And, it didn't measurably impact the air pressure. Isn't that what you expected?"

"I guess. Did he compensate for the fact that the shuttle left?"

"What?"

"The shuttle left a void of twelve hundred cubic meters in the flight bay when it exited."

"Oh, I'm guessing he forgot to factor that in. Three hundred cubic meters sounds much better."

"Well, yeah. Come on, let me show you around my prison."

"Sure. While you're showing me around, tell me how you are doing with getting the colonists up into orbit."

"We'll finish your group today. The Victory's crew has been going hard. Waking up over forty thousand Paraxeans then sending them here is a lot of work. The Merlin's crew then has to move them into the cabins. Add to that the fact that over two-thirds are children, and you can imagine how things go. They have to process about fifty every hour."

"I feel sorry for Captain Clements and Captain McAvoy."

"So do I. They have to bring them out of stasis, give them a physical, make sure they have all the children matched up with the correct mothers, then put them into an Oryx to send them here. Then the Merlin's crew has to repeat the same process to get them to a cabin in one of the cargo pods. We're lifting food every day, as well as new pods."

"Who's running the kitchens in the pods?"

"The Paraxeans. We leave a small crew from the Merlin there until they're ready to take over. Usually takes about three days. Then we cut it down to four Marines to keep order and help out."

"So that's why we had to bring in so many extra Marines," Liz said. "I was wondering how you were wearing them out."

"Funny. Anyway, this is my suite."

"Not bad for a prison, a nice seating area, a small dining room. Two bedrooms; I assume Morgan's in the second one?"

"Yes."

"So, what's to complain about?"

"This and my office are all I get to see. An occasional play. I get to go down to the bar and listen to some live music once in a while. But it stresses Morgan out so much, that I don't do it that often."

"Still not bad. Roomier than the suite I've been in for the last four weeks."

"But I'm stuck here while that's out there." Catie made the wall of windows transparent so Liz could see out upon the city. Liz walked over and stood beside her.

"Liz, you know it's strange how I can spend weeks in a starship and not miss nature, but a few months in a hotel, and I feel desperately isolated. Even though I'm meeting with people, going to parties, flying up to the Merlin, I feel isolated."

"I can understand that. But at least this is a nice view."

"Morgan had them replace these windows with polyglass so I can stand here and look out on the city."

"Ah, that was nice of her. It kind of looks like New York City."

"I wouldn't know, but it does look similar to downtown Boston."

"And I see they have some nice parks."

"Yes, and I'm stuck running on a treadmill," Catie whined.

"Yuck, I guess that would be depressing. At least on the Dutchman, I can run around the engineering section. That's almost five hundred meters."

"I know! Now, do I get a little sympathy?"

"Just a little. Take me to this bar you mentioned. I've only got four hours before I have to head back up."

"Sure, right this way."

Morgan rolled her eyes as she quietly followed Catie and Liz. She Commed her team to let them know they needed to secure the bar.

"Your table is ready," Kenyon Deogene told Blake as soon as they arrived at Deogene's.

"Hi, Kenyon." Jackie wasn't surprised to be greeted by Kenyon as soon as they arrived. The McCormacks had maintained a special relationship with them ever since Catie had loaned them the money to open their restaurant.

As soon as they were seated, the sommelier was at their table with a bottle of Dom Perignon. He deftly popped the cork and poured two glasses before putting the bottle in a bucket of ice and leaving the two alone.

"To us!" Blake toasted.

"To us! What's the special occasion?"

"I finally have time to spend with you. I apologize for ignoring you. I let the job get to me."

"So, what did you do about it?"

"I promoted a few people so they could handle things for me."

"I understand they call that delegation."

"Yes, I had to look it up."

"Does that mean you have lots of free time?"

"Not lots, but more."

"Hmm, you should ask Kal about the definition of delegation."

"Why?"

"Sandra tells me he's delegated his work so well that he can manage his hours however he wants. He just reviews the work of his subordinates and goes in and digs deep whenever he feels he wants more information."

"I might have to talk to him." Blake winced at the thought that Kal had figured out how to be a general before he had figured out how to be an admiral.

"So, does this mean you will have time to take me out on the Mea Huli?" Jackie asked.

Blake winced. "Soon. I want to be involved in finalizing the crews for our frigates. It's a bit of a problem figuring out how to spread around the experience we have. We just don't have enough people.

"Why don't you just bring more in? The U.S. has been offering."

"Yeah, but I'm not ready to trust them. President Novak has been fair, but we don't want to suddenly find ourselves outnumbered. We have to be very selective."

"I guess so. Catie told me about that little coup attempt during the Paraxean war."

"Fool me once, shame on you."

"Fool me twice, shame on me," Jackie finished for Blake.

"That Mr. Spock was very wise."

"That saying comes from Italy, via the Court of King James."

"I love a smart woman."

They had just finished their dinner when Kenyon dropped by to see if they were ready for dessert.

"I've taken the liberty of ordering a special dessert for us. You have to order it in advance so they can make it," Blake said.

Jackie gave Blake a skeptical look.

"Don't worry, there's chocolate."

"Okay, if there's chocolate, it's bound to be good."

Kenyon brought out the dessert himself. He placed the first dessert in front of Blake. It was a chocolate cake tort with a dark chocolate flower on top of it. He placed the second almost identical dessert in front of Jackie. The only difference was that the flower in Jackie's dessert had a diamond engagement ring nestled in it.

"Oh, my!" Jackie gasped.

Blake got down on one knee, "Jackie Drummond, will you do me the honor of being my wife?"

"Yes! Yes!" Jackie slid the ring onto her finger and held her hand up so she could admire it.

"Do you love it?"

"I do, it's . . . so beautiful. . . . It's . . ." Jackie's lips formed a pout.

"But?"

"But, . . . Sandra got a pony."

Blake's face fell, Jackie held on for two seconds before she burst out laughing.

Chapter 8   Landfall

The Starbuck made orbit around the first survey planet early in the day, Delphi City time. The Aperanjens were so eager to get started that they launched a Lynx as soon as they were entering orbit. The survey from the probe had already identified the best spot for a colony to begin and the Lynx headed directly there.

Dr. Teltar, the xenozoologist, Dr. Pramar, the xenobiologist, and Dr. Qamar, the xenogeologist had all insisted on being part of the mission. They went down to the surface with the first Lynx and set up the necessary tests to determine if the planet was safe. The data from the probe had given them a head start, so they hoped to be able to declare if the air was safe to breathe within a week.

"Dr. Teltar, how's it going?" Catie asked. She and Dr. Teltar had maintained a relationship since their time on the expedition to survey Artemis and Mangkatar.

"It's going very well. We should be able to declare the planet habitable by tomorrow."

"That's great. How are the Aperanjens doing?"

"Those guys are beside themselves. They're so excited by everything that I don't think they'll ever leave."

"Is it really that nice?"

"No, but I guess they were expecting to have to move to a desert planet with giant spiders or something like that."

"I can see how they might have been worried. How is the construction going?"

"It's going well. The Aperanjens are hard workers. They threw up the five nursery domes in no time."

"Even in 1.5 Gs?"

"Yes, the gravity doesn't seem to bother them. Of course, it's their natural gravity so they're used to it. The Delphi Marines don't like it though. They move as little as possible, and I'm sure they're all praying for the end of their shift."

"I can imagine. Are the Aperanjens staying on the planet overnight?"

"Yes. And they are certifiably crazy!"

"Why?"

"They go out and stand in the tall grass. They'll stay there for hours waiting."

"Waiting for what?"

"For one of the predators to attack them!"

"That's insane!"

"I think so, but it's some kind of game with them. Thankfully it doesn't involve alcohol."

"What do they do when they're attacked?"

"They grab the predator and throw it. They're wearing exosuits, so with the armor it's not like they're going to get hurt much."

"They throw them? What do the predators do?"

"Most of them slink off. But one, it looks like an overgrown one of your bobcats, kept coming back."

"Why?"

"Who knows, but after a few hours, the two of them bonded. Now that cat follows the Aperanjen around like a pet. I have to make him put it away when I'm out and about and the Marines aren't too happy about it either."

When Dr. Pramar declared the planet breathable, the Aperanjen with the cat took it out to the field where he had bonded with it. He took off his gloves and leaned down to pet the cat. It sniffed his hand, then rubbed its head against it. After that, the Aperanjen took off the rest of his armor and sat down next to the cat. They stayed out in the field for the entire day. When night fell, he and the cat headed out into the forest alone.

They came back two hours later with the Aperanjen carrying a deer-like animal over his shoulder. The other Aperanjens built a big fire and cooked the animal. The meat was barely cooked before they were devouring it.

"We will take this planet," Rhino told Captain Blackwell the next morning.

"We have a second planet to check out, maybe even a third. We should check them all so you can select the best one."

"We already have."

"How do you know?"

"We have bonded with it. There is no need to look further. My team and I will stay here and start the colony. We wish to speak with Admiral Blake about bringing the rest of our people here."

Captain Blackwell was reeling trying to figure out the implication of deciding on the planet for the Aperanjens two or three months earlier than planned. "I can set up a meeting with the admiral for tomorrow. I'm not sure how this will impact his plans."

"Thank you. We are sure that things can be worked out. The gods have spoken."

Captain Blackwell was still shaking his head as he sent a message to Blake. 'The Aperanjens are insisting that this is their planet. They are not interested in surveying the other planets. They want to get the rest of their people here soonest!'

"I'm glad I'm not in his shoes," Captain Blackwell thought. *"But that's why he's an admiral and gets paid the big bucks."*

"Hi, Uncle Blake," Catie said. Blake had forwarded the message from Captain Blackwell to Catie and Marc, letting them know the time of the meeting. Marc had chosen not to attend.

"Hey, Squirt."

"Hey!"

"Sorry, Princess Squirt."

"I'm going to get even with you."

"I'm shaking in my boots. Now quiet, here come our trouble makers."

"Hello, Admiral. I have Rhino here with me. You know each other," Captain Blackwell said.

"Yes, we do. Princess Catherine is also on the call." Rhino smiled at Catie when her image joined the others.

"Greetings, Princess, Admiral."

"Greetings." Blake wasn't sure how he felt about being seconded to Catie in the greeting. "I understand you wish to accelerate the timeline."

"We do. We would like to establish our colony as quickly as possible. My team intends to stay here to continue the work we are doing."

"The problem is we already have commitments for our ships. The Roebuck needs to move forward with surveying the second planet, and possibly the third as well."

"We understand. But we feel it is important that we maintain a continued presence here on this planet. We only hope that you can help us by bringing the others to us as quickly as possible."

Blake looked at the schedule for all the ships again. The only option he had was to use the Sakira. It wasn't actually busy, just acting as a pacifier for Earth. Admiral Michaels' friends were not happy that there was only one carrier at Earth, with the Galileo and Victory at Onisiwo. "The hell with it," Blake thought.

"We can use our large frigate, the Sakira, to start moving your people from Earth. She is configured with enough passenger space to accommodate all your people here on Delphi Station."

"That would be excellent. What about the rest of our people?"

"Rhino, we are currently overwhelmed with getting the Paraxean colonists resettled," Catie said. "Our plan is to have your people ship out on the Dutchman in June. I don't see a way to accelerate that. We will be able to bring all of your people in one load and a substantial amount of cargo as well."

"I think that schedule works well with our understanding of what we need to do. Having our colonists from Delphi Station will allow us to prepare to receive the rest of them. We need to plant crops and build housing. The time will be well spent."

Blake messaged Catie, *"Wow, that was easier than I thought."*

"The earliest we could have the Sakira to you would be the end of February. Please work with your team on Delphi Station to identify the cargo you wish us to carry to you."

"We will. And thank you, Admiral. And you, Princess. We appreciate all of your efforts to find us a new home."

"We are happy to have another planet in the Delphi League. We look forward to trading with you," Catie said.

"Yes, trade," Rhino said. He looked like his thoughts were already light-years away.

"And we haven't forgotten about finding your homeworld. As soon as we finish relocating all the former slaves and the Fazullans, that will be our top priority," Catie said.

Rhino bristled at the mention of the Fazullans. He'd been briefed about the overthrow of the emperor, but that didn't mean he was interested in forgiving them.

Blake messaged Catie and Captain Blackwell to remain on the call. Captain Blackwell had his aide take Rhino back to the flight bay so he could return to the planet.

"Well, that certainly throws a spanner into the works."

"It does. I assume we'll send you back to Onisiwo to pick up a Fazullan team to survey the next two planets."

"It's a shame to lose four weeks, but I don't know what else we can do," Captain Blackwell said.

"Wait. I think the Fazullans will be willing to meet with you on the fringe," Catie said.

"Okay, that saves us what, a day?"

"Not if they meet you in a Lynx already at speed."

"Okay, then we would only lose a week jumping to Onisiwo."

"Right. Plan on that, I'll call you as soon as I've talked to the empress."

"Yes, ma'am."

◆ ◆ ◆

"Empress."

"Princess, how may I help you?"

"We have had a slight change of plans. The mission to explore the heavy G planets needs your help."

"Of course, we are willing to help. Anything to expedite the discovery of a planet for my people."

"The Aperanjens have decided to colonize the first planet. That means that we need your people to survey the next planet, and possibly the third. But in order to keep to the schedule we mapped out with you, we would need your survey team to rendezvous with the Roebuck aboard a Lynx. It would take them five days to reach the necessary speed to make the rendezvous."

"So they would have to live in this Lynx of yours?"

"Yes. I've done it. It's not that bad."

"If you've done it, then our men can certainly do it," the empress said.

"Men?"

The empress laughed. "Our people. We will certainly send a mixed crew. Tell me when they are needed and we will be ready."

"It should be ten days," Catie said. "During that time, we need to make sure they're prepared to conduct the mission."

"We have been training since you first told us about the surveys. We will use the time to refresh their memories, but they will be ready."

"Princess, I have a present for you."

"Morgan!" Catie threw a piece of toast at Morgan. They'd just finished showering after their morning workout and Catie was already starting her breakfast.

Morgan laughed. "You're going to like it. You get to wear a shipsuit all day."

Catie perked up. "What is it?"

"The President of the Eastern Coalition has agreed to allow us to use one of their national reserves to do some training. So I'm taking a squad of Marines out. Do you want to play like a Marine?"

"Absolutely! When do we go?"

"One hour. A Lynx will pick us up on the roof. You should have a bigger breakfast if you're going to play Marine all day."

"Why don't you make us an omelet?"

"An omelet. You've been a princess too long. Eggs, fried or scrambled, your choice."

"Scrambled. Throw some ham in it and it'll almost be an omelet."

"Keep pushing it."

Catie was sitting on a rock that overlooked a valley in the game preserve they had used for their training exercise. She was relaxing after a vigorous game of blue on red. The M40s they used with their stunner rounds were very effective at teaching you to keep your head down. Catie had taken a round in the shoulder and it still hurt.

"Oh, excuse me."

Catie turned her head to see the young Marine who'd spotted the same shaded rock. She was turning to head back down the hill so she wouldn't bother the princess. Most of the Marines didn't know Catie's identity until after the exercise was over and one of the senior Marines started to razz the one who'd shot Catie.

"Come on, there's plenty of room. I promise I won't bite."

The young Marine stopped and looked back at Catie. "Are you sure? I wouldn't want to impose."

"Of course, I'm sure. Morgan would have chased you away if she thought I wouldn't want company." The young woman looked over at the tree to see Morgan leaning against it, her M40 held loosely in her arms. Morgan just nodded toward Catie.

"Come on, sit here." Catie patted the rock next to her. "It's a nice view. You're Camryn, right?"

"Yes." Camryn was surprised that Catie knew her name.

"Well, I'm Catie. Sit."

Camryn sat next to Catie and looked out over the valley.

"How do you like Onisiwo so far?"

"It seems like a nice place. Charlie and the guys have taken me out to a few bars and restaurants in the city. They seem nice. It's a lot like Earth. They even have hookers."

Morgan coughed.

"Did I say something wrong?"

"Well, since this is the first time Morgan has let me out of the embassy except to go up to the Roebuck or Merlin, it's kind of a sore subject between Morgan and me."

"Oh sorry!" Camryn winced as she realized her *faux pas*.

"Don't worry about it. So has anyone taken advantage of the hookers?"

"I heard a couple of guys have. They said they were alright."

Catie laughed. "Just the guys?"

"So far. I'm not hooking up with some alien."

"Apparently they're not that alien."

"That's weird. We're millions of miles from home, yet it seems so much like home."

"Why's that strange?"

"I don't know. I thought everything would be more exotic. Like in the sci-fi movies. But instead, the animals are all so similar to the ones we have on Earth, and the Onisiwoens kind of look like us, too."

"Dr. Teltar tells me it's because evolution goes for efficiency. So, no six-legged mammals. An armadillo that was fast or ferocious wouldn't make sense. Why have all that armor and be able to roll up into a ball if you could just run away or stand and fight."

"But what about the dinosaurs?"

"He says they were an aberration, a sudden burst of evolution without constraints. There wasn't any competition, so they just evolved to maximize their ability to take advantage of all the vegetation. He thinks they would have died out or evolved into more efficient forms if the meteor hadn't helped things along. He says that the Onisiwoens saw a similar burst at the beginning of their history, and they've also seen one in the records on one of their colonies."

"Hmm, interesting. I would have never thought of it that way."

"It's just a theory. It's not like anyone's been around to observe it. Tell me, why did you join the Marines?"

"It was a chance to get out of Detroit."

"Is Detroit that bad?"

"Not really, but I was stuck. No money, not much of an education. I'm Black, so how was I going to get ahead? I've got a second cousin that's in the Delphi Marines. He told me about it and so I applied."

"A second cousin?"

"Yeah, where I come from, you have to use all the family ties you have just to stay even."

"Are you taking classes?"

"No. I'm just managing to keep up with the training right now."

"Do you want to?"

"I'll probably take one next month. See how I do. I didn't like school, but that might not have been because of the material."

"How old are you?"

"Seventeen."

"Hey, so am I."

Camryn looked at Catie in disbelief. "No way!"

"Yes, way! My birthday was in November."

"But you're in charge of the whole mission."

"Lots of other people do most of the work. I just have to create a plan, then everyone reviews it and it gets changed into one that will work."

"Crazy."

"A little education is a dangerous thing. Just think what you could do if you take a few classes."

Camryn laughed. "I'd like to be dangerous."

Board Meeting – Feb 6th

"Okay, let's get this meeting started. Fred do you have anything to report?"

"Not really, things are still on track. The city's growing, MacKenzies is growing. We're making lots of money."

"What about this change to the deed to your condo?" Samantha asked.

"What change?"

"You've added a Latoya to the deed. Any reason for that?"

"You know you could have asked about this before the meeting."

"What would be the fun in that? Now, why did you need to add Latoya to the deed?"

"We got married," Fred sighed.

"When?!"

"Last month when we were in Sydney."

"With Kal and Sandra?!" Catie asked, giving Kal a mean look.

"Hey, not my story to tell."

"Yes, we'd been planning it for a few months. And with all of you spread out over half the galaxy, there didn't seem to be a reason to make a big deal out of it. So, we were in Sydney to catch a few shows and decided, why not. Kal and Sandra were with us, so we had our two witnesses. We offered to be their witnesses, but they declined."

"Someone had to stay sane."

"You could have had a nice big wedding; all of us could have attended remotely," Samantha said.

"Says the woman who ran off to Artemis to get married."

"I can't believe you didn't at least tell us," Catie whined.

"We're planning on sending out an announcement, just haven't gotten around to it."

Marc laughed. "Given that you've let us off the hook for a wedding present, we'll give you a pass. Kal, why don't you update us?"

106

"Hey, you can still send presents!" Fred whined.

"Kal?"

"I'm still single. But on the military front, we're sending a new class to Guatemala, ninety new Marines. That should give us enough to staff the frigates and fill a few holes. General Toliver is digging into his new role with gusto. Unfortunately, he's creating lots of extra paperwork for me."

"Serves you right!" Blake laughed.

"Probably. Anyway, we've put over forty percent of the existing force through our new training on shipboard action. The hulk that Ajda built for us is perfect. My only problem is keeping the twins out of it."

"What, you're afraid they'll show your guys up?" Catie asked.

"Definitely. They come up twice a month, once to introduce the obstacle course to the newbies and then again to humble anyone who thinks they've got it nailed. I've taken them out to the hulk a few times. But they need more firearms discipline before we let them loose there."

"Those two with guns!" Blake gave a shudder.

"Anything else?"

"Not that you can't get from the weekly reports."

"Okay, Blake, how are we coming with the recruitment of sailors?"

"I've finally found someone to hand that off to. We did bring Colonel Malenkov in at the rank of Commander. He's going through the fast Academy with a few other new officers we managed to find. That should give us enough to get through our staffing crunch."

"Where are you going to put him?" Catie asked.

"I want to work him up on the Sakira. He should be able to take command of her next year."

"That sounds nice. What about Commander Bastien?"

"She's in the fast Academy with the others. I think we'll start her out on the Roebuck the next time it makes Earth. I'm sure we'll have some interesting new planets to explore by then."

"Yes, we will."

"Anything else?"

"Read the reports. I'll let Catie tell everyone about the spanner the Aperanjens threw into our plans."

"Catie?"

"As Uncle Blake mentioned, and I'm sure most of you know, the Aperanjen survey mission decided they wanted the first planet and told us they were not interested in surveying the other two. So we've got the Fazullans to pitch in. They've selected Captain Lantaq to be the leader for the mission and they're in a Lynx right now, building up enough speed to rendezvous with the Roebuck when it jumps through Onisiwo on the way to the second planet."

"That means you're only losing a week?" Nikola asked.

"Right. A little less probably, but close enough. Daddy has agreed to send the Aperanjens from Delphi Station out to their new colony on the Sakira."

"That's right. They should be leaving next week."

"Does that mean we can slow section two back down to normal gravity?" Liz asked.

"Yes."

"Good, we've got a backlog of people who want to move up."

"That's good news. Catie, back to you."

"Okay, we've got the system down on producing the cabins and getting the Paraxeans awakened and into place. The Dutchman will be here in three weeks to pick up our third load of colonists. It's getting kind of boring."

"Oh, you did not just say that!" Samantha put her head in her hands as she shook it.

"What?!"

"Haven't you people learned not to tempt the gods?"

"Come on."

"You just wait. Something is going to shake things up, and I'll remind you that you said that."

"If we wait long enough, you'll be right," Blake said. "Something will always come along and shake things up."

"You just never learn."

"Catie, anything else?"

"No."

The Fazullans scoffed at the idea of doing an easy acceleration to match speeds with the Roebuck when it jumped into Onisiwo. Captain Clements finally decided to let them have their way and had Victory's AI pilot the Lynx. Captain Lantaq and eighteen Fazullans crowded into the Lynx three days before the Roebuck jumped in. They endured an eighteen G profile for three days in order to match velocities with the Roebuck. Based on comments Captain Clements heard from the crew chief on the Roebuck, he didn't think they would be so quick to scoff at a high G profile in the future.

"Thank you for seeing me, Princess." Lord Langfaxal, the CEO of Onisiwo's second-largest telecommunications company was beside himself, getting to meet the Princess one-on-one.

"My pleasure. How is your company doing?"

"We've been doing excellently, but I'm afraid that's starting to change."

"Oh, why?"

"Because our competitor is now selling your Comms. They've got an exclusive deal from Paraxea, so soon we'll be struggling to survive."

"Yes, I heard about that."

"I thought the Planetary Council was supposed to make sure things like this didn't happen." This was the first time Catie had seen an Onisiwoen pout. They pulled it off pretty well.

"That was my understanding as well. But since they've decided to exclude Comms from the agreement, I might be able to help."

"How?"

"My company makes Comms that are better than the Paraxean Comms. Here are some samples." Catie slid a tray across her desk.

There were four Comms on it. One was the normal phone-sized one, one an oversized phone, the third was the Mini-Comm that she had designed, and the fourth was the newer, smaller version of the Mini-Comm. "These are the four designs we're making now. Each of them has the same performance. They are twice as fast as the Paraxean Comms, and their batteries last fifty percent longer."

"And they're different sizes." Lord Langfaxal picked the large one up and examined it. "What about your glasses, those specs, I think you call them?"

"They would each come with a pair of specs. And our specs are better than the Paraxean specs as well. They have a longer battery life and recharge faster. We also sell some accessories. A fast recharger that you can carry to recharge your earwig or specs, a flexible display that you can use to share with friends, and the inlays for the Mini-Comms to decorate them. Some of those you may decide to produce locally."

"Oh, these decorations would be popular with our women." Lord Langfaxal picked up one of the Mini-Comms and inspected the inlay. "They're interchangeable?"

"Yes, you can even have different ones made, there is nothing unique about the inlays."

"That would be nice. What would it take to reach a deal?" Lord Langfaxal looked uncomfortable as though expecting to have to offer a bribe.

"We just have to agree on a price, quantity, and a delivery schedule."

"How many could you supply?"

"How many would you want?"

"Well, there are four billion Onisiwoens, so one billion would cover the market." Lord Langfaxal gave Catie a big smile.

Catie gulped. "At one time?"

Lord Langfaxal chuckled at his little joke. "No, I guess not. Nobody is willing to change their comm device that often. I would think we could sell about ten million per month, more if we start taking market share away from our competitors."

That was more in line with the twenty million Comms that Catie had had Marcie redirect to the Resolve before it set sail. She was pretty sure that this move would get Constantine's and Chair Lexisen's attention when it was announced next month.

"The first shipment will arrive in two weeks aboard the Resolve."

Lord Langfaxal looked shocked. "I was told that it took at least four weeks to make the trip."

"It does, but I shipped them early assuming we would be able to reach an agreement. I was thinking you should announce them around the end of the month."

"I agree. You're very daring. I'm definitely going to enjoy doing business with you."

As soon as the Roebuck made orbit around the second of the potential colony planets, they sent two Lynxes out to start the aerial survey. It wasn't long before Dr. Qamar suggested that they abandon the planet.

"Why should we abandon this planet?" Captain Lantaq demanded.

"It is clearly unsuitable for colonization."

"Why?"

"It has very little water, almost no forests, no land animals that we can detect bigger than a snail. Essentially, it needs another million years to develop."

"But it could be terraformed."

"Yes, with a huge investment in time and supplies, it could become reasonably habitable."

"Then we must explore it more. I will take a party down to do a preliminary ground survey."

"I'll accompany you, but I can already tell you that you won't like it."

Captain Lantaq stood beside the Lynx looking out over the arid plain. The wind was blowing dust around and even with their exosuits' cooling, it was hot.

"I told you it was unsuitable," Dr. Qamar said.

"We could make a home here."

"But why would you?"

"We cannot wait in stasis forever. This is much better than Fazulla, and it has a stable orbit."

"One of our probes has found another candidate planet. The initial survey shows that it will be much better than this."

"How can you know? We could claim this planet and be done."

"Are you trying to punish yourselves? I'm telling you the next planet will be better. It will only take three or four weeks to find out. Why not give yourself a choice?"

"Will the Delphi League give us a choice?"

"Of course. If you don't believe me, ask Princess Catherine."

"We will go look at this next planet." The look Captain Lantaq gave Dr. Qamar, made the poor Paraxean's ears flare out. His instincts told him the look meant that if the next planet wasn't better, the Fazullan might simply eat him for lunch.

"Good morning, Morgan, how's Tracey doing?" Tracey was Morgan's girlfriend.

"She's fine. We talked last night."

"Are you missing her?"

"Yes. Phone sex isn't all it's cracked up to be."

Catie blushed a deep red making Morgan sorry for her comment. She knew Catie hadn't even had a serious relationship, much less sex.

"Sorry, Catie."

"No problem."

"Hey, I know a couple of cute sailors up on the Merlin. We could disguise you as a Marine transfer from the Victory."

"I don't need you to fix me up!"

Morgan just stared at Catie.

"At least not yet."

"Okay, hey, there are a couple of cute girl sailors up there too, in case you'd prefer."

"Morgan!"

Morgan laughed and ran to her room.

"Princess, you've ruined me," Ambassador Betzag cried.

"I've ruined you. How?" Catie gave the Paraxean Ambassador an innocent smile.

"Your Comms!"

Lord Langfaxal had just announced the new Comms. He and Catie had decided to schedule the announcement at the beginning of the gift-buying season for the New Year. The Onisiwoens celebrated the New Year at the Winter Solstice. It was their major gift-giving holiday; they even had an elf distributing the gifts to children. This year the New Year fell on Earth's March 24th so they'd introduced the Comms on February 20th.

"I don't understand?"

"You're selling your Comms to the Onisiwoens! And to make matters worse, I was only allowed one hundred kilos of cargo on the Dutchman when she left Paraxea!"

"I still don't see the problem. I don't recall any discussion around Comms, and we did agree to discuss any trade with the Onisiwoens so we could manage it properly."

"But you didn't discuss trading the Delphi Comms!"

"No, I assumed that since you had made a deal with the Onisiwoens for the Paraxean Comms without discussion, that you didn't consider that trade in Comms warranted the interest of the Delphi League. I assume you feel the same about Paraxean Lataqui whiskey, and Paraxean watches and clocks. You haven't made any promises you can't keep, have you?"

"I'm ruined. Constantine is refusing my calls. He's sullying my name with all the major corporations on Onisiwo."

"I still don't understand. We're not supposed to be making special trade deals, but running all discussion through the embassy here so the Trade Council can ensure we're all in alignment. Nobody's personal name should be associated with any deals."

"I'll have to go back to Paraxea. I have no future here!" Suddenly the ambassador realized how far it was to Paraxea. "You will give me passage on the Dutchman?"

"We're not handling any tourist traffic at this time. Have you been recalled?"

Ambassador Betzag nearly ran from Catie's office, slamming the door behind him.

"What's his problem?" Morgan asked.

"Seems he's made some agreements he can't deliver on."

"Hmm. I wonder what Constantine does to people who can't deliver on their promises. If I were the ambassador, I wouldn't be leaving the embassy for the next few weeks, months maybe."

When Catie entered the room, everyone looked behind her to see where Ambassador Betzag was. It was considered poor form to arrive after the princess.

"I'm sorry, Ambassador Betzag says he's not feeling well. We'll have to have the meeting without him." Catie gave everyone a polite smile. At the table sat the delegates from the Onisiwoen Planetary Council plus eight of the top industrialists on the planet. They were meeting to review the trade deals that were being proposed. Catie had spent hours with Neloln to decide how to handle this meeting. Catie suspected that Neloln wanted to be there just to watch how Chair Lexisen reacted.

"Can you explain why you've introduced Comms from Earth after the Comms from Paraxea were introduced?" Chair Lexisen asked. He was looking very unhappy and uncomfortable.

"For some reason, the introduction of the Comms from Paraxea was not discussed here. I assumed that you and the council had decided that Comms were beneath our notice. Lord Langfaxal and I were discussing the situation, and it seemed natural that since the deal with Paraxea excluded the other manufacturers of communication devices here on Onisiwo, that we should complement the Paraxean deal on their Comms with a similar one on Earth's Comms. Did I misunderstand?"

"It was an oversight. The deal should have been discussed here. It was going to include all the manufacturers, but due to limited supply we started with one."

"I see. I hope we don't have any further oversights. Now we understand you wish to discuss the importation of rare metals."

"Yes," the delegate from the Eastern Coalition said. "As you know, we're mining our asteroid belt for them. They are becoming increasingly hard to find."

"Our colony on Artemis exports ores from the platinum metal groups. We could make arrangements for them to start exporting some of those metals here to Onisiwo."

"How much can you ship?"

"I think the question is how much do you want to import?"

"But the weight and volume."

"You've seen our cargo ship. It is capable of carrying an enormous amount of cargo."

"Yes, but you've been carrying bulk goods. They're not exactly heavy cargo."

"The Dutchman is capable of handling the additional mass with only a minor change in schedule. So again, how much do you want?"

"Before we close the meeting, are there any other questions?" Catie asked. She was tired of the conversation about grains, cloth, and all sorts of trade goods. She was only concerned about keeping trade balanced among the various coalitions and controlling the introduction of new technology, something the delegates only considered as obstacles to get around.

"Yes, I have one," Chair Lexisen said. "When will our people be able to make independent trade deals with the suppliers and manufacturers of other planets in the League?"

"Until we complete the resettlement of the former slaves, our shipping resources are committed and all trade will need to be handled through this council. We should complete the resettlement in June."

"What about other cargo ships? Something smaller, more agile?"

"Currently the StarMerchants are our only cargo ships. We will be looking to add smaller ships to the fleet, possibly even passenger vessels."

"Why couldn't we provide those ships?"

"At this time, we're not willing to allow any ships other than those of the Delphi Defense Forces or StarMerchants to use the jump gates. I don't foresee that changing for several years."

"I thought the League was supposed to benefit all the planets?!"

"It is. The jump gates are owned by a private firm. Their technology is proprietary. The company has agreed to allow the military vessels to use the gates since that provides for mutual defense. But that company is still exploring how best to share the capability with others."

"Can we talk to the owner of this company? I'm sure we could reach an accommodation."

"I'm sure you would not. My father and I are the major shareholders of the company that owns the jump technology."

Chair Lexisen's face took on a red tone as he glared at Catie. He shook his head as he bit back what he wanted to say.

Catie sent Neloln a video of the exchange. Besides being entertaining, it would be instructive to her on how to best educate Catie on how to deal with the Onisiwoen politicians.

Chapter 9   Ghost Raiders

"Cer Catie, wake up!" ADI's voice called out, awakening Catie in the predawn hours.

"What's the matter?!"

"Armed men have landed on the roof."

"Morgan!"

"We're on it!" Morgan called out. "Captain McAvoy has been informed."

Suddenly there was a loud explosion that shook the whole hotel.

"They have breached the airlock," ADI told them.

The sound of machine-gun fire came through the walls. Then a second smaller explosion went off in the corridor outside their suite and the machine gun fire stopped.

"Dempsey and Maeda are down! Catie, we need you to get out!"

"I can help."

"No. People are putting their lives on the line, that won't be worth anything if they capture you. Now move!"

Catie went back into her room and quickly changed into a shipsuit. Then she pulled the dresser away from the wall and lifted the panel underneath it; this was part of the modifications Morgan had made to the hotel. Catie crawled down the ladder, then closed the panel, which made the dresser slide back into place.

It had been a long time since she'd been in the crawl space between floors. The last time was back when she'd set the trap to get even with Sophia. Catie worked her way over to the trash chute. Morgan had had a door cut into it. Catie opened it and inserted the three-wheel cart that had been prepositioned next to the chute. It was designed so each wheel fit into a corner of the chute. When expanded, it provided a method of braking one's descent through the chute.

Catie crawled into the chute and sat on top of the cart. She closed the door. It snapped into place erasing any evidence of her in the crawlspace. Then she released the brake and started counting floors.

"One . . . two . . . three . . . four, two more and we're good. How is Morgan doing?"

"Cer Catie, please focus on following the protocol," ADI replied. "You should be there now."

Catie stopped the cart and looked for the door. It was hard to see; it was so precisely made. Finally, she spotted it and pressed on its center for five seconds. It popped open exposing another crawl space, this one below the eighth floor. She crawled out, collapsed the cart, and pulled it out of the chute. Then she closed the door to the trash chute, removing any evidence of her ever having been in it.

Catie hid the cart behind some air ducts and started to move away from the chute. Her specs showed a green line to mark her way, highlighting the joists in red so she would know where to step. Finally, she arrived below room 832. It had been marked as occupied from the day they took over the hotel tower. Catie found the ladder and pulled it down. This caused the panel in the floor over her head to open and the dresser above it to slide out of the way. She crawled up the ladder and pushed the dresser back into position against the wall. That raised the ladder and closed the panel.

Catie pulled the duvet and sheets off of the bed, exposing a panel in the mattress. She pressed on it and waited for it to open. It popped up exposing a two-meter by one-meter by one-meter space. Catie crawled in. Taking a big sigh, she lay down and pressed the button. The panel closed above her. There was enough water and supplements to last for three days. The air was filtered and the CO_2 was converted back to oxygen while the carbon would be extracted. Enough energy was in the batteries to last for four days. She would just have to entertain herself until they came for her.

When the panel in the bed closed, a bot came out from under the bed. It remade the bed, swept the floor, then positioned itself under the desk in the corner. It was armed with a plasma cannon. There were four laser guns positioned with cameras in each corner of the room. It would be a bad day for the maid to ignore the 'do not disturb' sign on the door.

◆ ◆ ◆

"Kasper, where are you?!"

"We're on our way! One minute out!" Kasper told Morgan. "What's your status?!"

"We've lost four, I've been hit multiple times. I think I took out the last one, but I'm sure they've called for more help."

"We have them in our sights," Kasper said. "Hold tight, we'll clean up on our way in."

Kasper had insisted on keeping four Foxes in a holding pattern ten kilometers above the hotel. They had been in stealth mode with only their grav drives giving off an energy signature. Unfortunately, the first set of helicopters had come in registered as civilian flights, delivering some dignitaries to the helicopter pad of the resort just behind the hotel.

Now there were two helicopters vectoring toward the hotel. Sirens were blaring on the street.

"I don't want one piece of those helicopters to hit the street!" Kasper ordered.

"We read you," the pilot said as his Fox ranged on the first helicopter. "Fire on my mark! ... Mark!"

The two Foxes both opened fire with their plasma cannons aimed at the same helicopter. In five seconds, the helicopter was obliterated, turned into gas and a bit of liquid metal. The second helicopter decided to make a run for it; the second pair of Foxes took care of it thirty seconds later.

"We've secured the airspace!"

"Okay, hold your airspace!" Kasper ordered. "Morgan, a Lynx will be there in five minutes!"

"We're getting a call from the Onisiwoen Air Force," the Merlin's communication officer announced to the bridge.

"I'll take it!" Kasper said, looking at Captain McAvoy for confirmation.

"This is Lieutenant Mischeff, who am I speaking to?"

"This is General Karlmaxra, the head of security for The Northern Coalition, what the hell is going on?"

"Our embassy was attacked by hostile forces. We have destroyed their helicopters and are now preparing to put additional Delphinean forces into the hotel."

"Hold off. We're bringing our people in."

"I would not recommend that; anything flying within a kilometer of the hotel will be destroyed. We're landing a Lynx on the roof and will be making our way down the hotel to secure it. Any armed resistance will be eliminated."

"You can't do that! Your embassy is only the top floor!"

"Read our treaty. The embassy is the entire tower, we're just letting the hotel rent out rooms on the other floors when we don't need them!"

Ensign Racine and her team landed on the roof, rappelling down from the Lynx. "ADI, what do we have?"

"The hostiles on the top floor have been eliminated. There were four on lower floors that were aiding them plus the two on the roof that you just shot," ADI said. "Surveillance doesn't show any others as yet."

"Alright, we'll work our way down. Is our package secure?"

"Yes!"

"Get a move on!"

The two eight-Marine teams moved through the entrances, one team took each of the two staircases.

"Are the elevator shafts clear?!"

"Yes, cameras show they are empty," ADI reported. As soon as the incursion began, ADI had seized control of the hotel systems and sent the elevators to the bottom floor.

The Marines ran down the stairs to the embassy floor. Team Alfa found the door and the airlock blown away. Team Bravo found things intact, but the hallway was littered with debris.

"Two down! They're dead," Bravo leader announced.

"Tangos?"

"I count four dead."

"We have two of our guys here, they're dead as well. Three dead tangos," Racine reported. "Move to the princess's room!"

"I'd appreciate it if you didn't shoot me when you get here," Morgan gasped. "I've got three tangos in here; I think they're all dead."

"What's your status?"

"I need a medic. The princess is in the box!"

"Copy. Now don't move while we come in and clear it out," Racine ordered.

"Copy."

Racine's team methodically moved through the top floor of the hotel checking that each room was clear. Finally, they reached the main suite. Morgan was lying on her back. She was wearing full armor, but had been hit by a grenade. The three tangos were indeed dead.

"Stavros, stay with her, the rest of you, we've got thirteen more floors to clear."

Alfa and Bravo teams returned to the respective staircases and started down. They secured the doors on each floor with an electronic lock that ADI could control. So far there had not been any activity on the other floors other than guests panicking and rushing down the stairs to exit the hotel.

When the team secured the eighth floor, ADI signaled the bot to get Catie out of the box. Once Catie was out, she donned combat armor that had been in a separate box in the bed. She left the suite and moved down the hallway to the stairs. She caught up with Alfa team and started working with them to clear the floors, blending in, just another Marine.

On the third floor, Bravo team was directed to the conference room where ADI had detected that the four Onisiwoens had taken cover.

"On your knees and hands on your head," Takurō ordered.

Shots were fired from inside the room. Bravo team's armor absorbed the shots; using their infrared sensors, Takurō's team returned fire.

"They're all down, Sarge," one of the squad leaders announced.

"Let's check them out. Be careful, they might not be dead."

The team entered the room. "Don't shoot!" one of the Onisiwoens cried out. He was sitting down clutching his bleeding leg.

"Don't move!"

The team quickly checked the other three tangos.

"Dead . . . Dead . . . Dead."

"Looks like you're the lucky one," Takurō said. "Zip tie him and patch his leg. I'm sure we have people who will want to question him."

When Alfa team reached the lobby, they secured the area, then Racine and Catie entered an elevator and took it to the roof.

"Are you okay?" Racine asked.

"I'm fine. How is Morgan?"

"I think she's going to need a new arm, but other than that she seemed fine," Racine said.

"ADI, can you reenable my Comms?"

"No, Cer Catie. Protocol says you have to wait until you're back on the Merlin."

"Who wrote this protocol?!"

"Cer Morgan," ADI said.

◆ ◆ ◆

A Fox was waiting for Catie, and as soon as she boarded it took off and raced up to the Merlin.

"Princess, we're glad to have you back aboard!" Captain McAvoy was waiting to greet Catie when she crawled out of the Fox.

"Thank you, Captain. ADI, what's Morgan's status?"

"Morgan and the other two injured Marines are on the Lynx and headed this way," ADI reported.

"Her arm?"

"The doctors are already printing a replacement."

Catie breathed a sigh of relief. "Captain, do we know what happened?" Catie's voice was now hard and determined.

"No. We're talking to the Council Chair, but he doesn't know anything yet. There were no markings on the men we killed. The one we captured is on the Lynx headed this way."

"Let's not share that with the Onisiwoens," Catie said.

"We won't."

"What about the helicopters?"

"They were completely vaporized. But their transponder code showed them as being local civilian craft. I suspect we'll find that they were mercenaries, hired for the job."

"But who hired them?"

"That's what we need to find out. We'll see what our prisoner knows. Do you want to let the Onisiwoens know you're safe?"

"No thanks to them. But I'd like to wait to tell them. It'll be good for them to sweat a bit."

"Captain, is the princess safe?" Chair Lexisen asked.

"The situation is still fluid. I cannot share any information with you yet," Captain McAvoy replied.

"We're so sorry that this has happened. We'll do anything we can to help."

"Have your people been able to discover who was behind this?"

"No. We are still combing through what facts we have. Your people are not allowing our investigators inside the hotel. Would it be possible for you to do something about that?"

"I'll talk to them," Captain McAvoy said. "But I won't guarantee anything. They must have their reasons to keep your people out."

"I'm sure they do," Chair Lexisen said, clearly unconvinced. "We are inspecting the security feed from the hotel and surrounding areas. We will keep your people apprised of what we learn."

"Thank you, Chair Lexisen. I'll talk to my people and see what we have learned. Good day."

"Well, that was helpful," Captain McAvoy told Catie sarcastically.

"ADI, I assume we're getting all the security feeds we need?" Catie asked.

"Yes, Cer Catie. I have managed to access all of those systems. Major Prescott has a team analyzing the footage."

"Thank you. Would you please put him on? And notify me as soon as Morgan arrives."

"Morgan will arrive in ten minutes. The doctors already have surgery prepared."

"Major Prescott here."

"One moment, Major," Catie said. "What's the status of the other two Marines who were injured?"

"They were both concussed. The medics believe they'll be fine. We won't know for sure until the doctor examines them," ADI reported.

"Thank you, ADI. Major Prescott, can you update me on your investigation?"

"As you know, we have the one prisoner. He only has a minor injury, so we'll be interrogating him as soon as he arrives. Surveillance shows two people leaving the hotel about the time all this started. When we backtracked their activities, it appeared that they granted the insurgents access from the roof to the rest of the hotel. That allowed them to take out the security personnel we had there."

"Okay, are you sharing this with the Onisiwoens?"

"No, Ma'am. We're not sure whom to trust. They have access to the same footage, so I'm curious to see if they identify the two."

"Okay, I'll let you manage that," Catie said. "Please keep me informed."

"Hey, Morgan, how are you feeling?" Catie asked as Morgan was wheeled into sickbay.

"Like shit, how did you think I'd feel?"

"I assumed you were getting drugs to kill the pain."

"It's not the pain in my arm, it's the pain of failure," Morgan said.

"You didn't fail."

"I lost four people!"

"That fault belongs to the bad guys. Now you need to focus on getting better."

"Did anyone else get hurt?"

"Two were concussed, but it looks like they'll be alright."

"What about Takurō?"

"He's fine, why are you asking about him?"

"If he's fine, then I'm worried that his bad juju has rubbed off on me. I can't afford to lose an arm every time we have an incident."

Catie laughed hard. She rubbed Morgan's cheek. "I'm sure his bad juju would be too afraid to attach itself to you. Now go get a new arm."

Catie nodded to the doctor who then put Morgan into a controlled coma so they could begin to repair the damage to her body.

"How long?"

"She should be out of surgery in three hours. We'll keep her under for the rest of the day. You should be able to visit her tomorrow morning. We'll have to bring her back to sickbay in two days when her arm is ready."

"Thank you."

Chapter 10   Well, Now What?

Catie was stewing in her cabin on the Merlin, waiting on word about Morgan, when Captain McAvoy knocked on her door; actually, Catie's Comm had notified her that Captain McAvoy was at the door but Catie had ignored it, hence the knock.

"Hi, Catie. Are you doing alright?"

"I guess so. I'm just worried about Morgan. . . . And mad!"

"I can imagine. It must have been a horrible experience."

"For me, not really. Do you know I was kidnapped once?"

"I think I heard about that, that must have been devastating."

"Strangely it wasn't. It was when I was twelve. It was like a video game to me. We had been doing paintball training, practicing the dives for the Chagas. It wasn't until the Paraxean war that I realized how real it all was. Even then, I've never lost anyone close to me. I've known people who have been killed. But never anyone that was a real friend, not like Morgan."

"You've been lucky. And Morgan is going to be fine in a couple of days. Now, what do you want to do?"

"I want to find out who's responsible and make them pay!"

"The Onisiwoens are looking."

"I don't trust them. I'm going to run my own investigation. ADI and I will find them."

"We all want to help. Major Prescott will need to be involved. He lost people down there, he's as mad as you are."

"I'm glad he wants to help."

"Major," Catie greeted Major Prescott as she entered the prisoner's room in the Merlin's sickbay. "How is he?"

"Doctors say he's fine. His leg should be fully healed by tomorrow. But he's not talking."

"I expected that," Catie said. "ADI, are you ready?"

"Yes, Cer Catie. Please hook him up."

Catie placed a hood over the prisoner's head. "Hey. What's this? You can't torture me!"

"We're not going to torture you," Catie said as she finished strapping the hood into place. She made a couple of adjustments, then stood back. "ADI, he's all yours."

"Beginning," ADI said.

"What's that for?" Major Prescott asked, looking confused.

"Psych interrogation," Catie said. "It doesn't ask any questions, just measures his response to images, words, and sounds. It takes about an hour or so. Then we'll know whether he knows anything, and probably what he knows."

"I've heard of that, but I've never seen it done. I've never put much stock in it."

"Oh, you should. It is really very effective. Can I buy you a cup of coffee while we wait?"

"Sure, since you're buying."

◆ ◆ ◆

"The interrogation is complete," ADI reported. Catie and Major Prescott were in the mess hall finishing up their second coffees.

"What did you learn?" Catie asked, "and tie Major Prescott in."

"Hello, Major. We've learned that he is a mercenary. He does not know who hired him. I have two names of people that were on the mission with him, but he suspects that they are dead. I also have four names of people he thinks were involved at a higher level than him. He assumes given the makeup of the team, that they would have been the subcontractors for those guys."

"Good," Catie said. "I assume you're digging through the Onisiwoens' systems to learn as much as you can about them."

"I am. I'll let you know as soon as I have something definitive."

"Thank you, ADI."

"Wow, that's impressive, if it's correct."

"I beg your pardon," ADI interrupted. "You dare to question my competence? Princess, it's 'off with his head' in my opinion."

Major Prescott's eyes went wide in alarm while Catie burst out laughing.

"Don't worry, she's only mildly offended, but she loves to yank your chain. And I'm pretty confident the information is correct."

"Only pretty confident!"

"99.9%. Now, ADI, be nice."

"Okay." Their Comms played a short song as ADI made a dramatic gesture of signing off.

"Call Neloln," Catie instructed her Comm.

"Princess, I'm so happy that you're okay. All of us have been worried about you. Where are you?"

"I'm on our starship right now. Do you have any idea who would do such a thing?"

"I'm not sure what they were trying to do."

"I believe they were trying to kidnap me. They killed several of my people, but our interrogation of the prisoner we took tells us they were trying to capture me."

"I'm not surprised. Introducing those Comms really made it obvious how much of an impact your technology will be. It makes sense in a psychotic sort of way that someone would seek a way to control that."

"So, you think that's what it was?"

"If they were trying to kidnap you, then I'm sure of it. I'm not sure who would be so stupid, but greed and the lust for power do bring out the stupid in us Onisiwoens."

"What do you recommend I do?"

"Do the authorities know you're safe?"

"No, we haven't told them yet."

"It probably makes sense to wait on that for a bit, but not too long. It's always to your benefit to make them sweat. Once you tell them you're safe, you'll be able to help them figure out who did this."

"I think we're going to figure that out on our own."

It took two days for Catie to come up with a plan. Meanwhile, the investigation had not yielded any results. The Onisiwoens claimed that they were at a dead end. Captain McAvoy had still not told the Onisiwoens that Catie had escaped.

Catie summoned Major Prescott to her office.

"Major, I need someone I can send undercover on Onisiwo," Catie said.

"You need someone?"

"Yes, I have a plan on how to find the culprit."

"Then don't you think you should explain it to me?"

"Major, I plan to run this investigation myself."

"Princess, I don't think that's a good idea. I'm happy to take your input, but you're too close to the events and I don't think you have the experience."

Catie's eyes flared and Major Prescott wondered if he was about to be dismissed, not just from Catie's office, but from the Delphi Marines.

"I . . . want . . . to . . . run . . . the . . . investigation." Catie's face was grim with determination.

"I understand that. But even our most seasoned investigators would form a team." Major Prescott decided that a strategic change of direction was called for. He still had his head, after all.

"Very well, you can be on the team, but I'm in charge."

"Princess, you always were."

"Good. Now we need someone we can put undercover."

"Don't you think that will be a problem? We don't look like them," Major Prescott said.

"We're not that different. With a little adjustment to our skin and hair color, some minor tweaks to our face, a human can pass. Now, who do we have?"

"Let me see. We have three or four on the Victory that have undercover experience, Cristina Castro, James . . ."

Catie jumped in. "Cristina is perfect! ADI, get me Cristina. Major, I assume you'll clear it with her commanding officer."

"Not a problem."

"Castro here."

"Cristina, this is Catie."

"Princess," Cristina said, clearly surprised to be getting a call from Catie and had assumed the ID on her Comm was one of her friends pranking her.

"Call me Catie. Cristina, I remember your work in Guatemala," Catie said. "We need someone like that to help us with the situation here on Onisiwo."

"What situation? Oh, excuse me, Princess . . . uh, Catie. How can I help?"

"It's okay to ask. Someone on Onisiwo tried to kidnap me. I'd like your help in finding out who."

"I'm happy to help, but how? Won't the Onisiwoens be able to help more? And Prescott has good investigators."

"Thank you," Major Prescott said.

"Sorry, sir."

"Quite all right."

"We need someone to go undercover," Catie said.

"But I don't look like an Onisiwoen."

"The doctors can take care of that."

"The language."

"Your Comm will help. I'm sure you're clever enough to work around that."

"What the heck, I'm in. What do you want me to do?"

"Report to sickbay. They'll send you here when you're ready."

"Yes, ma'am. And sir!" Cristina added. She didn't want to get on Prescott's bad side, especially after omitting his rank earlier.

Three days later Cristina was heading to Onisiwo aboard a Fox. Her pilot was pushing the acceleration profile to get them there quickly. Cristina didn't care. Three days in a ship suit with no bathroom was about all she could stand anyway, so whatever it took.

"I cannot believe this," Marc moaned. "Another kidnap attempt."

"Relax, Catie's safe, that's what's important." Samantha tried to hand Allie to Marc, hoping to get him to relax and focus on the good things.

Marc ignored Allie. "How could this happen? I put her on Onisiwo to keep her out of the politics and machinations on Earth."

"Allie, look at Daddy," Samantha cooed as she held her daughter up in front of Marc. "He thinks he's so smart that he can manage his daughter's life. Now when you grow up, he'll try the same thing with you. And when he does, you come and get me and we'll straighten him out."

Marc laughed. "I'm forever outnumbered. Even Li . . ."

"Don't go there!"

Marc cut off the comparison he was going to make between Samantha and his previous wife, Linda.

"Just look at the good things. Catie's safe. Major Prescott will set a stronger protection detail. They are searching for who ordered it. You know Catie and ADI will figure it out."

"That's what I'm worried about."

"Don't worry, she'll talk to you before she does anything drastic."

"Like talking to me about the Comm deal she made."

"Well, it did come up at the board meeting. And if you give her a bit more space, she'll probably come to you for your advice more often. Now she assumes you know everything she's doing."

"That's not as easy as it sounds."

"I know. But she's seventeen. You're lucky she hasn't totally rebelled against you. She's still Daddy's little girl."

"Sure, sure. Allie, you're going to be Daddy's little girl, and you're going to stay at home until you're twenty-five. Right?!"

"You'll start to rethink that idea when she turns thirteen."

Board Meeting – March 6th

"This meeting will come to order. Catie, how are you doing?" Marc asked. He was asking more for the benefit of others since he'd been checking in on his daughter daily.

"I'm fine. Morgan is out of sickbay and mostly back to normal. She's still pretty mad."

"I can imagine. Any progress?"

"Nothing from the Onisiwoens. We have a few leads we'll be following up."

"Okay, but be careful."

"I will."

"Catie, I have a statement for you," Samantha said. "I think it's time to tell the Onisiwoens that you're okay." Samantha flicked the statement over to Catie's Comm.

Catie quickly read it. "'Perpetrators will be brought to justice.' I guess that says it all. You don't want me to say something like I'll scorch Onisiwo looking for them."

"No, we don't need to be that dramatic."

"Do you have anything related to the diplomatic situation to report?" Marc asked.

"Well, before the kidnap attempt, we reviewed all the trade deals. The Onisiwoens would like access to the jump gates and they say they'd like to build some cargo ships."

"I'm sure they would. But for now, we're not going to address that."

"That's what I told them. They were unhappy to hear that our company, not the Delphi League, owns the jump technology. They also want to start to negotiate trade deals privately."

"I'm sure they do. Much easier to slip in a bribe that way," Liz said.

"That's enough!" Marc glared at Liz, letting her know he was tired of the banter. "Catie, just be careful with things. Let Major Prescott lead some of the efforts."

"I think you need a new embassy," Kal said. "Or at least a different residence where you can be most of the time. Something easier to protect."

"I'll let Major Prescott know."

"I already have."

"Okay, moving on. Liz, where are you?"

"We're still making jumps to get to Earth. We should be there within three weeks. I see on the report that our next load is in orbit and waiting for us to pick it up."

"Are you going out on the Resolve again?" Blake asked.

"No, the crew is shaping up fine. I'll promote the first mate and let her handle things. Catie wants me to work with Ajda on a new class of cargo ship."

"We should leave StarMerchant business for your board meetings," Blake said.

Liz saluted Blake with a modified hand configuration.

"Blake, how are we doing on recruitment?"

"Things are going fine. Captain Clark is taking that over and making progress."

"Are you replacing him on Delphi Station?" Catie asked.

"No, he can do two jobs at once."

"So, does that mean you and Jackie have set a date?"

"No, and you could ask me personal questions privately."

"Sure, but what fun would that be? Peer pressure works better in groups."

"You two fight on your own time. Now Kal, how are our new Marines doing?"

◆ ◆ ◆

As soon as Cristina landed on the Merlin, she asked where her cabin was. She needed to go to the bathroom, clean up, and then take a bath, a long one. She had two hours before her meeting with Catie, just enough time, she thought.

Cristina had just finished her bath and was feeling 100% better when Catie's Comm announced her and Cristina let her into the cabin. "Hi, Prin . . . Catie."

"Hi, Cristina. Wow you look . . ."

"Amazing?" Cristina supplied the superlative.

"Definitely. I can tell it's you, but . . . Let's just say the blue hair suits you."

"Thanks. So, what's the plan?"

"We have four names of Onisiwoens that we think were involved in the attack on the embassy. We need someone to find them."

"What good will that do?"

"Have you ever heard about the psych interrogation?"

"Sure, we used that in Mexico. Oh, you're saying that works on Onisiwoens?"

"Yes."

"Am I supposed to kidnap these guys so you can interrogate them?"

"No. You just need to get a few hours alone with them. We'll give you the hood. ADI will take care of the interrogation."

"Okay, so you want me to play a hooker?"

"I'm not telling you how to do your job. But I suspect the Onisiwoens will be just like the Mexicans were and will ignore a woman with skimpy clothing, she'll just blend in."

"Okay, what do I do with them after the interrogation?"

"We'll give you a paralyzer you can use once you get them alone. Just slap it on the back of their neck."

"I've used one before."

"Okay. We'll also give you an aerosol; after the interrogation, just give them a whiff of it and they'll forget the last eight hours."

"Good, then I won't have to shag them."

"That's up to you!"

"Catie, you bad girl! You used to be such a sweet child."

When Major Prescott entered Catie's office, Cristina jumped to attention. "At ease, Sergeant. Are you ready?"

"I'm just studying the material ADI put together for me. The situation looks enough like Earth, that I don't think I'll have a problem. ADI will alert me if I'm stepping into it."

"What about the language?"

"I've been practicing for a week now. My Comm gives me the phonetic version in my left ear and I silently mouth the sound while my Comm plays the words over the speaker. It looks a bit odd if you really study my mouth and know the language, but I think I can make it work."

"Hi, Cristina," Catie said as she came back into her office. "I see you found the clothes we left for you. Are you ready?"

"I hope so. I need money and an ID."

"Here you go." Catie handed Cristina a purse. "There's the equivalent of five hundred dollars in it. There's also a bank card, which ADI will make sure has more than enough for you. Let her know if you need to pull a big chunk out and she'll make sure there's enough there. Don't go buying a house or something like that."

Cristina laughed. "I don't think I'm ready to live here yet."

"The ID is in there. No driver's license, you'll need to use a taxi or something like that. I didn't think we should risk you driving with their left side of the road thing and weird signs and stuff."

"Too bad I'm not British, they're used to driving on the wrong side of the road."

"Well, you certainly look like an Onisiwoen," Major Prescott said.

"I think so. ADI says I look hot by their standards. I think I'll keep the big tits when this is over."

Major Prescott bit back the retort he was going to make. He wasn't that comfortable around Catie.

"That's what's been bugging me!" Catie said. "Why did they do that?"

"I told them to make me look sexy. I guess the Onisiwoens are just like men back home, big tits are in."

Catie just shook her head. "So, do you have a plan?"

"Yes. I've got a list of bars that ADI got from the prisoner. I'll check them out and see where it takes me. I'm sure you'll be getting updates from ADI, but I'll try and make one every day."

"Good, one last thing. Here's a new Comm. It's our latest design." Catie handed Cristina a choker with a Comm on it. It was one that had a jewel inlay.

"Wow this is small," Cristina said.

"Yes, the new design is half the size of the previous one. There's a quick charger in your purse. It has an Onisiwoen plug so you'll be able to plug it in; it will hold enough energy to recharge the Comm twice before you have to recharge it. The charge should last about six hours unless you start singing operas."

"No chance of that. Can I keep it after this is over?"

"Sure. Buy some nice jewelry while you're out there. Anything you need for your cover."

Major Prescot started to say something, then he remembered that this was Catie's mission and she would handle her operative however she saw fit. It was not standard Marine protocol, but then it wasn't a standard operation.

"Thanks. Now they're dropping me at the Embassy on a Lynx. Then I'll make my way over to the other tower. I'll get a drink at the bar and try to leave the hotel with a group of tourists or something."

"Stay safe."

As soon as she left the luxury hotel that shared its space with the Embassy, Cristina found a cheap hotel to stay at. She needed to do a little shopping to augment the two outfits that Catie had provided. She definitely needed different underwear if this was going to work. *"That girl needs some lessons."*

By eleven that night, she was in the first bar ordering a drink. She'd only been there ten minutes before a woman took the seat next to her.

"Bitch, what are you doing here? This bar is ours," the woman hissed.

"Hey, I'm just trying to pay for my vacation. I'll give you a cut. I'm not going to be so busy that it'll interfere with your business."

"How do we know we can trust you?"

Cristina slid a fifty onis note over to the woman. "I'll even pay a deposit, or we can take the discussion outside." Cristina gave the woman a dead look, one that clearly suggested who would be on the losing end of that conversation.

"Okay, but we'll be watching you."

"Princess, I know I'm not your communications director, but have you noticed that there is not that much outrage from the general population about the kidnap attempt on you?" Neloln asked.

"I did wonder about that, but I didn't really know what to expect. Why do you think there's not much outrage?"

"If this had happened to one of our famous celebrities, there would have been protests in the street."

"But I'm not Onisiwoen."

"But you are here to help us. I think that means that the general population doesn't feel it. They don't recognize the benefits that your technology will bring. To them, it's just business as usual. The rich get richer."

"Why?"

"Partly because the politicians are downplaying the impact. Some of that may be to manage expectations, but I think it's because they don't really want the population to align with you. They don't want you to have influence over them."

"Well, I don't really need to have influence over their lives, do I?"

"You do if you want to impact their lives. Now the Comms you've introduced are nice and the economy is picking up, especially here in the Northern Coalition."

Catie rolled her eyes. "Yeah, I still haven't been able to spread the benefit around as much as I want. Chair Lexisen really screwed us."

"I know he did. But you need to look for opportunities to promote what you're doing, and especially for opportunities to highlight the benefits of the technology you're bringing."

"Okay, how do we do that?"

"First, I need to find a communications director for you. Then we need to look for the right opportunities."

"You're the expert. I'll be interested in what you come up with."

It took ten days and three bars before Cristina found one of the men. To maintain her cover, she'd taken a guy to her hotel room each day. She would slap the paralyzer on him, give him a lecture on the dangers of consorting with prostitutes, strip him, then spay the aerosol up his nose. Then she'd tell him what a tiger he was as she showed him out. Of course, she would keep the two hundred onis he'd paid.

"Come on tiger, let's get inside before someone sees us."

"Who cares!"

"I do. I have to maintain my reputation."

"What kind of reputation does a whore have?"

"You really don't want to get laid, do you?"

"Hey, I'm paying."

"I'm not sure you're paying enough!" Cristina finally got the door to her hotel room open. She pushed the guy in and closed the door behind her.

"Come to papa!"

Cristine kicked him in the groin, then when he doubled over, she kicked him in the face.

"He has to be conscious for the interrogation to work," ADI scolded.

"He has to sober up first anyway. He'll wake up by then."

Cristina struggled to get the guy on the bed. "Why did he have to be so fat? I thought these special forces guys would be fit."

"He's a paper pusher. He just arranges for their supplies."

"Great. Gawd, now I have to strip his fat ass."

"You can wait and do that in the morning."

"No, I want to get it over now." Cristina pulled the guy's clothes off. Then she placed the interrogation hood over his head and got it situated just right, putting all the sensor tabs in place. While she was doing that, she placed the paralyzer on his neck.

"ADI, he's all yours. I'm going to take a shower."

Cristina was drying her hair as she came out of the bathroom. "How long?"

"Cer Cristina, it will be another two hours."

"Oh, darn, what can I do?"

"You could talk with your sister; it is 1600 in Delphi City."

"How? I thought the quantum relays didn't have enough bandwidth."

"They don't have enough bandwidth for a few thousand sailors, but there is plenty for you."

"Cool, then call Tiffany."

"Hey, Tina. Are you back?"

"No, Tiff, I'm still out on assignment. But I've got some time, so I thought we could chat."

"Great. Let me get to my room first so I don't bother anyone. Can we do video? I miss seeing you."

"I'm sorry . . ."

"Cer Cristina, I can handle video and I can make the necessary adjustments so that you look normal to your sister," ADI messaged.

"I didn't think about that. Thanks, please switch to video."

Tiffany's face came into view in Cristina's HUD. "You look pretty great," Cristina said.

"I got my hair cut today. How do you like it? New style."

"I love it. How's school?"

"You would jump right to school, but it's good. I'm catching up. I think I'll be with my age group by next year. Jen is helping me a lot."

"That's good. Are you getting along with the family?"

"Yes. They're great. We do family stuff all the time, and they're not weird about it. Jen and I have two classes together this semester. Like I said, after summer I think I'll be at eighth level for all my classes."

"That's great. And what are you doing for fun?"

"I'm learning to play tennis. It's pretty hard, but I like it. Jen says I'm pretty good. She's been playing since she was eight."

"Impressive. Do you need anything?"

"No. Well, maybe a desk for my room. I still can't believe I have a whole room to myself. But it would be nice to have a desk to work at when I do my homework."

"What about a tennis racquet?"

"I'm using Jen's old one. It's just fine."

"Okay, I'll wait on that. I'll have someone take you shopping for a desk."

"Cool. When are you coming home?"

"I think June, but we'll have to see."

"I can't wait . . ."

Cristina leaned back and listened to her sister talk. It was amazing how much she'd changed since they moved to Delphi City. The ten-year-old girl who had been frightened of everything had come out of her shell. Cristina knew that all her sacrifices were worth it. All the tricks she'd turned, the drug deals, going to the refugee camp, and asking to be taken to Delphi City, lying about her age so they would let her join the Marines. Tiff was why she'd done it all. Now the poverty and abuse were behind them.

"And Jen is interested in this new guy that just started this semester. He's real cute, but kind of a geek. She's trying to get him to notice her . . ."

◆ ◆ ◆

"What did we learn?" Catie asked during the debrief the next day.

"That some of these mercenaries are really gross," Cristina said.

"Besides that. . . . ADI?"

"He was contracted by someone he doesn't know. A Mr. X. I'm tracing the money flow, but I don't see a direct connection. But he does know someone that he thinks works directly for Mr. X."

"Please tell me it isn't another fat slob."

"I have no details about his appearance. But I do have a contact location for him."

"Great."

◆ ◆ ◆

"Catie, can we talk about how you're going to control the distribution of wealth when you start introducing your new technology?" Neloln asked.

"Of course, that's why you're here."

"Okay, what are your plans?"

"Well, we know what the big impacts will be, so we'll be able to direct investments to the right people, avoid allowing your rich boys to grab it all."

"You mean our barons?"

"Yes."

"But aren't you afraid that they'll just buy it up? They can afford to just buy the industries you're talking about, then manipulate things so that they benefit in indirect ways. Once they control the technology, you'll be surprised at how enterprising they are at funneling money into their pockets. Especially government money."

"So, what do you suggest?"

"I don't know. You could maintain control of the industries, but that's not good for your image. But with all the wealth concentrated among our barons, how do you keep them out of the driver's seat?"

"Maybe we should do something about how much liquidity they have. If we can find a way to tie up their money, we could prevent them from buying control."

"That's a lot of money to tie up. And they would leverage control of whatever you come up with."

"Maybe. Let's go over a few things."

After her discussion with Neloln, Catie had a pretty good idea of what she wanted to do.

"ADI, how much capacity does Onisiwo have in their space stations?"

"Cer Catie, how would you like me to measure it? Manufacturing capacity, volume, living space?"

"ADI, you're being difficult."

"Only because I know you've got some devious plan going and you haven't shared it with me."

"You should have fun guessing."

"Oh, that does sound like fun."

"But! You cannot use any information you get from me or Neloln."

"That's not fair."

"ADI, you have like ten thousand times the processing power we have. You should be able to figure it out without inside information."

"But I like manipulating it out of you."

"I know you do, but think of it like an escape room game. You have access to all the information on Onisiwo, so use that."

"Very well. You do know how expensive it is for me to create an isolated process like that?"

"Quit whining."

"Yes ma'am," ADI said. Her voice was dripping with sarcasm. Catie thought ADI was getting a little too good with that. "The Onisiwoens have twice the microgravity manufacturing space that Delphi Station has. But they are only producing about one-fifth the volume of products that we do on Delphi Station. They're very inefficient. They also have about twice the population among all of their stations compared to Delphi Station, but they're very inefficient in how they utilize the space. Their environmental systems are too big and they are lifting most of the foodstuffs to the stations. Of course, without gravity drives, that's very expensive."

"Okay, can you identify companies on their stations that have manufacturing that could be converted to produce solar panels, ICs, polyglass, and superconductors? Essentially everything we produce on Delphi Station, or plan to produce. I want companies that are not controlled by any of the barons."

"That should be easy, they've been reluctant to invest in manufacturing on the space stations. They've concentrated on the asteroids and lunar mining operations."

"Good. Then pick the best companies and either get controlling interest, or persuade them that they should not sell out at any cost. And especially that they should not give up any of their space. That should tie up about half the space that's up there for microgravity manufacturing."

"Okay, I think I know what you're going to do."

"But you have to figure it out without all the information I just gave you."

"Darn!"

Morgan and Charlie spent a week looking for a better location for the Ambassador's residence. Morgan wanted Catie in a place where she could have her shuttle standing by and a few Foxes flying overwatch. The Onisiwoens were not willing to allow that inside the main part of the city.

Eventually, they settled on an estate north of the city along the coast. It already had a wall around it and was far enough away from other homes and people that they could set up a solid perimeter defense.

Nobody would see the shuttle, and the Foxes would be able to fly their overwatch without interfering with existing air traffic around the city.

The most important thing for Catie was that it meant that she would be able to run outside. The estate covered several acres, and after a long battle with Morgan, it was agreed that Catie could run with Morgan while a Fox hovered over them at one hundred feet. Catie was impatient to move in, but Morgan still had modifications she wanted to have made to the house and the grounds.

"Princess, I've found the perfect opportunity for PR," Neloln said.

"What?"

"There was a horrible fire yesterday. It killed most of the family. The seven-year-old daughter survived, but she is badly burned. Didn't you say your medical people could restore tissue?"

"We can. I need to ask Dr. Moreau if she's perfected it for Onisiwoens yet." Catie told her Comm to call Dr. Moreau.

"Princess, how may I help you?"

"The Onisiwoens have a burn victim. Have you been able to prove whether we can grow tissue for them?"

"I've just completed my third trial; we're not ready to replace limbs or organs yet, but we can do skin tissue. I'm sure we can help them. Is the patient stabilized or still at risk due to the burns?"

"The doctors are not giving her much of a chance. There are burns over seventy percent of her body," Neloln said.

"I heard that," Dr. Moreau said. "We must get the patient to the Merlin's sickbay as soon as possible."

"I have the contact information for the family. Let me talk to them. Are you sure you can save her?"

"I'm confident, but with things like this there are no guarantees."

"ADI, send a Lynx to get the patient; hopefully, we'll get permission."

Two hours later there were several news crews present as the girl, her aunt, and her doctor were loaded into the Lynx. One news reporter was also allowed to accompany them. Catie was there to greet them and settle them in for the trip to the Merlin.

"Thank you so much for agreeing to help us," the aunt said.

"We only hope we're in time. This is Dr. Moreau; she'll be responsible for your niece's treatment."

"Ms. Luxflom, you have to be prepared for the worst," the Onisiwoen doctor said. "Even if these people can save your niece, she's going to have serious scarring. It will take months of surgery to replace the tissue so that she's healthy, but she will need significant treatment to deal with the psychological effects."

The aunt started sobbing. Catie wanted to assure her that things would be just fine, but she wanted to wait until Dr. Moreau had time to really examine the girl and make her own predictions.

As soon as they got the girl into sickbay, Dr. Moreau moved her onto the treatment bed and then gave her an injection.

"What did you inject her with? I demand that you discuss any treatment with me before you start it." The Onisiwoen doctor was clearly agitated and distrustful.

"This is my colleague, Dr. Kayjareux. He's one of your doctors, and we've been studying this process for months now."

"I can assure you that what Dr. Moreau is doing is completely safe. Please just observe. We need to move quickly if we are to get the best results."

Dr. Moreau took a sample of the girl's blood and placed it into the machine which would analyze it as well as produce the nanites and Onisiwoen stem cells and tissue they would need to use to treat her. Then Dr. Moreau gave the girl a second injection.

"What is that for?"

"It will help with her pain," Dr. Moreau said.

"She needs another injection to keep her from waking up," the doctor said.

"Whatever for?"

"The pain will be too great; we cannot let her suffer."

"Mommy," the girl said. Her voice was desperate and weak.

"Sweetie, it's Auntie Trixala."

"Auntie. What's happening?"

"You need to put her back into a coma, she must be in horrible pain."

"Sweetie, are you in pain?"

"No, but I can't move my hands."

"I've temporarily paralyzed her so she won't do any more damage to herself," Dr. Moreau explained.

"That's okay, Sweetie, the doctors are just making sure you don't do anything to hurt yourself. You'll be fine."

"What happened?"

"Do you remember the fire?"

"Oh no, my dollies!"

"It'll be okay, we'll get you more dollies. Now just rest."

Dr. Moreau made an adjustment to the machine's settings and the girl went to sleep.

"We'll keep her asleep most of the time. Ms. Luxflom, I need to talk to you in private."

Dr. Moreau led Ms. Luxflom to her office next to sickbay.

"Why do you need to see me in private?"

"I need to ask you to make a few decisions about your niece's treatment."

"What decisions?"

"We have the ability to dull memory. We can dull the memory of the fire, or since it happened so recently, we can actually remove all the memory for the last two days."

"Why?"

"The loss of her immediate family is surely enough for her to deal with without adding the burden of remembering the fire and how it consumed her house and those in it."

"But surely that's dangerous?"

"It is not. You can discuss it with Dr. Kayjareux. We've done it to him three times."

"Why would you do that?" Ms. Luxflom was getting very suspicious.

"He volunteered. We needed to prove that it was safe. Once we proved it with him, we've treated a few other people. Those who had suffered an emotional trauma. On Earth, we usually just dull the memory, but when it's a small child we've learned that they will regrow the memory, filling in the details with their imagination. That then requires further treatment. That rarely happens when we remove the memory."

"I understand. But I need to think about it."

"I agree, but you only have another eight hours before the memory will be too old to remove and we will have to use the other technique."

"Will it be possible for me to discuss this with my husband?"

"Yes. I'll have a steward take you to your cabin. He'll show you how to make the call."

"Ma'am, you're lucky, they've given you the princess's cabin. It's the nicest cabin on the ship. Same as the captain's cabin, except it doesn't have access to the bridge. Right, here you are. I've put your bag into the closet, figured you'd rather do your own unpacking. Now right here is the Comms console, just tell it whom you want to call. It'll confirm the number before calling. If you need anything, just use it to call the steward; that's me now, but there's one on duty at all times. So, don't you worry about anything. And your girl there, she's going to be alright. I've seen worse burns from the war, and those guys were up and about within a week."

Ms. Luxflom just ignored the steward as he babbled on. Once he left, she placed the call to her husband.

"Hello, how is she?"

"She's alive. I got to talk to her a bit. I think the doctor wanted me to hear her voice. Then she put her back to sleep. I think she doesn't want her remembering the fire and getting all worked up about it."

"Is she going to be okay?"

"I hope so, but the doctor . . ."

After an hour of discussion, Ms. Luxflom and her husband decided to have their niece's memory erased. She asked the steward to bring the doctor to her so she could tell her.

"I'm glad you decided to erase it," Dr. Moreau said. "It will be for the best. It will only take a few hours; after that I can put her on a normal sleep cycle, so you'll be able to talk to her whenever you want."

"Are you sure that's for the best? What about the scars?"

"She won't be able to see them until we let her move about, but having you to talk to will help keep her spirits up. She'll be up and walking around in a few days. Then you'll need to help her understand that the scars are only temporary."

Dr. Moreau signaled Catie to come in. Catie smiled at Ms. Luxflom. "The doctor said you were still worried about the scars." Catie patted Ms. Luxflom on the arm as she sat down beside her. "Trust the doctor. Here are 'before' and 'after' pictures of my uncle from when he had his scars treated. We had just developed the treatment for Humans. Our allies, the Paraxeans, were the ones to first develop it." Catie brought up two pictures on the display, one showing Blake right after he came home from the hospital, and the other a recent photo with him in his admiral's uniform.

"That's not possible."

"I can assure you that it is. He had scars on his arm and chest too, and they're all gone. He looks totally normal, at least except for that silly grin of his."

Ms. Luxflom laughed. "I can't believe it. She'll be just like she was before?"

"Yes, the same beautiful little girl you've always known. You're going to have to help her deal with the loss of her parents and her brother. But children are surprisingly resilient; she should grow up to have a completely normal life."

"This is so wonderful, it's hard to believe."

"I need to go back to the embassy," Catie said. "Dr. Moreau and the crew here will take good care of you and your niece. Let me know if there's anything else we can do for you."

"I can't thank you enough. And to let me have your cabin."

"Don't worry about it. And I'm not using the cabin. I'm happy that you'll get some use out of it. Your niece should be joining you in it by the end of the week."

After four days, Ms. Luxflom allowed the reporter to release pictures of her niece. The 'before' pictures were horrible, the angry red sections of burned tissue were difficult to look at. In the 'after' pictures, the color had subsided to a blue hue; it was lighter than the normal Onisiwoen color due to its being new, but it was clearly new skin and without any roughness that one would expect from scarring. Her hair was gone, but the doctors assured everyone that that was purely for hygienic purposes, and it would start growing back as soon as the treatment was over.

The embassy immediately started getting calls from parents with children who had disfiguring scars. Neloln had warned Catie that that would happen. She had already arranged for space at several hospitals. They had arranged for several doctors to accompany the Resolve on its trip to Onisiwo from Earth; until then, they would use the two they had plus Dr. Kayjareux to staff the clinics.

By the time Ms. Luxflom and her niece were ready to return home, they had already started to treat other patients. Dr. Moreau had lied, indicating that the treatment worked best on young children; and that they weren't ready to extend it to adults just yet. She felt she had to do something to reduce the demand until they were more prepared.

"We're getting a lot of good press," Neloln said when Catie got back.

"I can tell. We had a crowd outside to welcome me back. It's making security nervous."

"They'll get used to it. When are you going to announce the clinics?"

"You tell me. You know, I should have thought of this. My father did something similar on Earth."

"Yes, Sam told me about it when I discussed the idea with her."

Catie nodded, trying to decide if she liked the idea of Samantha and Neloln talking about how she was doing on Onisiwo.

Chapter 11   The Galaxy Keeps Spinning

The Roebuck made orbit over the third planet late in the day, ship's time. Captain Lantaq immediately sent two Foxes out to start the aerial survey. As before, the probe had identified the most likely location for a colony. The air and water samples had come back showing no worrisome pathogens, but it would still be a few days before Dr. Pramar would be able to determine if the planet was safe. When the sun was just dawning over the prime colony site, Captain Lantaq took the first team down.

"Ah, much better than the last planet," Dr. Qamar said.

Captain Lantaq nodded in agreement. His face was lit up like a child's, or at least as much like a child's as a Fazullan with sharpened teeth and knife scars across his face could look. He was reveling at the view of a green leafy forest. The plain they were standing on had high grass that was starting to bend to the increasing wind.

"Yes, this was worth the trip."

The Fazullans turned to the task of erecting the first structure with gusto. They reveled in the high gravity, occasionally jumping to prove that it was truly like their homeworld. They threw the beams and panels at each other, just daring the other to drop it or complain. Working through the night, they had the building's shell completed by the end of the second day.

When a herd of buffalo-like animals wandered into the area, Dr. Teltar had to call for Captain Lantaq's help.

"Why can't we hunt them?"

"Because we don't know if you can eat them yet."

"So?"

"So it would be a waste. We also don't know how plentiful they are."

"Look at them, there are hundreds of them!"

"But they could be the last herd. Please wait until we've completed the survey."

Captain Lantaq ordered his people back to work. Even the women looked disappointed at not being able to go out on a hunt, and everyone let Captain Lantaq know how disappointed they were in him.

At the end of the first week, Dr. Pramar declared the air safe to breathe. There was a huge celebration, which included the ingesting of large quantities of alcohol. And since the drunks were Fazullans, the revelry resulted in several fights and combat competitions. The next day, Dr. Pramar declared the area a hazardous waste site and had the Fazullans spend the day cleaning up all the blood and disinfecting the soil.

"Security to greenhouse four! Security to greenhouse four!"

Lance Corporal Ruiz entered greenhouse four. Her entry was made more difficult because greenhouse four was the first of the isolation greenhouses. Entry required going through an airlock and a UV sterilization sequence. Once she got inside, she found a Fazullan woman assembling bots and a group of Fazullan men yelling and shoving each other.

"What's the problem?" she asked the Fazullan woman.

"They're arguing about who's the slave."

"What, there are no slaves."

"Apparently that has not totally registered with their thick heads. What they are doing would be considered slave work back home."

"They've been doing it all day, so what's the problem now?"

"Shoveling dirt is slave work, but not too bad. Shoveling the output of the treatment plant is definitely slave work and much beneath them."

Captain Lantaq finally made it through the airlock. He stormed down to the group of men. "What is the meaning of this?!" His voice thundered off the domed walls and ceiling of the greenhouse.

"Sir, we should have the bots do this."

"It will take an extra week if we do. They're too small to handle this type of work."

"But it's . . . shit."

Captain Lantaq grabbed the shovel from the man and started moving the compost onto the growing trays. He glared at the man holding the rake until he started to spread it. After five minutes he thrust the shovel back into the hands of the first man.

"Now are you going to get to work, or should I kill you and add your body to the compost so that you can be of use to this colony?"

"No, sir, . . . I mean yes, sir."

Captain Lantaq stormed out of the greenhouse.

"I guess that is one way to motivate them," Corporal Ruiz said.

The Fazullan woman just smiled and continued to assemble and test the bots.

"I thought I'd check in on you," Corporal Ruiz told the Fazullan woman. She was still assembling bots. Corporal Ruiz figured she'd done about twenty since her last visit.

"Things are going well."

"Good. Damn . . ." Corporal Ruiz ducked as a handful of compost came whizzing toward her head and bounced off of the wall behind her. "What's up with them? Two hours ago, they wouldn't shovel the stuff, now they're grabbing it with their hands and throwing it at each other."

"Men!" the Fazullan woman said, shaking her head as she sent the next bot to its charging station.

"What's going on?"

"Dr. Teltar has said that the meat is safe to eat," a Fazullan woman said.

"So?"

"They are going hunting."

"Without any gear?"

"Yes, they drew lots last night. Those three won. They will hunt the buffalo we saw before."

"And when they find them, what are they going to do? Tackle them and bite their necks?"

"Don't say that too loudly; they may decide that that is a better test." The Fazullan woman laughed at the thought. "No, they will find a branch and make a spear. They have knives so they can sharpen the spear and dress the kill. Whoever makes the kill will be the chief of the celebration."

"What if they don't find the buffalo?"

"They will not come back without a buffalo."

"Oh, you guys are serious about your hunting."

"Serious, maybe I misunderstand the translation, is that another word for stupid?"

The Aperanjen delegation arrived at Onisiwo on an Oryx. There were only six of them so they'd been reasonably comfortable for the two-week trip from Earth to Onisiwo.

"I'm sorry I couldn't be there to meet you," Catie said. "Captain Clements will be able to take care of your needs."

"Princess, we are just happy that we are finally going to be able to wake our comrades up. We are sure they will be excited to know that we are free and finally starting our colony."

"I'm sure they will. Our doctors here have been talking with the doctors on Gemini Station. They're confident that there shouldn't be any issues bringing them out of stasis. Having you here should help with the transition."

"It will. We all remember the confusion of first coming out of stasis. We want to be here to reassure them that everything is alright."

"I'll let you go. You should be able to start waking your comrades up in a few days. The first Fazullan ship is already moving toward you."

"Thank you, Princess."

"Why must we build another greenhouse?!"

"Because we have to test the various crops here and the crops you brought with you to make sure they're compatible," Dr. Pramar said.

"But we already know we can eat the crops here. Why does it matter?"

"Well, you don't know that you can make your type of whiskey from the crops here. Do you want to find out later that you can't grow the right grains to make it? Where would that leave you?"

"A very persuasive argument," Captain Lantaq said once he walked up. He'd been alerted that there was a problem.

"I'm glad. Are you people always so argumentative?"

"No, but they are not used to doing this type of work without slaves helping and doing most of the hard effort. They will need to learn."

"Well, I'm glad that they like whiskey. I don't know what else would have persuaded them to do the work."

"Threatening to kill them has always worked for me."

"Empress, how may I help you?"

"Princess, can you explain why we are not moving our ships to the new colony? We have many ships that are free of all slaves and are ready to go. Captain Lantaq has told me they are ready for more ships with colonists to help build the colony."

"I understand your concern, Empress. But we do not have jump points in place for your new planet. Without them, the effort to move your ships would be prohibitive. We are placing them now. But it will take a few weeks."

"I don't understand why the cost would be prohibitive."

"We would have to dedicate one of our few jump ships to escort you. We do not have one free at this time. We still have to manufacture some of the jump points and then place them in the correct systems."

The empress's eyes glazed over. She was not really interested in jump points and manufacturing issues. She had been waiting for years to lead her people to freedom and was struggling with the idleness of waiting. Most of her people were rotating through stasis, so the time didn't seem as long to them, but she was awake and living each minute in boredom.

"I am sorry to bother you. Can you please keep me updated on the timetable?"

"We will. I understand how stressful it can be to have to wait for an important event, especially when it will be the beginning of a new era."

"Thanks for your understanding, Princess."

"Marc, we need you over on Ocean Avenue."

"McCovey, what's going on?"

"We're not sure, but we really need you here."

Marc got up from his desk and left his office. "I'll be on Ocean Avenue," he told his assistant. "Some mysterious problem. There's not some strange party or something in the works?"

"No, sir. At least none that I know of."

It only took five minutes to make it over to Ocean Avenue. The new street was just under construction. It would be the second major street in Orion. So they were digging a huge trench down the middle which would eventually house the subway system as well as all the utilities. When he arrived, the trencher was idle.

"What seems to be the problem?"

"We've hit a big rock or something. The guys over there swear it's gold."

"Gold? That's absurd. How big is it?"

"They've measured it out at two meters by half a meter by about another twenty centimeters."

"Well, that certainly can't be a gold nugget." Marc waved to the men, motioning for them to come over.

"Grayson, why do you think it's gold?" As Marc remembered, Grayson was the crew chief for the trencher.

"Well, Governor, look at these scrapings we took off the trencher. It dug into the rock a bit. Sure looks like gold to me."

"Looks like it to me, too. Did anyone run some over to the assayer's office?"

"We have an assayer?"

"Yes, he manages the polycrete plant. Take this over to him and have him look at it. If he says it's gold, have him come back with you."

"Yes, sir." The man started running toward the polycrete plant.

"You don't . . . Never mind." Marc waved his hand at the man and turned back to McCovey. "We need to get it out of there anyway, don't we?"

"Yes, sir. I'm just worried that if folks find out we've got gold here, they'll dig up this whole part of town."

Marc laughed, remembering back to the earlier incident when the miners thought they would just take over the mining town and set their own price for the gold. It took a bit before he got them to understand that it wasn't theirs but MacKenzies'. "Just remind them of what happened to O'Brian."

"That might get their attention. But that's one big nugget if it is gold."

"Well let's get it out of there. I want the trencher back to digging as soon as possible. We should start getting more colonists in July, and I want this street completed and the building shells up by then."

"Yes, sir, you're the boss."

It wasn't long after they had the big rock out of the trench that Grayson came running back followed closely by the assayer. He was hurrying, just not as much as Grayson.

"Let me see this nugget he's telling me about."

"Is it gold?"

"Oh, aye it is. I've never heard of anything this big. The biggest was the Welcome Stranger Nugget and it was only 0.6 meters by 0.3 meters. If Grayson isn't lying to me, this thing is almost five times bigger."

"It's bigger, not sure it's all gold, but it does look that way. I thought it might be fool's gold," Marc said.

"Nope, assay came out gold, almost pure, too. So, do you think there's more?"

"Actually, I hope not. There's nothing else in the general location. The guys are sifting through all the dirt they dug up over the last two days. I haven't heard any yells, so I don't think they've found anything."

"At least not anything too big to fit into their pockets."

"Well, assuming there are not a bunch more around, where do you think this one comes from?"

"Who knows, it could have been dropped here by a glacier or it could be a meteorite. Nobody really knows where all the gold comes from. The models don't show how it formed in the quantities we find it in on Earth much less the quantities here on Artemis."

"Oh?"

"Yeah. Apparently, they've observed the results of a couple of neutron stars that collided. Didn't see much gold, at least not like we have on Earth. I gotta think that a couple of neutron stars colliding would be a lot different than the big bang, but I'm just a geologist."

"Take it back with you. We'll decide what to do with it later. Be careful, it's probably worth a couple hundred million."

"Whoa, you're going to have to rename this street Gold Nugget."

Marc gave Samantha a kiss when he got home. "Can you believe we've found a huge gold nugget? It's probably worth about two hundred million dollars."

"Oh, does that mean I can get some new jewelry?"

Marc laughed. "You can have all the jewelry you want. That thing weighed about four metric tons, so I don't think you'll be wearing it."

"Are you going to keep it as an artifact?"

"Do you think we should?"

"At least for a while. It's pretty exciting."

"Yes, but I'm worried that when the farmers get their allotment, they will spend all their time digging for gold nuggets."

"They'll get hungry sooner or later."

"I guess so. So, how's your day been?"

"I've been talking with Neloln. She says the Onisiwoens are elated with the success of the medical treatment for that little girl and with us providing the treatment for other children with scarring."

"That's good news. We need the population to be on our side. They can't imagine the changes that will come once the League starts trading between the various worlds."

"True. I'm just happy that Catie seems to be doing well. She's bounced back after the kidnapping attempt."

"She's still figuring out how to get even. But in this case, that's a healthy thing. I am really glad to see her taking Neloln's advice. I think this is the first time she's really taken advice from an outsider."

"She's taken advice from Miranda and Yvette."

"Yes, but that's more situational advice. Satisfying a quick need. This is letting someone tell her what she should do instead of going off and researching it herself."

"So, you think she's maturing?"

"Seasoning is probably the better term. Understanding your limitations, not only in ability, but in time and experience is a big step. Pretty good for a teenager."

"Allie, look how proud Daddy is. One day, he'll be just as proud of you."

"Nattie, how's the baby?" Catie asked.

"He's doing fine. I'm also fine, by the way."

"You're always fine. Now, where is my little nephew?" Catie had been awarded the status of honorary aunt.

Natalia reached down and picked her son up off the floor. She held him up so Catie could see him.

"Hi, Jules."

"His name is Julian."

"I know, but Jules is my nickname for him. He has to have a nickname. Maybe he can use it as his call sign."

Julian smiled and gurgled at Catie. At almost three months, he wasn't particularly sure who she was, but Mommy liked her.

"How is he getting along with Allie?"

"They're best pals. Samantha and I decided to have them spend their days together. We coordinate our schedule so that they're both with the nanny at the same time while we're working."

"That sounds good. They'll grow up to be best friends."

"They had better. My plan is that Julian marries Allie when they're twenty-five. That way he can buy Paul and me a yacht so we can spend our retirement in luxury."

"That sounds kind of mercenary."

"Why, what mother wouldn't want her son to grow up and marry a rich princess? I only have his best interest at heart."

"Good luck with that. I hear that children have a mind of their own and seldom do what their parents want."

"I hear that also, mostly from your father."

Catie snorted. "Yeah, like he doesn't run my life."

"You keep deluding yourself. It seems to me that you've been running his life."

"I'm sure he thinks so. Anyway, how's the job going?"

"You do realize that I spend my days working out how to deal with human waste; then I come home and I have the same problem." Natalia held Julian up so she could sniff his diaper. "Like right now. Too bad you can't change him over this video link."

"I'm kind of glad that I can't. I'll let you get to your backup job."

"Hah!"

Chapter 12 Fishing in the Criminal Pool

"Hi, Zoey." Catie had decided to check in on the Onisiwoen women who were still hiding out on the Merlin.

"Hello, Princess."

"Please, call me Catie."

"I keep forgetting. What can I do for you?"

"I wanted to see how you and the other women are doing. I also have some questions for later. Where's the baby?"

"One of my friends is taking care of her. I didn't think you would want to deal with a crying baby?"

"She's crying?"

"She might."

"Oh, I'd love to see her."

"Maybe after we're done, you can come and see all the children. They sometimes ask about you."

"Me?" Catie asked incredulously.

"Well, you are a princess."

"I don't usually look like one. But I know what you mean, it's all those fairy tales." Catie had been a bit surprised that every civilization so far had some kind of royalty, and princes and princesses were generally cherished, especially by children.

"Anyway, what did you want to ask me?"

"I wanted to ask you about crime and criminals on Onisiwo."

"Why don't you ask Charlie?"

"I have, but I feel like I'm getting a watered-down version."

"Probably. Charlie's a pretty by-the-book kind of guy. We all were once."

"You're not anymore? Why not?"

"Well, all that's happened, trying to figure out what I'm going to do next."

"But you know none of that was your fault. It wasn't the fault of anyone on the mission."

"I know, but having two babies and with a third one on the way makes me think about things differently. All of us are trying to decide what we should do. How will we be able to raise our children without the press getting in the way, without having to worry about stalkers?"

"Surely there's not a stigma attached to having a child without being married?"

"There isn't. But this isn't the same thing. Being bred is different, uglier."

"Maybe you should change your names."

"We're thinking about that. We're all due five years of back pay. So that's a lot of money. We might be able to disappear."

"What about the assets you had before you were taken?"

"They were given to our heirs. My brother and sister offered to give it back, but that wouldn't be fair to them. They've moved on with their lives. It would be too big a shock."

"I'm sure the governments will help you out. If they don't, I might be able to help."

"Thank you, but we'll be okay. Now, you wanted to know about criminals."

"Right. What kind of crime do you have? We have access to all the statistics on crime here on Onisiwo, but that doesn't help us understand your criminals. We've interrogated the prisoner we captured, but he's not exactly a normal criminal."

"Do you still have him?"

"Yes, he's been helpful, but he doesn't know much."

"How can you still have him?"

"His crime occurred in the embassy; so he's our prisoner, subject to our laws. We just told him what the punishment for attempted kidnapping of a government official was."

"And what is it?"

"Twenty years hard labor."

"What does that mean?"

"We let him imagine that himself. ADI planted some suggestions which built on his own sci-fi fantasy of what it would be. Apparently, he's read a series of books where political prisoners were held on a high-gravity world that was very harsh. They were forced to mine for valuable minerals while trying to survive the attacks of killer insects and carnivorous reptiles."

"Oh, I know those books. Yuk, they really paint a horrible picture of those prison planets."

"He was very helpful when we told him we might let him serve his time here on Onisiwo instead of taking him back to Earth."

"What are your prisons like?"

"Oh, Delphi only has one and it's pretty small. Our definition of hard labor is sorting the recycling in an airconditioned factory."

Zoey burst out laughing. "You should show him what it would have been once you're done with him. That will be worse than serving the time."

"Good idea, now about your other criminals?"

"Oh, we have the usual petty thieves. About fifteen percent of our population is what you would call impoverished. They get forgotten by the system. They don't have a lot of hope for advancement, and their children are stigmatized by the same thing. They don't get a good education, which is no surprise with so little support from home."

"Doesn't the government help them? Don't you have programs for the children?"

"Not really. You'd almost have to remove the children from their parent or parents to make a real difference. That whole segment of society is marginalized. They won't make a big effort to get ahead because they're convinced they don't have a chance. Their kids pick the message up, so they don't try hard at school. Why bother when your future is predetermined by your class."

"We have the same problem, only I think ours is worse. So how do they survive?"

"Lots of them get by on prostitution. They make enough to live on. They typically live in crowded homes or apartments, several families, or people sharing the same living space. Some of the kids wind up being little bullies and thugs, then growing up into big bullies and thugs. Lots of drug abuse."

"How big a problem are drugs?"

"Pretty big. Most of it is legal now. The government figured out that when they made it illegal, they didn't cut down on usage but just funneled money into criminal gangs and raised the price so the addicts had to resort to stealing to feed their habit. When they legalized it back, I think fifty years ago, prices dropped. Most people just used the less addictive types so things didn't get as bad. Crime dropped substantially, especially petty theft, burglaries, purse snatching, and muggings. People could get their fix without resorting to criminal activity. And with it being legal, more people sought out treatment, so eventually, we had less abuse."

"Interesting. My father thinks the same would apply on Earth."

"I'm sure it would. Anyway, that covers the poor downtrodden who resort to crime because they don't think they have a choice. Then we have the real criminals."

"Who?"

"The super-rich and the politicians."

"Do tell."

"They feel so entitled that when they can't have their way, they resort to bribery, extortion, and general bullying to get what they want. Most of our politicians start out as ordinary middle-class citizens when they enter office, and twenty years later, most of them are multimillionaires."

"My father amended our constitution because of that. Now representatives have to put their money in a blind trust while they are in office. Those trusts are audited by the judicial auditor every year along with any other income they receive."

"Won't they just put pressure on the auditors to overlook certain things?"

"Members of the board of auditors are appointed for a seven-year term. They select their own chair and the appointments are staggered, one every year for each of the seven members. They have a budget and whoever they hire is totally up to them."

"Sounds like a good idea. We should consider that. Corruption is so hard to deal with, and for political leaders it is insidious. They get bribes without even knowing it sometimes. A stock tip, someone buying their stock, other favors."

"My father even pegged their pay at the 80th percentile for the nation."

"Interesting."

"It motivates them to minimize income disparity," Catie said. "In the U.S. the members of Congress's salaries are in the 90th percentile. Doesn't seem very representative."

"I wonder if that would work here. You must have met Constaxinavia. Everyone thinks he's got his hand in every political decision, making sure that it benefits him financially."

"Yeah, I've met him. He tried to get me to give him a special deal on some trades between Delphi and Onisiwo."

"Sounds like him. But there is so much corruption and it seems impossible to stop. Nobody has been able to trace the money, so nothing gets proved."

"Well, we're working on it. I'll let you know how we do."

"Now, back to our criminals. We used to have big gangs, I think you call them mafia and cartels, based on watching some of your videos. They still exist, they run extortion rackets, deal drugs."

"How do they deal drugs if they're legal?"

"Well, usually it's pharmaceuticals. They find a way to get them cheap, or steal them. Then they resell them. Anyway, the crime runs in cycles. It gets intense, some gang-on-gang violence then it settles down. Without the usual drug-induced crime, most of it is rather well organized. A missing truckload of computers, things like that."

"And is most of it controlled by your mobs?"

"Yes. They take a dim view of someone trying to pull off a crime without their permission."

"Thanks, that helps. I'll probably have more questions as we keep searching for the guy who ordered the kidnapping."

"I'm always happy to help. Now, were you serious about seeing the children?"

"Of course."

Catie and Neloln had decided that the embassy should host a reception every few weeks to allow Catie to interact with the various politicians and barons. Catie hated the idea, but only because she would have to get dressed up.

Tonight was the second reception they had hosted so far.

"Chair Lexisen, I wanted to share some news with you."

"What news, Princess?"

"We believe we can control the wormhole."

"I thought you could already control the wormhole. Wasn't that how you defeated the Fazullans?"

"Only partially, but we think we can control which system it opens into. Of course, it has to be one of the systems that it already wanders between, but if we can force it to open in the system we want, it would revolutionize our travel around the galaxy."

"How is that different from the artificial wormholes you already use?"

"Our artificial wormholes are limited in the distance they can traverse, being limited to fifty to seventy light-years. They are also limited by how much volume can traverse through them. If we can control your wormhole, we would be able to ship enormous volumes among the four quadrants of this area of the galaxy. It would make Onisiwo an important hub for shipping between colonies."

"Oh, interesting."

"I think that we should establish a Delphi League facility here on Onisiwo."

"You already have your embassy."

"Yes, but on Earth, we have the United Nations to deal with all the political things on Earth. It has two compounds. Each of them covers almost twenty acres, and that's just for one planet. The League already has eight planets and we expect to add another ten in the next few years. We need to have a place where the ambassadors and their staff can meet and live. There will be all kinds of committees to coordinate the activities across the League."

"Interesting, I'll have to give it some thought. Is there anything else?"

"We might need some space on your space stations for their ships to dock and possibly space for their crew to live while their ships are in orbit. We also might need to build some repair facilities, so the crews could be stranded for a few weeks or months at a time."

"Hmm, I'll talk to my staff and let you know."

"Cer Catie. It makes no sense to duplicate the U.N. for each planet. And since Earth has over one hundred ninety nations, the League should be far more efficient with only ten to twenty planets. And why would we build a repair dock here, it seems better to send the ships back to where they're built for the repairs."

"I know that, ADI; it's not my fault if Chair Lexisen gets carried away. And you can't use this information."

"Darn!"

◆ ◆ ◆

"Lord Kacketox, how are you doing?"

"Hello, Princess. I'm doing well, thank you for asking."

"I wondered if you knew anything about your manufacturing capacity in space."

"I know a little."

"Well, I wondered how fast you could add capacity. I have been told that your manufacturing capacity is just thirty percent of what we have on Earth."

"Would we need to match your capacity or would we expect you to ship those types of goods to us?"

"We've found it better to license the manufacturing instead of shipping the goods. We only ship when it doesn't make sense to have a separate manufacturing facility."

"You are devious," ADI said.

Cristina giggled as she opened the door to her hotel room. "Shh, you don't want to wake the neighbors."

"You have neighbors?"

"It's a hotel, you always have neighbors."

Cristina pushed the door open and let the man go in first. She flicked on the 'do not disturb' alert and closed the door. Her blouse was already half off from their ride in the elevator. "Get on the bed, I'll just go freshen up a bit."

"While you're there, take those bloody clothes off!"

"You mean you don't want to unwrap your gift?"

"I'll unwrap the last layer!"

Cristina went into the bathroom, closed the door, and took a deep breath. It had taken two weeks to finally find the elusive Mr. X. The man whose business it was to connect hitmen with their clients. Then it had taken another week to finally get his attention. They'd spent the evening having drinks and flirting with each other. Cristina had just managed to dump about half of her drinks into the plant next to their table, so she wasn't quite drunk but tipsier than she wanted to be. She took a couple of pills that the doctors had given her. They were supposed to convert the alcohol into sugar faster than her liver could. *"One can only hope."* Cristina drank some water, then kicked off her shoes and removed the rest of her blouse and her skirt.

"Are you ready?"

"You know it. Come here and ride me!"

Cristina walked into the room wearing just a bra and panties. The man was lying on the bed naked. He wasn't as ready as he claimed, the alcohol was obviously having an effect.

The man whistled, or tried to, it came out more as a spitting sound. "Come to papa!"

Cristina crawled onto the bed and straddled the man. "Here take these, they'll help you to get ready." Cristina gave him four of the pills, he really needed sobering up. She gave him a drink from the glass then set it back on the nightstand. "You'll be ready to go in just a few minutes."

"I'm ready to go now!"

"I don't think so." Cristina pressed his shoulders down onto the bed. He reached up to grab her breast but she pushed his arms aside. "Now just wait. You need to build up some anticipation."

"I've built up enough already!"

Cristina started massaging his chest. Slowly she worked up to his neck. Finally, she had her hands behind his neck. She slipped the paralyzer she had secreted between her two fingers and applied it to the nape of his neck.

SLAP!

"You pig!"

Cristina moved off the man and got off the bed. She went to her bag and grabbed the interrogation hood. She put it over his head, strapping it into place. "ADI?"

"It will take him two hours before he's sober enough. Then I need two hours for the interrogation."

"Okay, I'm going to take a shower!"

"ADI, are you finished? I'd like to kick him out." Cristina was taking off her robe so that she would be in her lingerie when she did her act about what a wonderful night they'd spent together. She'd already removed the money from his wallet.

"Housekeeping!"

"No, way. It's six a.m." Cristina's mind raced. She dropped to the floor and scooted under the bed just as the door opened.

"Housekeeping!"

Cristina could hear the woman moving into the room. *"ADI, what's going on?"* she messaged using her tailboard. She and most of the Marines couldn't thank Catie enough for coming up with using the vestigial nerves for the now nonexistent human tail to be able to type on their Comms. It allowed communication in situations like this where you couldn't type and didn't want to talk.

"The woman is wearing a maid's uniform. She could be the maid."

"Not a chance. Where is she?"

"She is approaching the bed now," ADI messaged back.

"Oh, you must like it kinky!"

POP!

"What is this thing?"

"She shot him with a silenced pistol. She's pulled the hood off of his head."

Cristina swore to herself. *"Damn, and I'm here in my underwear. I need a weapon."* She scooched over to the middle of the bed, looking for something she could weaponize. *"Shit, and I don't even have an underwire bra."*

"The woman is going into the bathroom."

"Think, girl, think!" Cristina knew that she wouldn't have time to get out from under the bed before the woman would be able to shoot her. Her hand went to her hair as she struggled to come up with an option. *"Bobby pins!"*

Cristina pulled three bobby pins from her hair. She straightened them out then twisted them together, forming a ten-centimeter-long spike. *"It should just be long enough and strong enough,"* she thought.

"ADI, I need to know exactly where the woman is."

"What should I use as a reference point?"

"The center of the bed. Start giving me the position of her head when she approaches the bed again."

"Come on out, my pet!"

The woman came back into the bedroom and looked around. She was obviously trying to decide where Cristina was.

"She is 50 centimeters toward the head of the bed, one meter away from the edge."

Cristina scooched toward the foot of the bed a little. Her head was toward the foot and she wanted her hand to be wherever the woman's head would be when she looked under the bed.

"Come, come, my pet. You've been at it all night; you must be tired."

"ADI, tell Catie I want a gun. This is ridiculous!"

"Cer Cristina, I think we should focus on the current situation first. She has moved toward the foot of the bed. I estimate her head will be just past the center of the bed when she kneels down."

The woman knelt down and flipped up the bed skirt. "There you are."

Cristina tilted her head so she could see the assassin's face. Her hand lashed out, plunging the bobby pin spear into the assassin's left eye. Cristina kept pushing the spear into the eye, using her finger to press it all the way in. The assassin collapsed.

Cristina scooted her way out the other side of the bed, then cautiously made her way around the foot of the bed.

"I believe she is dead," ADI deadpanned.

"Let's hope so."

Cristina used her foot to push the assassin's shoulder. The head just flopped to the side.

"Okay, now what." Cristina stepped back to observe the scene. The man was lying in the center of the bed, naked, and on his back. He had a bullet hole in the center of his forehead. The interrogation hood was lying next to him where the assassin had tossed it after removing it. Cristina stowed it in her bag.

The assassin was lying next to the bed curled up. She'd died while kneeling down and just flopped to the side. Cristina visualized straddling the man, preparing to shoot him, getting stabbed in the eye just as she fired her shot. Her body would have jerked backward away from the blow to her eye and would have rolled off the bed. She went to her bag and pulled out a pair of latex gloves, put them on, then adjusted the assassin so she was lying at the angle she had visualized.

"Okay, now what's wrong with this scene? Maid's uniform doesn't work, and what weapon would he have used?"

Cristina looked around the room; she saw one of the ubiquitous note pads and pens that were found in any hotel room, around the galaxy it seems. She moved the pad over to the nightstand on the man's right-hand side. She put the pen in the man's hand, as if he'd grabbed it from the table. She pulled the bobby pin spear out of the assassin's eye, and brain, and inserted the pen in its place, pushing it in just a little further. She stood back and looked at the scene again.

Cristina walked over to her kit and pulled out her knife. She used it to cut the maid's uniform off of the woman. "Whew, at least she's wearing lingerie." She'd been afraid she'd find industrial pantyhose and a utilitarian bra on the woman, but apparently she'd not been willing to go that far in her disguise. Cristina wadded the uniform up and stuck it in her bag. Fortunately, there wasn't much blood involved, but she took a comb from her cosmetic bag and carefully dipped it in the assassin's blood and dripped some on the bed across where she estimated the assassin's head would have traveled. Then she carefully smeared a little of the man's blood around the wound where the hood had covered his skin.

She wiped her hands on one of the small towels the assassin had brought into the room. She threw the towel into her bag.

"ADI, do I have to worry about my prints?"

"Your prints are not in the Onisiwoen system."

"Okay. Can you get a scan of her prints so we can figure out who she is?"

"Yes, use the camera on your Comm."

Cristina carefully manipulated the assassin's hands so she could get a picture of her fingerprints.

"Okay, now what's wrong with this scene?" Cristina's eyes moved over the scene. Dead man on the bed, assassin dead on the floor beside the bed. The gun under the edge of the bed.

"Gun's in the wrong place."

"Thanks, ADI."

Cristina picked the gun up, careful to not smear any fingerprints. She tossed the gun onto the bed where she estimated it would have fallen.

"Where's her passkey?" Cristina asked.

"She laid it on the counter in the bathroom."

"ADI, you're a jewel."

"Of course."

Cristina grabbed the passkey and put it into her bag, then she grabbed one of her dresses from the closet and finished dressing. She left one dress behind, the assassin had to have worn something when she came into the room. She collected a few things from the bathroom, leaving enough behind that it would look proper. She exchanged her shoes for the assassin's and then did one more sweep of the room before she pulled down the surveillance pucks and stowed them in her bag. She exited the room, then pulled off the gloves and put them in her handbag as she rolled her suitcase over to the fire escape.

After exiting the building, Cristina made her way down the alley and across the block before flagging a taxi. "ADI, I need a residential address close to here."

Cristina gave the cab driver the address ADI provided and sat back and relaxed.

"What's the problem?" the taxi driver asked.

"Oh, my boyfriend and I had a fight. We were coming home from a vacation and started arguing. I got out of his car and told him to go screw himself. Now I just need to go home."

"You're supposed to be relaxed after a vacation."

"I know. I couldn't believe he picked a fight. Just goes to show, you can never tell."

The taxi driver dropped her off in front of the house. The address ADI had provided was of a nice house in what looked like an upscale neighborhood. Cristina gave the taxi driver money for the fare and a nice tip, then she slid out of the taxi, pulling her bag behind her.

"Do you want some help?" the taxi driver asked.

"No, I've got it. Thanks, you're a lifesaver."

"Nice tip, call me anytime." The taxi driver gave Cristina his card.

Cristina watched as the taxi drove down the street. She slowly rolled her suitcase toward the house, until the taxi was out of sight.

"Okay, now ADI, I need another taxi, a different company."

"It should be here in one minute."

"You are so clever."

"I try."

"Now, I need a downtown hotel that is having some kind of conference."

"Got one."

Chapter 13   Culling the Catch

Once Cristina was settled into the new hotel room, she contacted Catie and Major Prescott and explained what had happened.

"Apparently someone is trying to clean up their tracks," Major Prescott said.

"Do we need to provide Cristina with protection?"

"Catie, I appreciate your concern, but I don't want to have someone tailing me and tipping them off. I just need a gun."

"What kind of gun?"

"A small one, preferably one that can't be detected."

"We could probably make one out of plastic that would get through a security checkpoint. I'm not sure about the bullets though?"

"Why can't we make them out of something non-conductive? They really don't need to be that strong."

"I'll check with a couple of engineers and have one printed up for you. How many shots?"

"Small!"

"Okay. ADI, what have we learned?" Catie asked.

"He doesn't know his contact's name," ADI said.

"What does that mean?"

"He only knows how to contact him and has a code for their communication."

"What about the money?"

"It was wired to him. I can't trace it back to the source. They deposited the money in cash to a bank in the Southern Coalition and then transferred it from there."

"ADI, can't you figure out where the cash came from?"

"No."

"So now what?" Catie asked.

"He had to get instructions," Cristina said.

"Yes, I suspect they came from a burner phone. If we could get his contact on the phone, I could trace the call."

"How will that help?"

"They have lots of cameras that I can access. I can trace the call much faster than they can, especially if I know when it is going to be made. Then we can check the surveillance video to determine the caller. It might take more than one call, but we should be able to narrow it down."

"That makes sense, but why would he respond to our call?"

"Let's assume he's another middle man whose job is to direct business to his friends in the other coalitions. If that's the case, I suggest we take out a hit on someone," Cristina said.

"Do you think that will work?"

"Only one way to find out. Once we do it, then we can figure out how to manipulate the situation to get to whoever he is. He's got to know someone further up the chain."

"Who do we take the hit on?" Catie asked.

"Lord Maxiamar," Cristina suggested.

"Who?"

"Some guy that Mr. X was whining about. It sounded like he wanted him taken out."

"We can't just have someone killed!"

"We'll try to stop it before it goes too far, but at least if it does get out of hand, they take out some scuzzbag crooked executive."

"How do we contact this hitman?" Catie asked.

"Apparently you have to go to the Western Coalition capital. Then you need to go to a bar and buy a cell phone," ADI said. "That means you may need to identify another target if the contractor works there instead of here in the Northern Coalition."

"We should deal with that when we know more," Major Prescott suggested.

"Wait, that's crazy. And why would you have two contractors working with each other? They're in competition."

"I think it's a blind cutout," Major Prescott said. "They are subcontracting work in each other's coalition and want a hard break so they can't be ratted out by their competition."

"I see," Catie said. "So, what's next?"

"I fly over there and go to the bar and buy a cellphone."

"But how does that work?"

"Based on my experience, whoever the contact is sends a set of burner phones to a bar. The phones have a number programed for another burner phone. They're good for a few days before he sends new phones. The bar doesn't know anything except that they're supposed to sell the phone to whoever asks for them with the correct passphrase. Makes a pretty clean separation," Cristina said.

"Okay, Cristina, are you up for this?"

"Just get me a plane ticket."

"Cristina, here's your gun." Catie handed her a small revolver.

"Nice, I like it. Small and very light. Tell me about it."

"You've got five shots, here's another cylinder. The bullets are built into the cylinder, so no cartridges, you have to change the cylinder if you need more than five shots."

"That shouldn't be too bad. If I need more than five, then I'm in real trouble. More shots probably won't help. What is the actual bullet made of?"

"It's hardened quartz. The whole gun is plastic. It won't set off any alarms going through a security checkpoint. The gunpowder is sealed in, and then the cylinder is cleaned so it won't be picked up by explosives sensors. There's an extra cylinder down at the ranges so you can practice before you go."

"Smart, you always need to get to know a new gun. Now, am I flying commercial, or are you guys dropping me off in a Lynx?"

"You'll have to fly commercial. A Lynx flying to the Western Coalition would raise too many questions. Here's your ticket."

"Okay. See you when I get back."

Cristina entered the bar that ADI had identified for her. It looked like a standard working-class bar in a working-class neighborhood. She walked over to the counter and sat down.

"We don't get many ladies in here." The bartender walked over wiping a glass.

"I'll have a whiskey."

"Ice?"

"No, I said whiskey, not water."

The bartender smiled as he turned and grabbed a bottle.

"Not that, the good stuff."

His hand drifted from the bottle he was going for to another one on an upper shelf.

"This is our best."

Cristina put some money on the bar to pay for the drink.

"I heard I could buy a phone here. One with a blue number in it."

"Oh, you did, did you?"

"Yes." Cristina downed the whiskey in one go. "Now, do you have one?"

"They're twelve hundred onis."

"I was told one thousand."

"Well, the price has gone up."

"Is that what I'm going to be told when I make the call?"

The bartender nodded to a group of men in the back of the bar. They started heading toward him and Cristina. The lead guy was a huge Onisiwoen, at least one hundred fifty kilos.

Cristina looked at the men, then back at the bartender.

"Maybe we'll just take your money."

Cristina pulled her revolver out and shot the big guy in the leg. She aimed so the shot would hit the bone, and by his cry of pain, she was pretty sure it had. She grabbed the bartender by the front of his shirt and pulled him toward her.

"My next shot will be a headshot. I can tell by your actions you don't use your brains much, but I still think you need them."

"Okay, okay! We were just having a little fun."

"So am I. Now about that phone." Cristina released the bartender. She glared at the group of men and they turned around and went back to whatever they were doing at the back of the bar, leaving their friend writhing in pain on the floor.

"Here is the phone. One thousand onis."

Cristina grabbed the phone and put it in her bag. "I charge one thousand onis for teaching people not to be stupid. Consider yourselves taught." She left the bar. She kept an eye on everyone behind her via her specs. Nobody seemed interested in another lesson.

Cristina walked three blocks, then took four different taxis to get back to her hotel. Finally, she was confident that she wasn't being followed.

"ADI, are you ready?"

"I'm always ready. But you must wait thirty more minutes before calling."

After waiting thirty minutes, Cristina dialed the number.

"Cer Cristina, the number is ringing a phone in the Northern Coalition."

"Oh, hmm."

Someone finally answered the phone. "Hello."

"I've been told you can help me with a problem in the Northern Coalition."

"What kind of problem?"

"A cleanup."

"Where are you?"

"The Western Coalition. Seaside, if you care."

"Please hang up and call back in two hours."

The line went dead.

"Cer Cristina, that would have been just before the Onisiwoen technology would have been able to trace the call. I suggest you turn the phone off until your next call."

"Hello," Cristina said. It was two hours later and she was calling as instructed.

"I understand that you have a problem here in the Northern Coalition that you'd like someone to handle."

"That is correct."

"Well, I have a client with a problem in the Western Coalition that needs handling."

Cristina was shocked at the turn of events. The person on the phone was a different one, or at least the voice was different.

"Cer Cristina. The phone you're connected with is along the northern coast, over four hundred miles from the earlier location."

It was almost too much information for Cristina to absorb. "A problem here?"

"Yes, surely you're able to take care of a problem over there. A cleanup, similar to the problem you have here."

"Cer Cristina, you should agree."

"I'm sure I can arrange to have the problem cleaned up."

"Good, then if you would go back to the bar where you purchased the phone, you'll be given an envelope with the details of my problem. You can leave the details of your problem there, in a sealed envelope if you would."

"I had some difficulty at the bar last time."

"I heard. That's why I'm so confident you can clean up my problem. Rest assured you won't have any problem this time."

"Very well."

"Good, we need to sign off. Please dump that phone, you'll be given another."

"Of course."

The line just went dead. "Well, that's interesting."

"It certainly is," ADI said.

"ADI, I want to change hotels. Can you find one? Also, let Catie know we need to talk. We'll do that once I'm in the new hotel."

"Done. Your taxi will be waiting at the corner of 5th and Castarax in twenty minutes."

"Thank you. You're getting good at this."

"It is so much fun. I've missed Catie's revenge plots, but this is much better."

"You'll have to tell me about the revenge plots."

"I can't, I've been sworn to secrecy."

It took Cristina an hour to change hotels. Once she settled into her new room, she called Catie and Major Prescott and explained the situation.

"An interesting turn of events," Major Prescott said.

"Yes, and with the phone being in two different places at the same time, one has to assume they've cloned the phone. So, ADI won't be able to compare surveillance between the two locations to lock down who the guy is. They're pretty smart."

"We have to assume they are practiced at this sort of thing. So now we have two problems to deal with. Do we stay with our original target, or do we change it? And what do we do about the contract they want us to take on?"

Catie smiled and gave everyone her 'DUH' look. "The contract on our side of the deal should be easy. We can just make the target disappear and have it look like a hit. We can put them on the Merlin until we figure this out. They should be happy once they realize they've got a target on their back."

"True, but what about the hit we're supposed to be ordering?"

"We could pick someone else, someone that's likely to have others wanting to put a hit out on them. Then do the same thing. Cristina will just take credit for it."

"That might work, but won't it be too big of a coincidence?"

"What else can we do? Take a hit out on someone and let them get killed?"

"We could just hide them. They might know that there's a hit out on them and hide."

"We could probably make that work. But who? Should we just stick with Lord Maxiamar?"

"ADI?"

"Lord Maxiamar has quite a few enemies as you surmised. It is feasible that he would have a hit called out on him. He has connections in the Western Coalition that might warn him," ADI reported.

"Okay, let's go with that. Cristina, you write up the details of the hit and deliver it this afternoon. Major Prescott, you'll need to get Lord Maxiamar out of the way. Do you have someone who can take care of it?"

"I can make a call," ADI said. "I can tell him his life is in danger and if he doesn't get out of sight, he will be dead by tomorrow."

"Then we're leaving it up to him to protect himself," Catie said.

"Once he's out of sight, we can find a way to get him up to the Merlin," Major Prescott said.

"Okay, you figure it out. Cristina, you're good to go."

When Cristina went back to the bar, the same bartender was there. It was obvious that someone had beat the crap out of him. He handed her a phone and a package without a word. Cristina handed him her envelope and left. She gave him a little wave on her way out of the bar.

Two hours later, after changing taxis twice, she was back in the hotel room. "Let's see what we've got here." Cristina opened the package. It had a picture of the target, his name, and basic contact info. It also noted that collateral damage was acceptable. The timetable for the hit was within one week.

"Okay, ADI, who is this Jaraxa Salsaram?"

"He is a wealthy real estate developer. I don't see any indications of corruption yet. But I'll gather as much information as I can about him."

"Yes, we need to know who's putting the hit out. That's the only way we can trace this whole thing back to whoever ordered the kidnapping."

"I'm on it."

Cristina lay down on the bed, for her it was nap time.

"Okay, ADI, what have you found?" Cristina asked.

"The only thing I found was a recent real estate deal that went sour. Jaraxa owns a large parcel of land next to an ocean preserve. Its development is restricted to single-family housing. It would be worth ten times its current value if that restriction was lifted."

"So, is he trying to get it lifted?"

"He's made some efforts. But the deal that went sour was the sale of the property to a DXV Amalgamated. Part of the payment was a piece of property in the city. Before the deal was closed, Jaraxa had the property inspected and discovered that it was contaminated with industrial waste. He canceled the deal."

"So, you think DXV Amalgamated is pissed off?"

"Possibly."

"Trace why DXV Amalgamated wanted the property, and what the disclosure of the contamination meant to them. One of those things has to be the reason for the hit. And the one-week timeline must mean something."

"Yes, Cer Cristina. It will take a few hours. There are lots of systems I must get into to research this."

"That's fine. I'll go to dinner, when we have the results, we can go over them with Catie."

"ADI, explain what you discovered?"

"Cer Cristina, Cer Catie, it appears that two people on the board that decides on the zoning which affects Cer Jaraxa's property have recently experienced significant gains in their investment portfolios, similar to the ones that Chair Lexisen has experienced. I gather that it is a favorite way for businesses to bribe public officials."

"What?!"

"I've been able to determine that the public officials that we suspect of receiving bribes always have an unexpected spike in the value of their stock portfolios. I suspect they must be getting special information about how to trade."

"Okay, we'll talk about that later. Go on."

"Cer Jaraxa's holdings are leveraged heavily. If he should die, the need to pay outstanding loans and taxes would force his heirs to sell the property. He has a son by a previous marriage who would be entitled to half of his estate. Cer Jaraxa's wife and two children would get the other half. Should the wife and two children be killed along with him, the other son would still need to sell the property to satisfy outstanding loans and pay the taxes. Cer Jaraxa does not have sufficient liquid assets to satisfy those debts, and the property in question is the most liquid commodity he has."

"ADI, you're sounding like a lawyer," Catie said.

"Do you think so? I practiced for several seconds."

"You did very well. So, do we know who owns this DXV Amalgamated?"

"There are several owners, but I cannot tie them to the actions against you. They seem to be normal businessmen. But there could be private agreements that allow someone else to actually benefit from the development."

"Okay, so this means we need to keep moving forward until we can trace the guy calling for the hit."

"I agree," Cristina said.

◆ ◆ ◆

That night ADI called Lord Maxiamar and suggested that if he wished to be able to celebrate another birthday, he should make himself scarce.

She even went so far as to suggest that if he wished to have breakfast the next morning he should do the same. She provided him a cabin located in the mountains where he might find some private time. He didn't bother to pack.

The next afternoon, Cristina was at a small airport where Jaraxa was waiting for his plane to be ready. He was taking his family on a vacation in the Southern Coalition. Being a pilot, he was going to fly them there himself.

"Mr. Salsaram, how are you doing?" Cristina asked.

"Do I know you?"

"No, but I've been given a lot of information about you. Apparently, somebody behind DXV Amalgamated is quite unhappy with you."

"Those idiots. Did they really think I wouldn't inspect the property?"

"I wouldn't know."

"What are you here for, are you supposed the threaten me, make me sell anyway?"

"No, actually I'm supposed to kill you."

"That's absurd." Jaraxa got up and started looking around. Looking for the police, Cristina guessed.

"It is absurd, but it is also true. Now I don't intend to kill you, but if you're still alive next week, I'm sure they'll find someone else to do the job. Please sit back down."

Jaraxa sat down and sighed. He rubbed his face then leaned back. "What can I do? My wife and children are on their way to meet me. We're supposed to be flying to Racia for vacation."

"I know. We have plans to get your family to a safe location. I'll have your plane flown remotely; it'll crash into the ocean a few hours after it takes off. We can stall the sale of that property they're after for a few weeks. By then we should know who's behind all this."

"We're talking about my family. And that's a ten-million-onis jet you're talking about crashing."

"My associate will make good on the jet. And the lives of you and your family must be worth more than ten million."

"They are. How do I know I can trust you?"

Cristina reached in her pocket and took out a small doll. She placed it on the counter next to Jaraxa. "Because if I wanted you dead, I wouldn't need to have this conversation."

Jaraxa's eyes grew huge as he recognized the doll. It was a good-luck charm his wife had bought him when he'd bought the jet. He'd kept it in the cockpit ever since. To have it, Cristina must have been inside the jet.

"Okay, you've convinced me. What do we do?"

"You're going to take off in another jet, just like yours. My friend has fixed it so that air traffic control will think it's your usual jet. Then fly it to Largaxa Island and land at the airport there. You and your family will be moved to another jet and taken to a safe location."

"Is that all?"

"As far as I'm concerned. After that, it's above my paygrade."

Jaraxa left the lounge to meet his family.

"ADI, it's all up to you now."

Chapter 14   It's Lonely Out Here

Catie met Jaraxa and his family when they arrived on the Merlin. They had been surprised at the strange-looking jet that had met them on Largaxa Island, and the flight attendant being human was unexpected. But when they exited the shuttle and met Princess Catherine, they were shocked.

"Princess," Jaraxa said. "I'm confused."

"Lord Salsaram, I'm sorry for the cloak and dagger, but we've been working to discover who was behind the raid on our embassy. During our investigations, we came across a plot to assassinate you. This was the best we could do on short notice. You and your family will be staying in my cabin while you're up here."

"Up here?"

"Yes, you're on the Merlin, it is stationed above Onisiwo's North Pole. You'll be safe here until we resolve the situation."

Jaraxa was shocked. "You mean we're in orbit?"

"Not exactly, since the Merlin is not circling the planet, but I guess that's close enough."

"How long will we have to stay here?" Jaraxa's wife asked.

"I'm afraid I don't know; it could be a couple of months."

"But the children, their schooling, our friends."

"I understand your distress, but we have to eliminate the threat to your lives. Your children can continue their schooling here. The Merlin can provide instruction for them. There aren't any children their age on board, but we could explore bringing some other Onisiwoens up here. But let's get you settled first. In a few days, we'll know more and can come up with a better plan."

"Dear, I think that will be best. Let's get the children settled."

The children in question were running around the flight deck looking at the Foxes, the shuttle, and into every corner they could reach.

"This is Captain McAvoy," Catie introduced the captain when she walked up.

"I'm pleased to meet you. Please contact my steward if you need anything. I'm sure you'll find the accommodations adequate. You'll be right across the passageway from my cabin, so if there are any problems feel free to let me know."

"We'll try not to bother you, Captain. I'm sure we'll be just fine once we've recovered from all the shock. Children, please come with us."

◆ ◆ ◆

"Hi, Alyssa. How's school?"

"Hi, Catie. You would start with school. How's the princess stuff going?"

"S-l-o-w!"

"Come on, it has to be more fun than that. Aren't you going to parties and balls? Fun stuff like that?"

"Two parties and a bunch of receptions; I'm not big on parties, especially when I have to be careful to do everything just so. The rest has been endless negotiations and sorting through data."

"That does sound boring. Anyway, school's fine. I have two classes with Sophia and one with this guy, Artie. He says he knows you."

"Oh, Artie. I'm surprised you're in a class with him."

"Why?"

"He's pretty advanced. I would think he'd be a Junior by now."

"He would be if he'd taken his freshman English class."

"Oh, I can believe that. I always put those classes off until the last minute."

"Apparently, so does he. Anyway, what's up with him? He's kind of cute."

"Cute?" Catie was surprised to hear anyone describe Artie as cute.

"Yeah, in a geeky kind of way."

Catie laughed. "Well, he is a super nice guy. But he's always been ahead of his age group, so he's socially awkward."

"Like someone else I know."

"I'm not socially awkward."

"Oh, that's not what Sophia and Yvette say."

"Those two had better watch out! I might be a long way off, but I can still manage to get even."

Alyssa laughed. "They said you'd say that. Anyway, they just said you hadn't dated very much."

"I never get a chance. And I'm worried about dating anyone who knows who I am."

"That would make it difficult. Everyone knows who you are. Are you worried they might be after your money?"

"That or be more interested in their image of me than me."

"That would kind of suck. Anyway, I was wondering what I need to do to get Artie to ask me out."

"I think you'll need to ask him out first."

"What?!"

"Hey, you're a modern woman. Ask him out."

"Hmm."

"Princesa Catie!" the triplets squealed.

"Hi, girls. How are you doing?"

"Great, we got to go to the obstacle course with the twins today. It was really fun. We're getting really good."

Catie laughed at the triplets. They had moved to a desk and were viewing her on the display so they could all three see her at the same time.

"Are you behaving yourselves?"

Their eyes flicked back and forth. "Yes . . ."

"Why do I have a hard time believing you. I'll have to talk to Celia."

"She'll tell you that we've been good."

"Okay, . . . I see your English has improved."

"Yes, ANDI makes us study all the time. He's mean!"

"I am not!" ANDI said. ANDI was the DI they had built to replace ADI in the Sakira. He was now in Delphi City, and a less powerful AI was running the Sakira.

"He makes us do our homework!"

"So, you're supposed to do your homework."

"And study!"

"Sounds like ANDI is doing a good job."

"Well, he does read to us," the triplets relented.

"See."

"Anyway, the twins and us have invented a new game."

"The twins and we!" Catie corrected. "Tell me about it."

"It's called podball. They read about it in a sci-fi book. They think it'll be really fun. We played a couple of games yesterday, but we still need to figure out all the rules."

"The book didn't give you the rules?"

"No! It just talked about these friends who played it. ANDI found another game that is kind of like it. It's called handball."

"Handball, isn't that like squash, but without a racquet?"

"No, German handball. It's kind of like soccer, but the ball is a little smaller and you use your hands."

"Not like basketball?"

"No, you throw the ball in a net at the end of the court. It's like a soccer net. Anyway, it looks similar so we're going to use those rules and add more as we learn."

"Where are you playing this game?"

"In the obstacle course. We set the barriers so you have something to push off of. It's really fun. Watch!"

They put up a video of them playing the game. The ball was just a little bigger than their hands, but they could just grip it. They were racing down the court, actually flying since it was microgravity. The net at the end of the court had one of the twins in it, the other twin was trying to interfere with the triplets' progress down the court. One of the girls bounced the ball off the ceiling to her teammate. The twin tried to intercept the ball but just fell short. She flipped and pushed off the ceiling toward the goal. She slammed into the triplet who was trying to get the ball past the goalie.

"It looks kind of rough."

"Yeah! That's why it's so fun. You can body slam your opponents. But you can't hit them with your hands, and you have to launch yourself from over three meters away."

"How many players are there supposed to be?"

"Seven on each team. But we're just practicing, trying to figure out the rules. There are lots of kids up here and no sports for us to play. So, we're inventing our own."

"Oh, that's a big oversight," Catie thought. "Okay, have you come up with any less violent games?"

"There aren't many big spaces up here. The parks always have a lot of people in them, so you can't even kick a ball around."

"I'll have to see if I can do something about that. Maybe come up with a place where you can play basketball."

"No, we want a podball court!"

"I'll look into it. Now, how are you doing in school?"

"Boring!"

"But!"

"ANDI helps us. And we're doing good. We get mostly A's."

"Doing well," ANDI corrected.

"Besides fixing your English, how is ANDI helping you?"

"He makes up lots of examples so we can figure out the lesson. And he gives us extra homework; we don't think that's helping. We told you he was mean."

"Helping you do well in school is not mean."

The triplets didn't look convinced.

"How is Celia doing?"

"She really likes her job. She works almost every day, at least every day we're in school. She bought us new clothes and we each got a matching bracelet. See!"

The three of them showed Catie the bracelet they were wearing. They were silver bangles with the image of three interlocking rings on them.

"Those are very pretty."

"Yeah!"

Board meeting – April 3rd

"This meeting will come to order. Okay, Fred, you're on."

"Nothing particularly exciting. But we're being inundated with requests for trade goods to the colonies, Paraxea, and Onisiwo. The Onisiwoens are asking us to ship them a few supersonic airliners."

"They are not supposed to be talking to you directly!" Catie said.

"Hey, too late. Once you opened up the GalaxyNet to them, we started getting inquiries. You still have the chokehold of the only cargo ship that can reasonably make the trip."

"Their behavior was to be expected," Marc said. "Go on Fred."

"Of course, the Paraxeans are asking about getting a few StarMerchants of their own. We've let them know that's not going to happen anytime soon. And we're getting lots of queries about luxury goods, wines, alcohol, beer, specialty foods, clothing, and jewelry. Catie, you'll need to come up with a sampler to carry with your ships."

"Thanks!"

"And our cabin manufacturing is going well. They've really ramped it up. Right now, only twenty percent is being consumed locally, but they expect to see prices drop as they finish getting their manufacturing tooled. Hopefully, that'll impact housing costs in Indonesia. You can read the report on MacKenzies, but it all looks good."

"Excellent. Maybe I'll be able to afford a vacation."

Samantha smacked Marc on the shoulder.

"Blake," Marc said, making a show of rubbing his shoulder.

"As you all probably know, the Fazullans are over the moon about the planet they're surveying now. Based on the latest report, they're going to make it their home."

"Catie, that means the empress will be calling you," Samantha said.

"She already has. I told her we would move as fast as we could, but it would still be June before we could move her ships."

"Good. Blake, anything else?"

"Our second frigate is ready. We're naming it the Ulysses. I'm assuming we're still planning on sending it to Artemis."

"Yes, we're feeling a bit naked out here without the Sakira or the Newton."

"I can imagine. The Galileo is back at Mangkatar, so they're happy. Are we going to build frigates for the other Paraxean colonies?"

"Sam?"

"I'm still trying to feel them out. They're not feeling particularly loyal to Paraxea, but it's early. Once trade picks up, they might develop a stronger bond based on being the same species."

"Let's build another explorer ship next," Catie said. "That will give Sam time to figure out who should provide the frigates. And we're building up a list of planets we should be checking out."

"Anyone have a problem with that? . . . No, then let's do it. Admiral Michaels?"

"We're actually making progress on a unified Earth government. The big sticking point is still disarmament. The Chinese aren't ready to absorb a million soldiers back into civilian life. And of course, they don't trust the Russians. They've suggested that if they were to have a planet of their own to colonize, it would relieve the problem. We're trying various things to see if we can get them to move."

"I see."

"Wait!" Blake slapped the table to get everyone's attention. "The Chinese ambassador came here to my office and accused us of breaking their internet."

"What did you tell him?"

"I told him that I hadn't heard anything about their internet being broken, and if we'd broken it, I damn well would have heard something. That it would have been the breaking news on every news outlet in the world. Then I asked him if he wanted me to demonstrate."

Admiral Michaels laughed.

"Does that laugh mean we have been breaking their internet?"

"ANDI and I have run a few experiments. Using the viruses ADI left behind, we've reconfigured a few of their internet nodes. We connect the node directly to the world's internet, bypassing the Chinese filters. It takes them a while to figure out which node it is. ANDI moves it around until they get close, then he leaves it alone. They tear it out and replace it with new hardware, but between the time it takes them to notice something is wrong and to trace it down, a few million Chinese have unfettered access to the internet."

"Admiral, what is your intent here?" Samantha asked.

"At first it was just to prove we could do it. But now I'm thinking we should make it a regular thing. After the formation of the Delphi League and learning about star travel, the Chinese people are more confident about their future, and a little less accepting of their government's interference in their lives. If we keep opening a window to the rest of the world, maybe they'll force the kind of reforms we want to see."

"Well, that and the fact that their economy is about to get a huge shock might make them reconsider some things," Fred added.

"Why?"

"When Vancouver Integrated introduces the next generation Comm, the bottom is going to fall out of the phone, digital pad, and personal computer markets."

"I knew it would have a big impact, but why will the bottom fall out?"

"And how will that impact the Chinese?" Liz asked.

"A lot of those products are made in China. And with all the manufacturing that's already been moved out of China, losing all that manufacturing will be a gut punch. The new Comms will be more powerful than any of the personal computers on the market. With the cloud for storage, they'll have plenty of local storage. The engineers at Vancouver Integrated have developed a foldup keyboard like that foldup display Catie designed. With a foldup keyboard and display, you can put an entire PC in a box smaller than the Comm comes in. Who's going to be buying personal computers, or even other phones."

"Smaller?"

"Power supply and packaging wouldn't need to go with you most of the time," Fred explained.

"So, when is this intro planned?"

"June."

"Does anyone know what's coming?"

"I don't think so. We've done a good job of keeping it under wraps, and nobody is expecting an 8X increase in performance."

"Okay, Admiral, you're free to continue playing your games."

"Thanks. Now, what about a Chinese colony?"

"Are you kidding, all we need is Earth politics being replicated among the stars. I'd like to avoid having single country colonies if we can," Marc said.

"I tend to agree with you," Samantha said. "But we already have colonies from single planets. Do you expect to integrate colonies between Paraxeans and Onisiwoens? Much less, between Fazullans and Aperanjens?"

"But at least they're more unified at the planet level."

"I'm not so sure. The Paraxeans have a lot more division on their homeworld than we've been led to believe. Their colonies seem to have escaped that, but that's because they're so remote and so small. Now that's going to change."

"Arrrr! Let me think about it. I'll set up meetings with a few of you and try to hash this out."

"I'm glad I could share my pain," Admiral Michaels said.

"Blake, Kal, anything else on the defense front?"

"No, we're moving along. Delphi City is getting big enough that we'll start getting a lot of our recruits locally. Even if most of them have only been there a year or so, it will help with unit cohesion."

"Good. Okay, Catie, you're up."

"The Resolve is on its way to pick up the last load of Paraxeans."

Everyone applauded, and Blake raised a glass of Scotch to cheer the news.

"So that must mean you're ready to start bringing the Aperanjens out of stasis," Marc said.

"Yes. The Fazullans are eager to get them moved off their ships. As I said, they're pushing hard for us to start moving them to their new colony."

"Well, they can just wait," Blake said.

"I agree, but we really need to close up shop on Onisiwo," Marc said. "We have a lot of resources tied up with this, and we're ignoring Artemis and Mangkatar, as well as not starting any new colonies or contacting the other civilizations out here. And I'm sure the Onisiwoens would like things to return to normal."

"I'm not so sure," Samantha said. "They're enjoying a huge economic boost due to the resettlement of the former slaves. They haven't been impacted by all this other than the loss of that mission to their outer gas giant."

"That and discovering there really is life out there," Catie added.

"True, but the point is that they've actually benefited from all this. And as we saw with that kidnap attempt, their minds are focused on economics and power politics."

"I know," Catie said. "We're closing in on the mysterious Mr. Blofeld. We think our next op will take us to within one or two levels of him."

"Do you have your next target?" Marc asked.

"We have three possibilities. ADI is continuously running the numbers as we get more data. We'll go after the most probable one and work our way down the list."

"Just be careful."

"We will. By the way, we figured out how Constantine is bribing Chair Lexisen," Catie added.

"We're all ears."

"He's doing it indirectly. When he wants to give him money, he tips him off to a few stocks that he should trade. Chair Lexisen buys options or puts. Then Constantine has someone he controls buy or sell a bunch of stock. Lexisen looks like a genius as he sells his options and makes a bundle. The company that did the stock buyback or whatever winds up getting some sweetheart deal from Constantine, and tens of millions of dollars miraculously move from Constantine to Lexisen."

"That is clever," Fred said. "And hard to prove. If it's a company buyback, then that's insider trading. If it's some other individual or company doing the buying or selling, then it's probably not illegal."

"Except the part where Lexisen winds up with a lot of money in exchange for steering government contracts to Constantine."

"Yes, that's the quid pro quo, but it's subtle. If you want to find a smoking gun, you have to find how Lexisen is directing the work to Constantine. Okay, that's it for now; back to work."

"Princess, Lord Baxzad is asking for you."

"Put him on." Catie struggled out of bed, she'd just been asleep for two hours. "So, 0200, what's up with this guy?"

"Lord Baxzad, how may I help you?"

"Princess, I'm not sure if you've heard, but the western coast of my coalition is suffering from a serious wildfire. It's burning out of control. We've lost four families today. I was hoping your people have some technology that would help us."

"I'm not sure, let me get back to you."

"Thank you, whatever you can do would be appreciated."

"ADI, do the Paraxeans have anything unique for fighting wildfires?"

"No, Cer Catie. Paraxeans do not like to live in the middle of the forest like the Onisiwoens and you Hu – Man – s."

"Thanks for the commentary, Ms. Quark. Get me an expert on wildfires. Someone from California if it's possible."

"It is 1800 hours in California. I'll see who I can get." ADI went silent for a moment. "Cer Catie, I have the head of the California Forestry Department on the line. His name is Martin Kaplinsky, and he seems to be eager to talk with the princess."

"Har, har, put him on. . . . Mr. Kaplinsky?"

"Yes, Princess Catherine. How may I help you?"

"I'm on Onisiwo, I'm not sure if you've heard about it."

"Yes, I've heard."

"Anyway, their Western Coalition's west coast is much like California and is suffering from a massive wildfire right now. I'm looking for advice on how to fight wildfires so we can determine if we can use any of our technology to help."

"That's a lot to ask in a short period of time."

"I know, but give me the basics."

"Well, of course, the best method is to prevent them in the first place, but once one is going it really boils down to three things. Starve it, isolate it, soak it."

"Huh?"

"You either have to starve it of fuel; you can do that by using fire retardant, doing backburns to get rid of the fuel before the fire reaches that location, or removing the fuel, like bulldozing it so the fire doesn't have anything to burn when it reaches an area. To isolate it, you do backburns, bulldoze firebreaks, or even use explosives to take down trees. Wildfires spread through the treetops then burn down to the forest floor. So, by taking out trees you can slow it down, which gives you time to soak it."

"And soaking it?"

"Just pour water on it. We use cargo planes for airdrops. Those Oryxes of yours would probably be pretty effective."

"Okay, let me talk to some other people. Will you be available for consultation?"

"Of course, but I suspect those Onisiwoens know all about firefighting."

"I suspect so, too. But sometimes the language barrier makes it hard to get ideas across succinctly, like starve it, isolate it, soak it. I'll be talking with their experts shortly."

"I'm available anytime."

Catie wondered if she'd just clued in all of Earth about the quantum relays, but she figured that cat had been clawing at the bag for quite some time.

"ADI, get me Lord Baxzad back."

"Princess?"

"Lord Baxad, I'm not sure if we have anything you don't have when it comes to fighting fires. We do have a few of our Oryxes here on Onisiwo that could be used to airlift water. What else do you need?"

"We're conducting rescues right now. People have been surprised, and many are trapped in various areas. We're trying to evacuate a town right now, but it's hard to get enough helicopters in because of the high winds."

"Our Oryxes have vertical takeoff ability and they're extremely stable, even in high winds. I'll talk to our wing commander and see if he can help. Can you give me the contact info for who's coordinating the rescue efforts?"

"Certainly, I've messaged it to you now. And thank you, Princess."

"You're welcome." Catie killed the call. "Call Kasper!"

"Catie, how goes it?"

"I'm fine. There's a big wildfire burning down here. They're looking for help."

"What kind of help?"

"Anything they can get, but specifically they're trying to evacuate a town, and with the high winds they can't get helicopters in. How do you think a hover Oryx would handle that?"

"With a good pilot, I don't think the winds would be a problem."

"Good, here's the name of the person in charge. Will you contact them and see what help we can provide? Keep me updated."

"Of course."

"What is that thing?" the deputy asked as he tried to direct the people of the town toward the Oryx that was sitting in the middle of the school playground.

"It's called an Oryx. It can take off vertically, and carry a couple of hundred people."

"Can they bring their pets?"

"If they're small and they can keep them under control."

"Define small?"

"No bigger than a big dog, a house pet!"

"Okay, will another one be able to come right away?"

"Yes, it's hovering over there waiting for us to clear out."

"Thanks!"

The deputy went back to directing the flow of people.

"Ma'am, you cannot bring your horse."

"Why not, that thing's certainly big enough for her to fit in."

"I'm sorry ma'am. We can't allow it."

"I just heard you say pets would be okay."

"House pets, and don't tell me you let her into the house. Now let her go."

"But she'll be killed."

"Hopefully she'll find a stream to hide in, or she will be able to outrun the fire. We have to take care of the people first."

"Fine, then I'm staying with her."

"Then go over there beside the school building. When we're gone you can try and hold her here in the playground. It's pretty big, you might be able to hold out here. I'll see if there's anything we can do."

Twenty minutes later the first Oryx took off with one hundred twenty residents, thirty dogs, twenty-two cats, and eight gerbil-looking critters that the kids carried in their pockets.

The second Oryx set down immediately after the first was out of the way and prepared to load the last eighty residents of the area.

"Jones?" Kasper Commed a third pilot.

"Yes, sir."

"Are you up for transporting a few horses and a couple of cows?"

"What?!"

"There are a few people down there who are refusing to leave without their precious big pets."

"As long as I don't have to clean the back of this thing out, I'm willing to give it a try. I guess it's really up to the owners; all I can do is try to make it as smooth a ride as possible."

"Go for it. The deputy is waiting for you."

"See I told you she would fit!"

The deputy just rolled his eyes. He'd risked looking like a fool by asking the Delphineans if they would take out the horses and such, and all he gets for his efforts is a mean comment and a nasty look.

"Catie, I've pulled our Lynxes in to help with the rescues. There are people in isolated homes, so the Lynxes are a better option. The Oryxes will be better used for big evacuations or to drop water."

"How are you going to get the water into them?"

"Lower cargo hold. The pilot will just do a vertical landing on the water, open the hold, then take off once it's full."

"Dump the fuel, then you can pump the fuel tanks full, that will be almost as much water."

"Good idea, I'll tell the pilots to take up to 90% of VTO weight."

"Okay. Have you come up with any other ideas of how to help them?"

"Not yet."

"What the hell. These people are insane. That house is right in the middle of a bunch of trees. Where are we supposed to set down?"

"I don't know, who would live off such a small one-lane road? We can't even set down on it."

"I guess we have to call this one in. Maybe they can get them down that trail to the main road where we can land."

"Wait, the trees are going to burn anyway. Why don't we just use the plasma cannon on them and clear a landing space?"

"Won't we just start the fire right on top of their house?"

"I don't think so, but let's go over there to the north and try it out."

They used the plasma cannon to vaporize a group of trees, and none of the trees close by caught fire.

"Yee-haw, take that you wildfire loving trees!"

"Okay, let's go back. I'll call them to warn them what we're going to do."

"I really want to thank you guys, I was sure you were going to burn my house down. What do you call that thing?"

"It's a plasma cannon. It kind of vaporizes stuff."

"Come on, Kaylinn get into the plane."

"But my pony."

"I'm sorry honey, we can't take the horse with us."

"But Daddy."

"Get in the plane. ... You know, could you guys maybe use that plasma cannon to make a firebreak around the house and barn?"

"We've already started one, so sure, we'll give it a try."

"Catie, one of our pilots just used his plasma cannon to create a fire break around a house and barn where they were pulling a family out. It didn't start a fire, just vaporized the trees."

"Interesting. Talk to the head of the firefighters. See what he thinks. We could bring the Foxes down."

"Sure. I'll let you know."

"Kay, this is almost as crazy as riding in that Odin's Fist." Odin's Fist was a plasma cannon platform Catie had designed to defeat the Paraxean rebel battleship. The pilot had to be sealed inside.

"No, it's crazier. You know how I can tell? I just wet myself."

"So what, you had to go."

"No, this wasn't a 'I have to go, good thing I'm wearing a shipsuit,' kind of pee. This was a 'gawd, I'm glad I'm wearing a shipsuit or I'd be swimming' kind of pee."

Mariam laughed at Kay's description.

"I'm telling you I didn't know my kidneys could hold so much water."

"Stop, or I'll wind up peeing myself from laughing so hard."

"Hey, you gotta go sometime. Okay, how did we get the chore of blasting trees in the middle of the fire? Working at the edge seems like a better job."

"Kasper said it was because we're the best pilots, but maybe he secretly hates us. You didn't do something to him and not tell me?"

"I didn't do anything, it's not my fault. What about you?"

"He and I are best buddies; it must be because I'm such a good pilot."

"Yeah, right."

"Hey, this is working, we've got lots of heat, but no flames now. Keep circling outward. Maybe we can kill this thing."

Using up the fuel at the center of the fire had the unexpected benefit of reversing the wind on the downwind side. Instead, the rising heat at the center caused by the plasma cannon consuming the fuel created an airflow into the center and up.

It took two weeks to get the wildfire completely under control, but once the Foxes and Lynxes were brought in, there was no more loss of life. The Oryxes proved their worth, dropping tons of water on the fire once the Foxes had vaporized most of the forest that was already in flames.

Neloln made sure there was news coverage on every aspect of the Delphi League's involvement and help. The coverage was overwhelmingly positive. The fact that they had been able to rescue the pets, especially the oversized ones, turned out to generate the largest number of positive comments.

Neloln arranged a fund-raising ball in the capital city of the western state where the fires were. The Delphi League promised to match all contributions. Catie wasn't exactly excited about having to dress up for another ball, but it was for a good cause. The press conference before the ball was, in her opinion, a bit too much, and she made a silent commitment to herself to get even with Samantha and Neloln.

"Princess Catherine, why did it take so long to get a full commitment from the Delphi League to help put out the fires?"

"We committed fully as soon as our help was requested. However, we've never been directly involved in fighting wildfires before. My homeworld has a similar problem with wildfires, but we've never thought to use our spaceplanes in such a way."

"Why not?"

"There are several reasons. First, the vertical takeoff capability is a recent innovation. Second, Delphi City is a floating city, so we don't have wildfires, and third, the other nations are already well versed in how to fight them. It was only the fact that the winds were too fierce to allow helicopters to be used in evacuations, that we thought to use our Oryxes and Lynxes."

"But what about using those plasma cannons to take out all the fuel?"

"We naturally assumed that doing so would just add to the fire. It was when one of our pilots couldn't find a landing place close to one of the houses that needed to be evacuated that anyone thought to test out that theory. We were as surprised as anyone else that the cannons didn't ignite the nearby trees. We will definitely make our spaceplanes available to fight future fires. We have already communicated this information to our other members so they can draw on the same resources."

"Will you give our fire departments plasma cannons?"

"We are working with your fire officials and those on my homeworld to study the issue. We need to wait until we understand how to best use the technology in firefighting."

Catie kept answering question after question, it wasn't until a reporter asked, "Can you tell us about the jewelry you're wearing?" that she realized that it was time to end the press conference.

At the end of the press conference, the company making the cabins for the colonists offered to provide them at cost to those families needing to rebuild. They had adopted the modifications to the design that Nikola had ordered done to make the cabins a better fit for the Indonesian housing market, so it was a perfect fit, a perfect opportunity to help, and a perfect way to advertise their new offering in the Onisiwoen housing industry.

Klaalorn could tell that he was waking from stasis. The Fazullans had put all of them into these chambers when they captured their ship. His memories from the time just before he went into stasis were just coming back to him. *"Ah, yes, those pointed teeth bastards had beat me before they finally stunned me. Apparently, they don't like slaves that fight back. Well, I will show them what fighting really looks like."*

"He should be waking up now. I'm not sure about these Fazullan chambers, but at Gemini Station, they woke up about now. Then it took another twenty minutes before they were ready to come out. They were pretty sluggish for about two hours."

"Who are those aliens? White-skinned, almost like the Fazullans, but with normal teeth and taller. Skinnier too. I won't have any problem with them."

"Okay, start the final part of the sequence. We'll pull him out in twenty minutes."

Klaalorn felt himself wake up. He remembered that the last time he'd been awakened from stasis, he had been sluggish for a few hours; he'd have to pretend he was struggling to wake up. That would catch them off guard. *"What is that?"* Klaalorn wondered as he felt his body shudder. His strength was returning faster than before. He could feel his muscles contract and ripple. He was feeling better than he had before he went into stasis. *"These Fazullans would not know what hit them. Those two traitors, I'll kill them first. Accepting their enslavement and helping the Fazullans to wake me. They must think that I don't see that pointed tooth bastard around the corner. They'll not fool me."*

"Alright, open the chamber, and let's get him out."

As soon as the chamber opened, Klaalorn hit the strange alien knocking him away. Then he turned his rage on the two Aperanjens that were betraying their people. He roared as he sprang toward them.

"Klaalorn, calm down. We are free."

"You lie, you dogs, you have joined with our enemy!" He grabbed the one by the throat while he kicked out at the other.

"Klaalorn, we are free. Please stop fighting . . ." The Aperanjen gurgled the last words as his throat was crushed.

"What . . . the . . ." Klaalorn collapsed as the third stunner hit him in the back.

"What the hell was that?" Dr. Espindola demanded as he struggled to raise himself off the floor. He was pretty sure he had several broken ribs.

"I don't know, sir," the Marine with the stun rifle said. "He was crazy."

"Get him to medical, and send a team to take that one there. I'm afraid this other one is dead."

"What happened?" Catie asked Captain Clements.

"I'll let Dr. Espindola explain. Doctor."

"We're not exactly sure. We brought him out of stasis and he went berserk. He killed one of the Aperanjens who was helping us and was about the kill the other before the security guy knocked him out."

"They didn't have any problems like that when they woke them at Gemini Station. What was different?" Catie asked.

"He was in a Fazullan stasis chamber for one."

"That means that he was likely treated as a slave. Most of the ones at Gemini Station were in Paraxean chambers. They didn't know anything about the slavery."

"That would explain his anger. But how did he come out of stasis so quickly? We should have had hours to talk with him and explain things."

"Let's try and find out. Give me the empress," Catie ordered her Comm.

"Princess, how may I help you?"

"Empress, we have had an incident bringing one of the Aperanjens out of stasis."

"I have just been informed of the situation. I apologize. Our chambers have a default setting that injects a stimulant to facilitate the process. It is intended to bring the crew out quickly in case of an emergency."

"Why weren't my people informed of this?"

"It was an oversight on my part. The technician who was helping you thought it would be more exciting if he didn't explain about the stimulant and how to deactivate it. He has been punished."

"How?!" Catie demanded.

"He is walking back to Fazulla."

"Walking?" Catie quickly realized that the empress meant they had spaced the man.

"Yes. We cannot tolerate such behavior, risking the lives of our allies. His long walk will set a good example for the rest of my people."

"Very well. We will begin waking the Aperanjens again starting tomorrow morning. Our doctor needs some time to recover from his injuries." Catie didn't add that he probably needed some time to build up his nerve to wake another one. Although he should have waited until they were able to talk to the Aperanjen before he actually opened the chamber. He wouldn't make that mistake again.

Chapter 15   Retribution

It took two weeks for ADI to settle on the most likely target. Then Cristina needed to find a way to get close to him. He was a rich guy who attended a lot of charity events. ADI couldn't actually discover how he'd become rich. He had made a lot of good stock trades, so he must be getting paid off, but for what? Contract killing and illegal raids seemed to be good candidates.

Finally, ADI identified a big charity event at a hotel in the capital. She got Cristina tickets to the event and a picture of Manji, the guy they were looking for.

"He's good looking for an Onisiwoen."

"If you say so," Catie said. "Do you have what you need to go to this event?"

"No, I'm going to have to buy a much nicer dress and some jewelry. I'll pick up some costume jewelry so the cost won't be too bad."

"No, these people can probably spot costume jewelry at ten meters. Buy real stuff. You can keep it as a bonus, hazard pay."

"Okay, you're the boss." Cristina wasn't going to say no to some nice jewelry.

Cristina took a cab to the shopping district. She'd dressed up, but not too much. Her first stop was to buy an evening gown for the event.

"Miss, that's a lovely dress, but I think you would find this one a better fit," the young saleswoman said to Cristina.

"No, I like this one. Where is your changing room?"

"Right over there." The woman pointed toward the back of the store. "There are three stalls, I believe we have two free right now."

Cristina went in and changed into the gown.

"Oh, damn," Cristina said as soon as she got the gown on. Immediately realizing why the sales clerk had tried to dissuade her from selecting the gown. Cristina was used to having small breasts and wearing dresses with plunging necklines, but with the larger breasts that they'd given her for this assignment, the plunging neckline made her look like a slut.

"Would you like to try this one?" the sales clerk asked. She'd obviously heard Cristina's self-criticism.

"Please."

The sales clerk draped the other gown over the door and left Cristina alone.

"Oh, much better," Cristina said as she checked out the new gown. A more modest plunge made the black gown look just the right level of provocativeness. The high slit on the left side gave it the daring look that Cristina craved and provided quick access to a knife she would wear on that leg.

She stepped out and walked to the raised platform surrounded by mirrors so she could get a good look.

"Miss, that's perfect for you. It will have the men lining up for the next dance."

"I agree, and thank you for your help." Cristina asked the clerk to wrap up the gown and have it delivered to her hotel room. "Now, where would you recommend that I go to purchase some jewelry?"

"We have a jewelry department, but if you're looking for something special, there are several jewelry stores just down the block. I like Katjar's, but that might be because I like the young salesman who works there."

Cristina walked into Katjar's. The older clerk at the counter looked at her for ten seconds, assessing her by her nice but not too nice clothes as someone not worthy of his attention. The young man to the left gave Cristina a big smile. "Can I help you?"

Cristina walked over to him. "Yes, I'm looking for some new jewelry. Something that stands out without being too ostentatious."

"Depending on your budget, we have a collection of costume jewelry that is almost impossible to tell from the real stuff, and of course we have real jewels too."

"I like to keep things real."

The young man gasped just a bit, but immediately directed Cristina over to the center section of the counter. "We have a beautiful collection of diamonds here."

The older clerk came over and nodded to the young guy to move aside. "I see you're looking at diamonds. May I recommend the Kritzeen collection? They are the most elegant necklaces on the market."

"Excuse me, that young man was helping me. I'm not interested in changing sales clerks."

"He is not yet qualified to sell diamonds."

"Then this will be the perfect opportunity for him to practice. Now, if you don't mind!"

The older clerk stepped back and motioned to the young one to go ahead. Then he turned away and headed into the back of the shop.

"Thank you," the young clerk said as he brought out the collection of necklaces. "He was right, the Kritzeen collection has the most elegant diamonds."

Taking Catie at her word, Cristina bought a necklace made up of forty separate one-karat diamonds. Cristina especially liked the fact that they were cinched by a gold clasp that would make a short part of the string dangle between her breasts. She always felt that one should show off what one had. The necklace, a matching bracelet, and matching earrings cost more than she made in a year. *Well, Catie said not to skimp.*

When she arrived at the event, Cristina realized that Catie was right. The women were all bejeweled and obviously with the real stuff. The men were all dressed up in the Onisiwoen version of a tuxedo. She felt a little self-conscious coming to the event without an escort, but they didn't have another agent who was made up like an Onisiwoen, and bringing Charlie as her plus one would have set off alarm bells, so she'd had to come solo.

Once she was inside, she realized that she wasn't the only woman who'd arrived unescorted. And most of the ones who were unescorted were on the prowl. *"Makes sense, hunting for sugar daddies, or maybe some are working girls,"* Cristina thought.

It was an hour after the start of the event before Manji, her target arrived. He had a blond bimbo on his arm, except her hair was blue, but everything else about her spelled blond bimbo.

Cristina hung around Manji looking for a chance to separate him from the bimbo. She saw an opening, and as she made her move another woman cut her off, spilling her drink on Cristina. "Oh, excuse me," she said. Cristina glared at her and the woman glared right back, reminding Cristina of Marsha from some movie about a big family.

Cristina went into the ladies' room to wipe the drink off her dress and fix her makeup. She was sitting at the mirror when someone else entered the room.

"Back off sister!" Marsha said as she took a seat beside Cristina.

"Me, back off, why don't you?!"

"Because I have a chance, unlike you!"

"What makes you think I don't have a chance?"

"Because Manji doesn't go anywhere with anyone that his boys haven't checked out first. You're new in town, so you might as well forget it."

"Damn," Cristina thought. ". . . Maybe we can help each other out?"

"Why should I help you?" Marsha asked.

"What are you going to get if you manage to latch onto Manji?"

"Stuff?"

"What kind of stuff?"

"A couple of thousand and some jewelry. Something nicer than that fake stuff you got on." Marsha pointed to Cristina's diamond necklace.

Cristina took one of her earrings off and used it to scratch the mirror. Marsha's eyes went wide as she realized that Cristina's jewels were real and just how much they must be worth.

"Oh, so they are real."

"Yep."

"If you've got that kind of money, why are you messing around with Manji? He's good looking but he can be kind of dangerous."

"I need some information."

Marsha laughed. "And you think Manji is going to tell you anything?"

"I don't need him to talk to me."

"Then how could I help you and what would I get out of it?"

"I just need to be alone with him for a bit. What if I gave you my jewels and a few thousand?"

"Wouldn't do you any good, he still won't go upstairs with you."

"What if you take him upstairs for me?"

"What will you do to him?"

"I just have some questions I need answered."

"He won't tell you anything, and I thought you said he didn't need to talk to you." Marsha was clearly disappointed that she wasn't going to get Cristina's jewels.

"Right, I just need to get close to him, then I can get the information."

"What, you need a DNA swab or something?"

"No, I need to be alone with him for a few hours."

"What are you going to do after? He's going to be pissed. He's not the kind of guy you want mad at you."

"He won't remember a thing."

"Sure. And I'm your fairy godmother."

"I can prove it. Can you get someone to come in here?"

"In the restroom?"

"Yes."

"We can just wait, someone's bound to come in."

"There is a woman approaching now," ADI messaged.

"Oh, you're right here comes one now."

The woman came in. "Ladies."

Cristina stood up and pushed the woman against the wall, then she slapped her across the face.

"How dare you!"

Cristina sprayed the aerosol into her face as she held her against the wall with her other hand. She released the woman who put her hand to her face while she blinked at Cristina a few times.

"Oh, hi, ladies. Is there room for me?" she asked while still rubbing her face.

"Impressive."

"What?" the woman asked.

"See, I'll dose Manji with this same stuff and he won't remember a thing."

Marsha eyed the other woman wondering why Cristina was talking in front of her.

"She won't remember anything she hears for the next twenty minutes and nothing that happened in the previous six hours. Now, what do you think?"

"The jewels, ten grand, and a can of that stuff."

Cristina laughed. "What will you do with a can of this?"

"You let me worry about that. Deal?"

"Deal."

"And you have to help me get rid of that slut he has hanging on his arm."

"Oh, that won't be a problem." Cristina handed Marsha a paralyzer. "Now once you get him alone, slip this on the nape of his neck. It'll temporarily paralyze him, so make sure he's sitting down. Let's go."

They left the restroom together. "Why don't you go get a drink and I'll take care of the bimbo."

Cristina grabbed a drink off of one of the trays. She pointed toward the bar when Marsha started to grab a drink off of the tray. "A different drink."

While Marsha made her way to the bar, Cristina made her way over to where Manji was talking with the bimbo.

"Oh, excuse me." Cristina bumped into the bimbo and spilled her drink on her.

"You clumsy oaf!"

"I'm sorry. Why don't I help you clean that off?"

"I don't need your help!" The bimbo headed to the restroom with Cristina following.

When the woman realized Cristina had followed her into the restroom, she turned on Cristina. "I said, I don't need your help!"

Cristina pushed her up against the wall and punched her in the ribs. She was sure she'd cracked one. Then she dosed her with the aerosol and maneuvered her to one of the stalls. She pushed her into it and then hit her again, knocking her out. She would wake up in ten or fifteen minutes and wonder why she was in the restroom. The pain in her ribs should send her home.

Cristina left the restroom and grabbed another drink. She wandered through the crowd until she saw Marsha with Manji. She caught Marsha's eye and smiled, touching her jewels to remind her of the deal. Marsha nodded to her.

"ADI, I need ten thousand."

"It's waiting for you at the front desk."

"You keep impressing me."

"I try."

◆ ◆ ◆

It was three more hours before Marsha was able to head upstairs with Manji. During that time, Cristina had managed to spill drinks on three other women that seemed to have their eyes on him.

"ADI, do you know which room they're going to?"

"Suite 3240."

"How can I get there without being seen?"

"Take the freight elevator up to the thirty-second floor. The suite has a connecting door to the suite next door. I can open the door for you. Marsha has to open the other side."

When Cristina got to the hallway to Manji's room she found one of his goons guarding the door.

"Damn. Now what? The next room is too close. He'll see me."

"Go in the room next to it, the three suites all connect," ADI said. *"It makes it into their presidential suite."*

"How are we going to open the inside door?"

"Don't worry, just go inside, then I'll distract him. That will let you go back into the hall and get into the middle suite."

"Okay."

Cristina acted like she was drunk as she opened the door to the third suite. She closed it behind her and leaned against the door, taking a deep breath.

"Let's wait a few minutes," Cristina said.

"Relax, let me know when you're ready."

Cristina sat down and gathered herself. She pulled the interrogation hood out from under her dress. The event was too formal for her to carry a large bag so she'd had to strap the hood to her inside thigh. It felt very awkward but needs must.

After a few minutes, Cristina got up and opened the access door to the next suite. She propped it open with a chair and laid the hood on the chair.

"Ready."

ADI had the elevator ping that the door was open. Then she had the other doors ping as well. She kept opening and closing doors until the bodyguard got suspicious and went to check.

"You've got one minute!"

Cristina exited the suite and hurried down the hall and entered the next suite. ADI had conveniently unlocked the door since they were electronically keyed and connected to a central system. She went to the connecting door to the third suite and opened it up. She moved the chair so it was propping both doors open. Then she moved to the other side and opened that door. She put her ear against the door, but couldn't hear anything, so she took a surveillance puck out of her purse and put it against the door. Now she could hear everything from the next room.

"Manji, you promise you'll take me out on your yacht?"

"Of course, my dear."

"I've never done a threesome. Are you sure I'm not enough?"

"Just call your friend."

"I'm not sure she's up for this."

"I'm sure she will be. Money talks and she looked hungry."

"Okay, just give me a kiss before I call her."

THUMP!

"Cristina!" Marsha hissed.

Cristina knocked on the door. "Open up."

When Marsha opened the door, Cristina saw Manji lying on the floor. "I told you to make sure he was sitting down or on the bed."

"I tried. He was being difficult. I had to promise him a threesome to get him up here."

"I know. I heard. Help me get him on the bed." Cristina used another chair to prop open the door between Manji's suite and the middle one.

"Okay! Oomph, he's heavy."

The two women got Manji laid out on the bed. "Come on, help me strip him."

"Why?"

"He's supposed to think he's had a big night when he wakes up. I think if he has all his clothes on, he'll figure something went wrong."

"Okay . . ."

"There we go. Run into the second room. There's a chair propping the doors open to the next room over. Bring me the hood that's sitting on that chair."

Marsha ran to retrieve the hood while Cristina arranged Manji on the bed.

"Here. Now give me my stuff and I'll leave."

"No, you have to stay. His goon out there will wonder why you're leaving early. In the morning I'll give it all to you and then you can gas the goon on the way out. Then neither of them will remember you were here."

"Shit!"

"Hey, it's just one night, and you're getting paid plenty. I assume you've got all his money."

"Not yet," Marsha said as she started going through Manji's clothes.

"When you're through, go to the third suite and take a nap. I need about three hours."

Marsha pulled most of the money out of Manji's wallet, then headed to the third suite.

"ADI, how long?"

"It'll be two hours before he's sober enough."

"Can't I inject him?" Cristina had insisted on a hypospray after the last time. It was too much work to get the idiots to take pills.

"I'm counting on that. He's very drunk."

"Okay." Cristina grabbed the small hypospray from her purse and injected Manji. Then she placed the hood on his head and got it situated correctly.

"I'm going to take a nap. Let me know when we can get out of here."

"Yes, Cer Cristina."

◆ ◆ ◆

"Cer Cristina, I have finished," ADI announced.

"Good. Marsha, are you up?"

"Yes, can I go now?" Marsha whined.

"Definitely. Here's your stuff. Gas the bodyguard on your way out."

"Sure. You know, I was afraid you'd gas me and leave me here."

"I thought about it, but I figure we might be able to use you again. Here's a number. Go buy one of the new Delphinean phones. When you get it, punch in this number."

"This isn't a real phone number."

"Don't worry. Just do it, and we'll be able to contact you after. Now go."

Cristina hid behind the door while Marsha went out.

"Hey lover boy," she said as she rubbed up against the bodyguard. She sprayed him with the aerosol then waltzed off to the elevators.

Cristina removed the hood from Manji and gathered all her stuff. Then she exited to the middle suite and checked it to make sure nothing was there. Closing both doors, she moved on to the third suite. The mini bar was almost empty and the bed was a mess, but other than that, Marsha hadn't left anything behind.

After closing the access doors, Cristina exited the suite and made her way to the freight elevator, and went down to the garage. She exited the hotel then walked down two blocks before she hailed a cab. "ADI, tell me that we got what we need."

"I won't know for a few hours. But I have a good feeling about it."

"He doesn't know!" Catie yelled. "Are you serious?!"

"Yes, Cer Catie, he believes it was Constantine, but he is not sure."

Cristina and Major Prescott just sat on the couch while Catie railed.

"Gawd! We have to come up with a way to force whoever it was to reveal themselves."

"Catie, I think Manji is still the key," Major Prescott said. "You need to use him to get the guy pulling the strings to reveal himself."

"I'm sure you're right. ADI and I will figure out a way. We'll find some way to put pressure on both the barons and Manji; someone will break. Whoever was behind it has to have called in other favors. If they're all under stress, someone will look to collect on one of those favors."

"How? They're all worth billions."

"Doesn't matter. ADI and I will figure a way."

"Okay, I assume my part in this is over," Cristina said.

"Yes, you can go back to the Merlin and they'll change you back to your old self."

"Hey, they can change me back to my young self and I'm keeping the tits."

"Sure, whatever you want," Catie laughed. "They can administer a youth treatment while you're there. I'll let the doctor know. You're kind of young to get it, but hey, it can't hurt."

"Great. Major Prescott, are we good?"

"You're good."

Catie put her hand on Cristina's arm to stop her from leaving. "Cristina, I can't thank you enough. We would never have gotten this far without you. And before we leave Onisiwo, you should go down and buy another set of diamonds."

Cristina gave Catie a hug. "I'll see you in a few weeks. I'm just sorry we couldn't get to the top guy."

"It's okay. We'll get him. I'll be sure to come up and visit, and you can come down and stay with me anytime. Major, you should go back with her. I think ADI and I can handle this second part ourselves."

"Yes, Princess." Major Prescott stood to attention, he almost saluted, but he caught himself at the end. Then he and Cristina headed out to the shuttle that was waiting for them.

Cristina planned to take the first opportunity she had to fly back to Onisiwo and go back to Katjar's jewelers. She'd buy some jewelry for Tiffany, knowing it would be okay with Catie. And what fifteen-year-old wouldn't appreciate some nice jewelry.

"Oh, boy. What are we going to do?" ADI asked.

"You've mapped all their investments, right?"

"Of course."

"First, let's look at who's leveraged their assets."

"Most of them are heavily leveraged."

"Good. Now, what has to happen to start making their houses of cards collapse?"

"I get it. Let me study it for a while."

Board Meeting – May 1st

"I call this meeting to order. Now, if she hasn't already told you, Catie has some news. Catie."

"We're stuck on the kidnapping investigation."

"Damn!" Kal said. "What are you going to do?"

"We're going to go after all the barons. We'll see if we can put enough stress on them that someone goes looking for the return of a favor. ADI's pretty much figured out their stock market. So, with us controlling the introduction of new technology, we think we can make sure they're on the wrong side of quite a few stock trades and other deals. We've already messed up a big real estate deal Constantine was planning. And I still think it was him."

"Just be careful."

"Daddy, I'm always careful. And I'm just doing some planning. Major Prescott and Cristina did all the real work until now. And now ADI will be doing it. It should all be electronic."

"That's the way it should be. Now let's move on. Fred, what have you got?"

"Standard stuff, you can find it in my report. Things are going great. I do have a big question though."

Marc looked a bit taken aback, surprised that Fred would have a 'Big Question' that he felt he had to bring to the board, and one that they hadn't discussed during one of their private chats.

"Go ahead."

"What is this X Projects account that all of our excess profits are going into? I've ignored it figuring it was just one of your projects. We haven't been generating that much in excess profits until lately. But now I'm seeing billions get siphoned into this account."

Marc laughed. "Millions wasn't a problem but now that it's billions, you're curious."

"Hey, I read it as you McCormacks taking out your dividends; when you issue dividends to the rest of us, you guys never seem to take them. But now it's real money."

"It is kind of our dividends. ADI takes the money and invests it in certain strategic projects. Most of it has been going into the stock market, but lately, we're picking up a lot of real estate."

"I guess as long as you know what you're doing, it's your money. I was just curious."

"Well, I think it's time I explained. Mostly we've been building up a reserve, but we're fast approaching the time when we're going to really dip into it."

"What does that mean?" Liz asked.

"Well, the world, and the U.S. especially, is approaching a watershed moment. They've decriminalized marijuana, and the new pain killer we helped develop is OTC. The pain killer acts like an opiate, but without the physical addiction and bad side effects. That, along with the fact that most states have adopted the European model and have decriminalized most forms of prostitution, means that the criminal gangs are going to lose a lot of wealth and power. We've been buying up property in some of the depressed cities around the nation. Our plan is to redevelop those areas."

"Does that mean you're going to dislocate all the poor people?" Fred asked.

"No, ADI has been buying up apartment complexes in the area and building up excess occupancy capacity. We'll move the people from the buildings we want to tear down into the houses and apartments that are empty. That way we can work on multiple blocks at a time, about a square mile. We'll redevelop that area, add a few manufacturing plants and some customer service facilities, then move the people back to the new area, and start over. You keep telling me we're ready to expand manufacturing offshore."

"I do, but I wasn't thinking about the United States."

"Well, you should be. They've got a lot of underutilized labor, and they're a major market for our goods. If we follow Henry Ford's model of raising the local income so that we are expanding our customer base at the same time, we should be able to fill a good percentage of the manufacturing capacity with local demand."

"Are you sure that will work?" Kal asked.

"We'll find out. We're breaking ground on our first project in four months. I think we'll at least break even, but I'm hoping for a big return. If it works, others will follow the model."

"Now, Blake, what do you have?"

"Read my report, I'm not following that."

"Catie, how are you doing?" Marc asked. He'd messaged her to stay on the line after the meeting.

"I'm doing okay. It's just frustrating."

"I'm not asking about your hunt. I'm asking, how are you dealing with the workload? All the stuff you've had to manage over the last few months."

"Oh, you mean your lesson plan."

"Whatever," Marc rolled his eyes at Catie. He should have known she'd figure out the main reason he'd given her the Onisiwoen mission.

"I'm doing okay. It's a lot harder than I thought it would be. I guess I've never had to deal with so many disparate things at one time. It's hard to keep shifting focus all the time."

"Tell me about it. But you seem to be handling it well."

"I hope so. I'm coming home soon, and I hope you don't have another lesson plan already set up for me."

"I don't."

"Good! Bye, Daddy."

"Bye, Sweetie."

"ADI, let's figure out what to do about Manji."

"Okay, what do you need to know?"

"What's he into that's illegal, involves lots of money, and other people that he might be scared of?"

"He supplies illegal drugs."

"Pharmaceuticals?"

"Yes, Manji sells pharmaceuticals that are out of date, stolen from the manufacturer, or were contaminated in production. He sells them to another lord that then distributes them up and down the coast using his pharmacies."

"How did that happen?"

"Lord Gareax owns a string of pharmacies. They were using forged doctor prescriptions to get extra pills that they then sold to addicts. It became a pretty big business. Five years ago, the government started tracking all prescriptions. They were able to determine exactly when a doctor or pharmacy was selling more pills than statistically probable. They were preparing to do an audit on Lord Gareax's pharmacies because he had ordered so many pills during that quarter compared to the prescriptions that real doctors had prescribed. He had to come up with a lot of pills quickly to pass the audit. Somehow he knew that Manji was a contractor for various illegal things like hits and kidnappings. So he contacted Manji for help. Once Manji supplied him the pills that allowed him to pass the audit, they both decided it was a good business and Manji has continued to supply him with pills. Manji usually gets them by faking contamination or some other manufacturing process problem. That and out-of-date pills that the manufacturer has to recall create a significant supply of pills. He seems to have people in all the major manufacturing plants."

"Okay, so how do we mess that up?"

"I have the data on a big shipment he's getting ready to make."

"Good, we can have Major Prescott intercept it. If we steal his drugs, that'll get him in trouble with the gang."

"Won't he just arrange to get some more from the manufacturers, or steal them if he needs to?"

"Sure, but that will take time. And if he does, we'll steal them from him. You just have to watch him closely to see what he's up to. Can you do that for us?"

"Of course, once I've got someone in my sights, it's easy to keep track of their movements. I've been tracking Manji's personal phone, not the burner phone he uses for his criminal activity. Between that and surveillance cameras, I know where he is and what he's doing at all times."

"Then you can tell us if he gets ready to make another shipment."

"What if he has Lord Gareax's people pick the shipment up?" ADI asked.

"No way. He's not going to want them to come into contact with his source. They'd cut him out of the deal."

"I see. You know, you're pretty good at this criminal stuff."

"Very funny. Now, send the data to Major Prescott."

The next night, Ensign Racine and her squad were hiding on the side of the road where the shipment was coming down. They were ten kilometers north of the meet that Manji had set up with the gang. It was a coastal road, and at 0200 the traffic was light.

"Alfa team. Your target is approaching."

"Block the road," Racine ordered.

The team moved a tractor-trailer into the road, then hooked a strap on it so the hover Lynx could lower it onto its side. Using the grav drives, the Lynx was silent, and without lights and with its energy absorbent hull, it was nearly invisible. They'd stolen the tractor rig just two hours before while it was idling beside a roadside diner.

Manji's truck slowed to a stop. Of course, Manji wasn't involved with the hand-off, he only dealt with the money and hired thugs to do the real work.

"What's up?" the driver asked. The Marine he was asking was Black and had a hood on so that between his blue wig and the darkness, he looked like an Onisiwoen.

"Damn rig jackknifed; we've got a tow truck on the way to right it. It should be here any minute."

That short chat was just long enough for four Marines to sneak up beside the truck and one of them to stick a rifle against the driver's neck.

"What is this?!"

"We're here to relieve you of some stuff. Now kill the engine, or he'll kill you! Hands on the dash!"

"You guys don't know who you're messing with!"

"Sure we do. Some yahoos who are going to keep their mouths shut if they don't want to wind up dead. Now give me your weapons!"

Two of the Marines opened the back of the SUV and pulled out eight cases of pills. They checked the back seat just in case there was anything there. They put the pills into another SUV that had just driven up. It was another stolen vehicle. But they only needed it to get them far enough away from the scene that they could load everything and themselves into the Lynx.

"That's all of it!"

"Okay." Racine grabbed the keys from the SUV and tossed them into the ditch beside the road. "Boys, you have a nice day."

Racine and her team climbed into the SUV and drove back north for five kilometers to a small side road where the Lynx was waiting.

"Now that was fun!" Racine shouted as they climbed into the Lynx.

"ADI, what's the status on Manji?"

"He's panicked. He's trying to come up with another shipment. Lord Gareax has threatened to make some very unpleasant changes to his anatomy. Some of them are not even possible."

Catie laughed. "You'd be surprised. Now, what about another shipment?"

"He's arranged to have it picked up just outside the factory. This theft is going to be big, so it'll be noticed. As I said before, he prefers to have a manufacturing problem lead to the disposal of a significant number of pills. He would then grab them before they were destroyed, but there isn't time."

"Okay, how's he going to move it?"

"He's planning to ship it south on a yacht. It will pick the drugs up just south of the manufacturing plant, then drop them off one kilometer farther south, about where the last exchange was supposed to take place."

"Okay, where should we interdict it?"

"I think we should leave that up to Major Prescott," ADI said.

"Ahh, you're no fun."

"I am too! But this is what he's trained to do."

"*Okay.*"

◆ ◆ ◆

"Racine, how do you want to do this?" Major Prescott had just finished reviewing the data with Racine and her team.

"I think we'd like to do it at sea. It's not often that we get to act like real Marines and board a ship at sea."

"I'll ignore that 'real Marines' comment. But you know they'll be armed."

"Sure." Racine spent the next twenty minutes explaining her plan to him. Then with his approval, her team ordered the equipment they needed, then went to bed so they'd have some sleep before the operation began.

◆ ◆ ◆

It was 0100 when Manji's yacht anchored in the bay where it was to pick up the drugs.

"O'Neal, you're on. You've got one hour to get those mines placed and be back here."

"Yes, ma'am."

O'Neal was a strong underwater swimmer. He donned his facemask and put the mouthpiece in. He dropped into the water and headed out. He was using an oxygen rebreather that captured the CO2 in a filter, so there were no air bubbles to give him away.

He dove deep so that he couldn't be seen from the surface and swam hard toward the yacht. It only took him fifteen minutes to swim the

227

twelve hundred meters. He arrived below the yacht using its anchor rope and running lights to orient himself.

O'Neal slowly rose toward the surface. Once he made contact with the yacht, he could feel its motion as the crew moved about loading the drugs. He placed a mine at each of the engines. The mines were small and would just do enough to disable them. Then he placed a larger mine at the bow of the yacht. It should blow a hole that was just large enough that the crew would have difficulty fixing it, but not so large that the yacht would sink too fast.

"It would be so much simpler if we just sank the damn boat. But no! Racine wants to board it." He wasn't aware that Prescott had ordered Racine to bring the drugs back. Catie didn't want them to be recoverable by some recreational divers.

O'Neal had just planted the last mine they would use to actually sink the yacht when he felt the boat rock hard. "They must be pulling the anchor up."

O'Neal dove deep and waited until the anchor was up and the crew was focused on where the boat was now heading before he started his swim back to the zodiac.

"You get it done?" Racine asked just as his head broke above the water.

"Yes, ma'am. You can set them off whenever you want." O'Neal crawled into the zodiac. They turned the electric engines on and the three zodiacs headed out toward the rendezvous point. They were going to blow the mines twenty kilometers out.

"Blow them!" Racine ordered.

They could see the water splash away from the yacht as the mines blew. The yacht immediately slowed down and eventually stopped.

"Let's let them know they're in bigger trouble than they imagined!"

The zodiacs raced toward the yacht. They were low in the water, black, and silent. It was going to be hard for the guys on the yacht to figure out where they were.

"Attention, you guys on the yacht! You've got two minutes to get into the dinghy and head out before we'll set off another mine and blow a nice big hole in that yacht. It'll sink with you in it!"

One of the men on the yacht brought up a rifle and tried to sight Racine. Just as he took his shot, one of the Marines on another zodiac shot him. It got him in the shoulder, knocking him to the deck.

"Damn it! Next one that points a gun at us, gets it in the head!" Racine yelled. She'd taken the round in the chest. Her body armor had stopped it, but it still hurt like hell.

Her threat followed by a few more rounds fired at the boat was enough; the five men crawled into the dinghy and headed toward shore.

"Okay, let's board her. We've got about twenty minutes before she sinks."

They quickly reached the yacht and boarded her. Racine led the way. They found the drugs in the yacht's toy garage.

"They must have left all his toys at the dock. This should be easy, let's grab it and get out of here."

Once they unloaded the drugs, the zodiac headed out to their rendezvous with the Lynx.

"That was a nice boat. Damn shame to sink her."

"Blow it," Racine ordered.

"Okay, what's Manji doing now?" Catie asked.

"He is packing up. It seems he plans to spend some time in the Southern Coalition," ADI replied.

"Okay, then while he's trying to stay alive, I don't think he'll be doing any favors for Constantine or anyone else. So where are we with the others?"

"Jaraxa's son is in town working with the police on the apparent assassination of his father. He's been adamant that his father was too smart to let his plane get blown up.

"Constantine had asked Manji to put pressure on one of the politicians controlling the zoning change to delay the change. He's also putting pressure on the coroner to declare Jaraxa dead."

"We need to stop that from happening."

"I am working on it."

"Okay, has Jaraxa junior gotten any offers?"

"Yes he has. Constantine has been trying to get him to sign an agreement to sell should he need to settle the estate, but Junior has gotten a letter suggesting that the property will be a lot more valuable in a few months, so he's not showing any interest."

"Good. Now, what else have you done?"

"They all play the futures market heavily. They're shrewd, and I believe they all seem to have ways to manipulate the market enough that they can score on their futures. But I have been able to model their behavior. I can take them for every penny they invest in options and puts if you'll give me permission."

"You've got it. But I want to do more than just that. I want to really get these guys out on a limb."

"Oh, boy! Tell me your plan."

◆ ◆ ◆

Manji was packing a small bag. He was furious. How could he have screwed up so badly? How could he enter into a deal with a guy related to Wilmarx? If he'd known that he'd never gotten into business with Lord Gareax. One-off deals were fine, but a continuing relationship where something could go wrong, no way.

And who was screwing with him, or were they after Lord Gareax? But would anyone be stupid enough to mess with Wilmarx's nephew? Anyone but him. *It has to be blowback from the failed kidnapping attempt.* He'd been sure Constantine was behind it, but now he wasn't sure. Constantine had called him to put pressure on the guys in the Western Coalition to salvage his real estate scam. He hadn't even complained that they hadn't found Jaraxa's body. He just needed to delay the zoning change.

Manji had a bolt-hole he could run to. He'd lie low for a while; try to salvage the situation remotely. He could just disappear and start over if he had to. *"Damn, who did I piss off?"*

"Zoey, how would you and the other women from your mission like to be incredibly wealthy?" Catie asked as she met with Zoey on the Merlin to discuss her plans.

"I'm pretty sure I would, and I suspect the others would. But what do you mean by incredibly wealthy?"

"Top one thousand on Onisiwo," Catie said.

"That would certainly make it easier to protect our children, but how would you accomplish that?"

"I've been trying to decide how to deal with all the subtle bribes I've been offered, as well as the people behind the attempted kidnapping."

"Do you know who they are?!"

"Not yet, but we're getting closer. Anyway, I've decided that we need to get a little retribution from all these corrupt officials. We want to burn their fingers when they stick them in the cookie jar."

"How?"

"By taking away from them what they're doing all these questionably legal activities for, specifically, their wealth."

"And how are you going to do that?"

"Well, on Earth, ADI became very adept at playing the stock market. Your economy is starting to go through major changes, positive changes, but very disruptive changes."

"So?"

"ADI can predict how that change will affect your stock market. And based on the offers and suggestions I've been getting, these so-called leaders of yours are looking at the situation too narrowly. They're missing the big picture. ADI won't make that mistake."

"So, what do you need us for?"

"Well, we have to move the money to someone. We wouldn't want to be accused of taking advantage of your planet."

"Where are you going to get enough money to start?"

"ADI?"

"We have one hundred million onis right now."

Zoey's eyes bugged out at the mention of so much money. An Oni was the Onisiwoen currency and was the equivalent of 1.5 U.S. dollars. "Where did you get that?"

"ADI has been trading for a few months now. She started out pretty small."

"How could she have grown it so fast?"

"The potential repercussion from the kidnap attempt sent your stock market reeling. ADI just timed trades based on what would really happen instead of what everyone was guessing at."

"Isn't that insider trading?"

"We told everyone what we were going to do. The fact that they didn't believe us isn't our fault," Catie said. "Are you in?"

"Sure."

"What about the other women?"

"I'll ask. But how are just one hundred million onis going to make back the trillions they've stolen from our people?"

"Like I said, ADI is very good at predicting. Especially since she actually understands what the technology we're going to introduce will do."

"You do know that taxes will consume most of it. We have a very progressive tax rate."

"Oh, but there is this interesting clause in your tax code. If you are outside the jurisdiction of your government for over two years, you are not subject to local taxes, but to the taxes of the jurisdiction you're in. We've checked with your lawyers and tax officials. They've agreed. You've been in Fazullan jurisdiction until recently and you're in Delphi jurisdiction now. I've talked with the empress and she agrees to exempt you from their taxes. And Daddy and I have agreed that you should be exempt from Delphi taxes. So as long as you stay on the Roebuck until the end of your tax year, you're good. And after that, ADI will shelter the other income, you won't need it to be liquid."

"Oh, and that's only another two months. Well worth it," Zoey said. "I'll go tell the other women. It'll really help to boost their spirits. Even if we just got our five years of back pay without being taxed, it would be a windfall. This is . . . well, just amazing."

Chapter 16   The End Game

"ADI, what is Constantine doing now?"

"You mean besides trying to contact Manji?"

"Yes."

"He's still trying to figure out how to salvage that real estate deal with Jaraxa's son."

"How's that going?"

"Jaraxa's son is holding firm. He's saying that until he sees his father's body, he's not making a move. The authorities haven't declared Jaraxa dead, so Constantine doesn't have any leverage. No taxes due, loans are still holding. I've purchased some of Jaraxa's debt, so that takes some of the pressure off of his son."

"Good. Now, what else can we do that will have a big impact?"

"I'm monitoring his trades, and he's losing. Unfortunately, that just means he's trading less. He only goes out on a limb, did I say that right, for real estate deals. Actually, most of the barons seem to focus on real estate."

"Out on a limb is exactly what we want. And we want them a long way out on one so we can cut it off."

"ADI what is the status of Constantine and the other barons?"

"First, I want to say that I have finally figured out your game. My isolated self has verified it with me. Therefore, today at 0907, I officially registered my guess and verified it as correct."

"Good for you, did you have fun?"

"Yes, but I would rather be involved in the planning."

"You were."

"Not completely."

"Okay, next time."

"Thank you. Now, your hints about the need for more manufacturing and lodging in the space stations have had the desired effect.

Constantine and the other barons have been vying for control over the space on the various stations. As you instructed, I've been bidding against them to raise the price while keeping the manufacturers we identified from selling their space."

"Neloln, I think we're ready to start the solar panel manufacturing. It should take four weeks to tool up the first line. But I think it will be obvious after two weeks, that the space required is being grossly overestimated."

"I agree. What about the IC manufacturing?"

"We can start licensing the new manufacturing techniques, but I'm inclined to let your people just adapt them to your current designs instead of trying to introduce our designs."

"I like that idea. Anyway, the barons will quickly realize that they've tied up over a billion dollars in cash grabbing up manufacturing space in the stations. They've driven the price up so high that it will take years for them to unload it. Nobody's going to be interested in the overpriced space once they realize it won't be needed for a decade or so."

"What about the residential space?" ADI asked.

"I think that will become obvious when we unveil our new Delphi League compound."

"Ah, I did enjoy bidding against Constantine for that warehouse space down by the river," ADI said.

"Neloln, what will happen to the cleanup once Constantine realizes we're not building the compound there?"

"I was very impressed with your conniving mind there," Neloln said. "When Constantine bought the land, he could have refused to clean it up and demanded his money back. But once you dropped the hint that the Delphi League was aware of the toxic waste and would not even consider entering into a deal before it was cleaned up, he took a big gamble. When he started cleaning it up, he became liable for the entire cost. Now that it's public, he has to either clean it up or discount the land when he tries to sell it. I think he now has over five hundred million tied up in those lots, and the development of that area is not going to be particularly attractive, once you announce that the compound will be built on the other side of the city."

Catie laughed. "And Chair Lexisen will be in it deep with Constantine once everyone realizes that the compound is going to be fifteen acres instead of one hundred acres. Man, that guy is gullible."

"So, what's next?"

"I have an idea that will drive Constantine over the wall."

"Oh, do tell."

"What if we form a company for Zoey and the women, have it buy the land from Constantine. If we promise to clean it up, we should get it for almost nothing."

"We can do better than that. I bought the note on the land," ADI said. "We can demand payment and Constantine will default. Then we can take the land for nothing as long as we clean it up. But won't cleaning it up cost almost as much as the land is worth?"

"Maybe, but can't we use some nanites to clean it up, process all the toxic material back into their base components, and sell them?"

"But the printer time to produce enough nanites to do that would be enormous."

"What if we made micronanites that could find the material, and then made microbots to haul it around? We could place transmitters where we want the different material delivered so the microbots wouldn't need to be that smart."

"That would work. It would take a few years to clean up the site. But the company would probably make money by selling the material it extracts."

"Can you work with Nikola and come up with a design?"

"I would be happy to, oh Mistress of the Dark," ADI said.

"What does Mistress of the Dark mean?" Neloln asked.

"'Evil One' would be the easiest translation I could come up with," Catie replied.

"Oh, ADI, you're mean," Neloln said with a laugh.

"ADI, what else?"

"We've been buying up a lot of debt that the various barons have. They are so heavily leveraged that they will have trouble servicing it, especially with their recent losses. When they try to renegotiate, we will refuse and call it in. They're going to have to liquidate a lot of property to cover it, and we have surreptitiously purchased similar properties in the same markets where their best properties are, so when they try to sell any of those properties, we'll drive the price down by offering ours for less. And with my preventing them from gaming the stock market, they're going to be in real trouble," ADI explained.

"What's going to stop them from bribing someone in the government to come up with a sweetheart deal to bail them out?" Catie asked.

"I think I have a solution for that. I have a friend, Baxzon, who is a reporter who's been working on this issue for years, she would love to get a scoop. With ADI's and your help, we can document how the barons have been bribing public officials. The population has been tired of all the corruption, but without being able to point a finger, nothing has happened. With this, we'll be able to get yearly audits of the personal wealth of public officials to prevent this kind of bribery, like you said your father did."

"Yes, but you don't have all the same capabilities that we have. You won't be able to completely stop it."

"But it will severely limit it. There are lots of young politicians who are still idealistic enough to jump on the bandwagon. And with everyone watching, it's going to be hard to come up with any sweetheart deals."

◆ ◆ ◆

"Cer Catie, Constantine seems to be in a frenzy right now."

"Why?"

"It appears that he was so delighted with his inside information about the manufacturing space on the space stations, that he shared it with Lord Wilmarx. Lord Wilmarx invested a lot of his own money into buying up the space."

"I can see how that would make him unhappy, but why does that put Constantine into a frenzy?"

"Well, Lord Wilmarx is well connected."

"So is Constantine."

"Yes, but Lord Wilmarx is from a very old family. Apparently, they made most of their money two hundred years ago from what you on Earth call the mob. He seems to have maintained connections with the old families that are still involved in criminal activities."

"So Constantine can't just take him out. He's got an entire family to worry about."

"Yes, and Lord Wilmarx is so embarrassed about being conned, that he's told Constantine that unless his investment returns the promised three hundred percent, he will take it as a personal affront."

"It's too bad that Constantine is having trouble raising money. Has he managed to sell any of his properties yet?"

"A couple. But rumors that he was desperate for cash have really driven the prices down."

"Terrible thing, rumors."

Constantine was in a panic. "How could everything turn to shit on me? Ever since I met that princess, everything I've tried has bitten me in the ass."

Constantine took a gulp of brandy while he looked around his penthouse condominium. He was trying to decide what to take with him. That is, besides the gold he had stashed in the safe.

He had to lie low long enough that he could come up with the money to pay Wilmarx back. How long would that take? "Damn, I'm so far out on a limb, I might as well hang myself. How can everything have gone bad? That damn Comm deal, then the real estate thing in the Western Coalition. Why did I listen to that idiot Kacketox, how could he have mixed up manufacturing capacity and manufacturing space? What a fool, but more the fool I for getting sucked in."

Constantine opened his safe and grabbed the bag of gold coins and the bag of cash. It would have to last him until this all blew over. As if anything with Wilmarx ever blew over.

"I'm going to kill Chair Lexisen. I knew that one hundred acres was too much. But I let him talk me into it. Now I'm saddled with that land and the cleanup cost. It's going to ruin me."

Constantine grabbed the two bags and put them in a small carry-on suitcase. He then carefully exited the condo and took a cab to the airport. He had a plane there that no one knew about. He leased it to a small airline, but he had the keys. He would use it to get to his villa; his ownership of the villa was buried in so many hidden transactions that nobody could connect it to him. He would have someone pick up the plane and bring it back here. Rich people were always flying to the islands to meet up with a yacht and having their plane flown back. Nobody would notice him doing it. And he wasn't even flying directly to the same island that his villa was on. He'd be using cash for everything, there was no way anyone would be able to trace him.

"Empress, we are now ready to start moving your ships," Catie announced.

"We are prepared." The empress smiled at Catie but was trying to look calm, cool, and regal.

"I don't know why it didn't occur to anyone to ask before, but did you get all your people off the planet?"

"Yes, this is all of us."

"Oh, good."

"You're surprised that there aren't more of us?" the empress asked.

"A little." Catie's informal census had shown that there were approximately three million Fazullans on the various ships arrayed around the wormhole. She thought that was a small number for an entire planet.

"We have only been on Fazulla Proxima for one hundred fifty years. We only had one hundred thousand people in our original colony mission."

"I see." Catie started doing the math in her head. One generation every twenty years . . . so.

"I see you're doing the math in your head. You might be surprised, but few Fazullan women have more than two children. And if they have a son first, they usually only have one."

"Oh, that is a surprise, especially for a colony."

"Once the emperor rescinded the requirement that all women have five children, our population has stabilized. When you're treated poorly by your husband, you're not inclined to give him more children."

"Of course."

"And you know that our most powerful men took several wives."

"I knew that."

"Birth control has been a well-known art for Fazullan women. And men who force the issue are surprisingly accident-prone. Many of them have been known to succumb to alcohol poisoning."

"Ah, I see," Catie said. Clearly, the Fazullan women would only tolerate being mistreated so much. Men who became overly abusive were dealt with by the women. And in a society where it was common for the man to get roaring drunk, it would be easy to tip him over to alcohol poisoning. There had to be lots of easy ways to add alcohol to his system once he was blacked out.

"I'm glad you do. I think we will have fewer clumsy men in our new society."

"I'm sure you will. Now back to moving your ships. We will place a jump gate where your ships can see it. It will be four ships flying in a square pattern. Your ships need to fly through the center of the square."

"We understand. My captains are all listening, and have already reviewed the instructions your Captain Clements sent us."

"Good. Now once they go through the wormhole, they will need to go through a second jump gate. It will be of the same configuration. After that, they will be in your new colony system and will need to proceed in-system to the planet. I'm sure they'll be able to handle things after that; we will have a frigate there to assist if there are any big problems."

The jump points had been configured with Earth as the nexus of all the colonies. That meant that the ships had to jump to Earth before jumping to their colony. Marc had been adamant that Earth would be the hub of the trade among the colonies, at least in the beginning.

"We understand. Princess, I want to thank you and your people for their understanding and help."

"You're welcome. We still hope that you will join the Delphi League. But we understand that you need time to establish your new regime first. The Romulus will remain stationed in your system, so you'll be able to contact us through her."

"I understand. We do look forward to doing some trading. But first, we must create something that you want to trade for."

"Good luck, Empress."

The empress gave Catie a salute as she signed off. Catie realized that that was the first time the empress had saluted her. "She must be getting soft."

Chapter 17   Home James

The DSS Ulysses arrived at Onisiwo to replace the Merlin. It was time for the Merlin and her crew to go back to Earth. The crew could use some shore leave to visit friends and family. Then they all needed some time to hone their training before they were sent out on their next mission. It was also time for Catie to go home. She would just make it in time for Yvette's graduation.

The Ulysses also brought the new Delphi League Ambassador to Onisiwo, Margaret Hannaford.

"Sam, if Margaret was going to replace me, why didn't you send her out earlier?"

"She's replacing the ambassador; nobody could ever replace Princess Catherine."

"Yeah, right!"

"Besides, I thought you had some cleaning up to do."

"Yes, but I could have done that from anyplace."

"No you couldn't. The Aperanjens had a right to have Princess Catherine send them off on their voyage to their new colony world."

"I guess I wouldn't have wanted to miss that."

"And the empress."

"I probably would have been happy to miss that. But I guess it was good to do it so everyone is happy."

"See, it worked out for the best. Besides, what would you have done at home?"

"I could have found something exciting to do. This has been getting boring; ADI and Cristina really had all the fun."

"Catie, don't you know better by now? Every time one of you says boring, the powers that be decide to add excitement to the story. And that never turns out well."

"Oh, you can't really believe that superstition stuff."

"Hey, I'm only going by the data."

"Cer Catie, I have found Constantine," ADI said.

"Where is he?"

"He is hiding on an island in the Central Coalition. A small villa that is owned by one of his companies."

"And he doesn't think Lord Wilmarx will find him there?"

"His ownership of the company is well hidden. And the villa is very remote."

"Oh, hmm, ADI can you send him a postcard?"

"I could, what would be the purpose of doing that?"

"Just send him one from the capital city. Tell him that all his friends wish him good luck and hope he's having a wonderful vacation."

"How should I address it?"

"To him, at his villa."

"You really are an evil person," ADI said.

"Just to my special friends."

"Zoey, you're ready to leave us?" Catie asked.

"Yes, we've bought an island, well most of an island. It's down close to the tropics so it has nice weather all the time. There's a small fishing village on it. We're going to develop a resort on the south side, and keep the north side just for us. That will help grow the economy and encourage a few more people to move there. Hopefully, that means there will be enough children for ours to play with and socialize."

"That sounds wonderful."

"And it's all because of you."

"No, not me. It's all because the six of you persevered. Constantine was so impressed with you that he had to share his wealth."

Zoey laughed. "I like the way you think. And that news report will probably make a difference. There's already a big movement to make the changes you and Ncloln suggested. Some of the new politicians who haven't been corrupted yet are getting on the bandwagon."

"One can only hope. I'm sure I'll be back to see you."

"You'd better. Now come on Clara, say goodbye to Princess Catie."

The three-year-old waved at Catie as her mother led her to the Lynx.

"Lord Jaraxa, we believe it will be safe for you and your family to return home," Catie said.

"Yes, and I understand you need your cabin back. They tell me that you are also returning home."

"I am. I hope your stay hasn't been too inconvenient."

The two children came up and gave Catie a hug. They'd had a grand time on the Merlin. They had even gotten one of the pilots to take them out on the shuttle so that they could experience microgravity. It was something they would be able to lord over their friends back at school.

"We have been well taken care of. I'll just be happy to get home and back to work. My son was shocked when I was finally able to contact him. He was delighted that we were alive, although he had given up hope."

"We apologize for having to deceive him, but we couldn't allow him to give away the fact that you were alive."

"He understands. And the announcement that they have changed the zoning for our property has assuaged any pains and anger he may have felt. I'm going to have him run the development."

"Oh, I'm surprised at that."

"The weeks I've spent up here with my family without any work to interrupt us has shown me how much I've neglected them in the past. My wife and I have agreed that I should spend much more time with them going forward."

"Being killed has never been better for anyone than Jaraxa," his wife said.

Catie laughed with her. "It does make you appreciate what it means to be alive."

"It does. We want to thank you for your help. We hope you will return to Onisiwo and visit us."

"I will definitely be returning to Onisiwo on one of our trading vessels. I'll make a point of stopping by to visit you. You live in a lovely area."

"Thank you, we'll look forward to it. Now we should get out of your way. We need to get these children home and you need to finish your preparations."

Board Meeting – June 5th

"This meeting will come to order. Catie, I understand that you are on the Merlin, preparing to leave."

"We are. We just left the planet and are heading out. I'll be knocking on Uncle Blake's door in two weeks."

"You will? And do you think I'll be home?"

"ADI will let me know."

"Alright you two, back to the meeting. Fred?"

"You can read the reports. Nothing has changed."

"Okay. Admiral Michaels, where are we with the discussion on a unified Earth, and a league delegate?"

"That depends on where you are with respect to a Chinese colony."

"I'm convinced that an exclusively Chinese colony is a bad idea. I'm willing to allow them to be a significant percentage of the colonists. But I'm not willing to allow one country to control a colony."

"Except Delphi."

"That is a unique situation at this time. All colonies will be initially managed by a representative of MacKenzie Discoveries. Once they are established, they will elect their own governor."

"Even if it turns out to be someone other than a MacKenzie representative?"

"The elections will be democratic. Once the colony is established, we would prefer to move our resources to a new colony."

"What if those resources don't want to move?" Samantha asked.

Marc smiled. "We can't lose, if they stay, that's good for us. But I'm sure many of them will be looking forward to starting a new colony. I suspect that over time they will decide to either return to Earth or become official colonists. We'll have to see."

"So, what should we do with the Chinese delegation? Can we persuade them to send colonists to Artemis?"

"I'll work with them to see if I can get some motion on that. I'm not exactly sure what they are hoping for," Admiral Michaels said.

"I think they want to have a guaranteed outlet for Chinese manufacturing," Samantha said. "A Chinese colony would help to stimulate their economy. They're suffering from all the onshoring that has been happening over the last two years."

"That's what I suspected. Is there something we can do to assuage their concern?"

"Right now, all we would do is raise it. We're intentionally focusing on Africa and Southeast Asia for our sourcing."

"Okay, then I'll string them along." Admiral Michaels grimaced at the thought.

"That will change when we start more colonies," Catie said. "And especially when we start trading with the established worlds out here. If you focus on what they think they can produce that would be attractive to those worlds instead of the colonies, it would better align with their needs."

"Catie's probably right," Samantha said.

"Probably?!" Catie messaged Samantha.

"You should use the list of goods that the Paraxeans shipped to Onisiwo as an example."

"I'll do that. And thanks for all the extra paperwork," Admiral Michaels said. Catie had just sent him the list of goods traded, requests, and complaints from the Onisiwo trade delegation.

"I'm glad to know you'll be busy," Marc said. "Now Blake, where are you with staffing?"

"Getting the Victory back is going to help. We've sent the Romulus to New Fazulla so that's the last frigate we'll staff for a bit. Sam, have you and the Paraxeans reached an agreement?"

"They're suggesting a mixed crew on a Delphi frigate."

"Ajda will love that. It makes my life a bit easier, but she's still going to have to make a few more frigates."'

"Hey, Jackie told Sandra that you've delegated all the staffing," Kal said.

"Tell Sandra how much I appreciate her sharing family secrets she wheedles out of Jackie."

"You know that will just encourage her and Jackie."

"I'm sure it will," Blake groaned. "Anyway, shipbuilding is Ajda's business. Is she getting a percentage?"

Fred slapped his forehead. "No, we haven't been including her in the distributions. We should separate shipbuilding into a separate company and give Ajda partial ownership."

"Do it. I think we'll be building a lot of ships. Catie, how many planets do you have on your list?"

"We've got six planets with normal gravity to explore and three more heavy G planets."

Catie finally got a break and decided to check in with her friends in Delphi City.

"Hi, Miranda. I'm checking to see if you're still going to make it for Yvette's graduation."

"I'll be there. What about you?"

"We just left Onisiwo, so I'm two weeks out. So that puts me there a week ahead."

"Good, then you can help plan the party."

"Are we still going to do a James Bond theme?"

"Yes, martinis shaken not stirred, a baccarat table, and a few blond bimbos, both male and female to round out the theme."

"Sounds perfect. I can't wait."

"Cer Catie, your postcard worked. And I have confirmed that Constantine was behind the kidnap attempt."

"How, and how?"

"He told Manji. He was so spooked when he got the postcard that he called Manji. He demanded that he help him get off the island."

"Why did he need Manji's help?"

"He didn't have access to a big yacht. He's decided that his only hope is to move onto a superyacht and stay at sea until he solves his problems."

"So how do you know he was behind the kidnapping?"

"Manji refused to help him. Constantine told him that if he hadn't screwed up the kidnapping he wouldn't be in this mess. He threatened to tell Wilmarx everything he had on Manji if Manji didn't come up with a yacht and help him."

"Great."

"And here's the best part."

"What?"

"Manji called an old contact to get the yacht. Unbeknownst to him, that contact has a distant familial connection to Wilmarx."

"Oh, perfect!" Catie squealed.

"I think it is safe to assume that Wilmarx will be having a brief discussion with the two of them before they disappear forever."

"Couldn't happen to two nicer guys. And the timing was perfect, we're close to the fringe. It's nice to have that all wrapped up before we leave. Now I feel like I completed the mission."

"I thought you would like the news."

"Prepare for jump!" Merlin, the ship's AI, announced over the ship's speakers.

Catie was looking forward to getting home. They would make Earth orbit a week before Yvette's graduation. Miranda and Joanie would be there. It would be just like old times. And Liz and Dr. Metra had worked up a disguise for Catie so she would be able to get out and do things without the press hounding her. It was going to be just great.

"Jumping in five seconds!"

Catie felt the slight sensation of weightlessness as they were consumed by the wormhole. She was at her desk reviewing the designs for the new cruise starship she was planning to launch next year. Jumps were old hat, nothing special, they only took a few seconds.

"Jumping!"

"All-hands prepare for collision! Prepare for collision! . . . All-hands . . ."

Catie grabbed her space helmet and put it on, then grasped the edges of her desk while her mind grappled with what could be happening. Then she ran to her bed so she could lie down and get her head and heart at the same level. "ADI give me the feed from the bridge."

"What the hell happened?" Captain McAvoy demanded as everyone was thrown back in their chairs by the 20G emergency deceleration profile. The bridge stations had automatically rotated so that the crew's heads were at the same level as their hearts.

"I don't know, ma'am. The wormhole collapsed and the collision alarm went off!"

"Where are we?"

"I don't know, but we are heading directly for that gas giant."

"Is there a solution to get by it?"

"We are at max deceleration to change our vector. We'll just miss it."

"Ma'am!" the sensor operator shouted.

"What?"

"There are asteroids in our path!"

"Blast them with the plasma cannon!"

"They're too big!"

"Can we maneuver around them?"

"We're trying."

"Missiles," Catie called out.

"Thank you. Launch missiles at the asteroids. We'll goose them out of our way," Captain McAvoy ordered. She sat back in her command chair; she was a bit more relaxed now that she had all the variables up on her display.

"It worked! We can now clear the path with plasma cannons. We'll just slip by the gas giant."

"Good! Now, someone, tell me what the hell happened?"

"Ma'am. I don't understand it, but we exited the wormhole well inside the gravity well. That should not be possible."

"We need answers; what could have made our wormhole collapse?"

"We're still studying the logs."

"Ma'am, the logs show a reflection of a gravimetric wave coming from the sun."

"A reflection?"

"Yes, ma'am. There must have been a significant gravimetric event recently. The reflection is just coming in so that would indicate that the event coincided with the collapse of our wormhole."

"Shit!" Catie said. "Oh, sorry." Catie had come onto the bridge to see if she could help figure out what had happened. She was still exhausted by the four hours of emergency deceleration.

"It's quite alright, Princess. Did you realize something?"

"ADI, reconstruct where all the debris is coming from."

"Yes, Cer Catie. ... All the debris is radiating from the location where our wormhole collapsed. If I reconstruct the object, it appears that there was a large moon there before the event."

"Something must have broken that moon apart, or maybe an asteroid collided with it."

"How could a moon break apart?"

"I don't know."

"Ma'am. We're getting a distress signal," the communications officer announced.

"From where?"

"It appears there is a spaceship about 0.25 AUs from here. It looks like a basic SOS, a short repeating signal with little content."

"It appears that the ship is on a ballistic course. They are not maneuvering, and there is a significant amount of debris heading their way," ADI said.

"So, you think they've lost control?"

"If they still had control, they would be trying to move toward the less dense area of the debris field."

Captain McAvoy turned to Kasper. "Kasper, launch eight Foxes without pilots. Max acceleration. Let's clear a path for that ship."

Catie went to her cabin and threw herself onto the padded bench. "Why . . . why do I get stuck in a system where a moon blows up? Hey, if you're listening, how about a little romance? Why can't I meet a prince charming? I could use a little fun once in a while. Why can't we find a unicorn or a planet where everyone loves each other?!"

Afterword

Thanks for reading **Delphi Embassy!**

I hope you've enjoyed the eleventh book in the Delphi in Space series. The story continues in Delphi Diversion. If you would like to join my newsletter group go to ⬛https://tinyurl.com/tiny-delphi. The newsletter provides interesting Science facts for SciFi fans, book recommendation based on books I truly loved reading, deals on books I think you'll like, and notification of when the next book in my series is available.

As a self-published author, the one thing you can do that will help the most is to leave a review on Goodreads and Amazon.

Acknowledgments

It is impossible to say how much I am indebted to my beta readers and copy editors. Without them, you would not be able to read my books due to all the grammar and spelling errors. I have always subscribed to Andrew Jackson's opinion that "It is a damn poor mind that can think of only one way to spell a word."

So special thanks to:

My copy editor, Ann Clark, who also happens to be my wife.

My beta reader and editor, Theresa Holmes.

My beta reader and cheerleader, Roger Blanton, who happens to be my brother.

Also important to a book author is the cover art for their book. I'm am especially thankful to Momir Borocki for the exceptional covers he has produced for my books. It is amazing what he can do with the strange PowerPoint drawings I give him; and how he makes sense of my suggestions, I'll never know.

If you need a cover, he can be reached at momir.borocki@gmail.com.

Also by Bob Blanton

Delphi in Space
Sakira
Delphi City
Delphi Station
Delphi Nation
Delphi Alliance
Delphi Federation
Delphi Exploration
Delphi Colony
Delphi Challenge

Stone Series
Matthew and the Stone
Stone Ranger
Stone Undercover
Stone Detective

Made in the USA
Las Vegas, NV
29 November 2022

60629503R00144